Savage Land

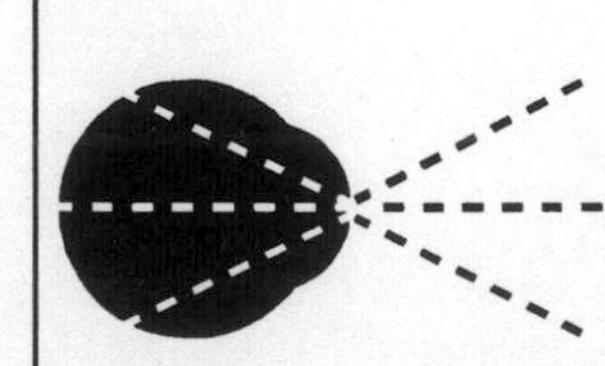

This Large Print Book carries the Seal of Approval of N.A.V.H.

SAVAGE LAND

WESTERN STORIES

FRED GROVE

with a Foreword by
Jeanne Williams

THORNDIKE PRESS
A part of Gale, Cengage Learning

GALE
CENGAGE Learning®

Detroit • New York • San Francisco • New Haven, Conn • Waterville, Maine • London

Thorndike Press, a part of Gale, Cengage Learning.

Thorndike Press® Large Print Western.
The text of this Large Print edition is unabridged.
Other aspects of the book may vary from the original edition.
Set in 16 pt. Plantin.

LIBRARY OF CONGRESS CATALOGING-IN-PUBLICATION DATA

Grove, Fred.
Savage land : western stories / by Fred Grove with a foreward by Jeanne Williams. — Large print edition.
pages ; cm. — (Thorndike Press large print western)
ISBN-13: 978-1-4104-5906-0 (hardcover)
ISBN-10: 1-4104-5906-3 (hardcover)
1. Frontier and pioneer life—Fiction. 2. Large type books. I. Title.
PS3557.R7S28 2013
813'.54—dc23 2013008695

Published in 2013 by arrangement with Golden West Literary Agency

Printed in the United States of America
1 2 3 4 5 6 7 17 16 15 14 13

FOREWORD BY JEANNE WILLIAMS

Fred Grove and I met over fifty years ago at the University of Oklahoma where we both studied with Walter S. Campbell and Foster-Harris. Since then, Fred and I have shared ups and downs of our personal and professional lives, let off steam, and encouraged each other. He was generous with his knowledge, practical in his advice, staunch in his friendship. I treasured his letters, often signed Big Chief Rolling Thunder, right down to his last scrawled note written a few months before his death when he told about the beloved "kid horse" he had ridden through the Osage Hills where he grew up in the 1920s.

The infamous Osage murders, when oil-rich Osages were being killed to benefit white heirs, had a lasting impact on Fred. He was living in Fairfax when an Indian's house was blown up with nitroglycerin, killing two people. He never forgot the terrible sight. His skill as a reporter enhances his gifts as novelist in the three books he wrote about this violent time: *Warrior Road* (Doubleday, 1970), *Drums Without Warriors* (Doubleday, 1976), and *The Years of Fear* (Five Star Westerns, 2002). The last book especially is based on solid fact, how Bill Hale, "King of the Osage Hills", was brought to justice by dedicated FBI officers and a few brave local lawmen who risked death to win justice. I remember Fred's long struggle to get this novel into print and how pleased he was when it was published.

My favorites of Fred's rich panorama of the West are the match racing novels, two of which won Spurs from the Western Writers of America, *The Great Horse Race* (1977) and *Match Race* (1982), both from Doubleday. These are funny, with the most likeable trio of rascals I've encountered in Western fiction, especially the Comanche jockey, Coyote Walking.

Fred's dry humor flavors even his serious books as in *Phantom Warrior* (Doubleday, 1981) when he writes of a Tonto scout and his watch. "He would gaze endlessly at the leaping stag engraved on the gold-filled hunting case. He seldom wound the watch or looked at the face and its Roman numerals, simply, Ewing supposed, because Archie knew where the sun stood and when the moon rose, unlike the puzzling *blancos* who were to be pitied because they seemed not to know and, therefore, had to depend on this ticking thing."

The match race Spurs keep company with two more won for short stories, two Western Heritage Awards from the National Cowboy Hall of Fame, a Levi Strauss Golden Saddleman from WWA, an Oklahoma Writing Award from the University of Oklahoma, and a Distinguished Service Award from Western New Mexico University.

Fred could write with deep understanding of both Indians and whites. His mother was born on the Sioux reservation at Pine Ridge, South Dakota, and his father rode on trail drives from Texas to the north. It's fitting that the stories in this last harvest of Fred's work speak with many voices about what Fred's old teacher and mine, Foster-Harris, who once wrote stories for the same magazines where Fred saw his early work published, used to call the Hoof Trail People. "The Mystery Dogs" concerns a Navajo slave boy. He believes he will die as his Spanish masters threaten, if he dares approach their horses, yet he painfully works up the courage to mount one, and instead of death experiences the incredible glory of riding to freedom.

The plains changed utterly in less than a warrior's life span. Even before the Civil War, gold strikes lured thousands across the prairies to California or to the mountains, or to claim land in Oregon. By the 1860s, there was noticeably less game. Buffalo Bill Cody alone killed 4,280 buffalo to feed workers for the Kansas Pacific Railroad. Indians and buffalo got some relief from the inexorable spread of settlements and railroads during the Civil War, but once it ended, troops were sent West to protect settlers, and hide hunters swarmed in to slaughter the shaggy beasts and leave their flesh to rot. A million a year were being shot by 1870. Five years later, the southern herd was all but gone. Another ten years destroyed the northern herd. With them vanished forever the free-ranging way of life of the Indians in Fred's stories: Pawnee, Kiowa, Comanche, and Cheyenne.

Also Hoof Trail People were the cavalry officers who face cruel choices in three of these stories. "The Deadly Friends" has a lieutenant new to the frontier, who escorts a Cheyenne hunting party from the reservation and runs into big trouble with hide hunters. A brave young woman in "Satan's Saddlemate" opens the eyes of a lieutenant who doesn't see why anyone would want to stay in what seems to him a desolate land plagued by Comanches. "Hostage Trail" presents a captain charged with delivering a supply of uniforms to Fort Sill who is also escorting surrendered Cheyenne warriors to lure in other hold-outs. The small column is challenged by an army of vigilantes who wants to kill the Indians. The captain's first desperate maneuver fails and the posse is attacking when everyone gets a huge surprise. Like the beleaguered officers, under Grove's incisive handling, the hard-bitten, experienced sergeants grow from stock figures into real men.

Reservation times continue in "Comanche Son" when a father, returned from the Civil War, at least physically regains his child who's been reared as a Quahada Comanche. Winning the boy's heart is a harder war than the one the father just fought. "Price of the Bride" has a beautiful Cheyenne girl entrusted by her father to a white man he believes will cherish her, although a rich and sore loser offered more ponies.

First appearing as a two-part serial in *Boys' Life* (3/68–4/68), "The Ravaged Plain" tells about a boy who leaves Missouri and works his way West to find adventure and his fortune hunting buffalo. He finds the plains littered with bones but presses on. He encounters a famed former hunter with a professor representing Eastern zoological societies. They tell him the vast herds are slaughtered but he won't believe it and scorns an offer of a job helping them try to save a remnant. When he blurts out this secret to unsavory "wolfers", he instantly regrets it and risks his life to help rescue the last herd.

Four stories detail the settling of the region and shift from hoof trails to wagon trails and railroads, from the law of the gun to the law of the court. The greed and hope of those who made the land run in April 1889 power the action in "Gun Loose" when a wanderer who had planned to file, make a profit on his claim, and ride on, decides to stay put and build a life. "Paper Bullets" shows a newspaper editor and an aging lawman battling for a new town's soul as it's overrun by rowdies who are driving out the honest businesses and genuine home-seekers who would make it a good place to build and live. "Killer's Medicine" forces a sheriff to confront neighbors intent on a lynching. In "Summer of the Big Die" drought and outlaws set on vengeance compel a hard-pressed rancher to send his wife back to town and teaching for her own safety, but she has other ideas.

"Hide Hunter's Prize" begins: "Time-worn, the hills still shoulder up from the rolling face of the prairies." This story of a hunter yielding a white calf and its herd to the Pawnees is a fitting epitaph for those days of Indians and buffalo, soldiers and first settlers.

When urged to write a long "big" novel, Fred would grin in his boyish way and say he was best with the quarter mile. He was indeed, but his short stories and novels create a rich panorama as wide-ranging and spirited as the West he loved.

Ride on, old friend, through those ancient hills.

The Mystery Dogs

He lay slumped against the rocky wall, sweat runneling his slim brown body, naked to the waist, his heart laboring heavily, his legs and arms strengthless. He ran a hand through his straight black hair, now cropped short, and gazed about him. In the fitful light of the torches, he could see the forms of his young Navajo friends, like him, becoming weaker day by day, some already unable to stand. Soon they would all die in this dark hole where they dug out the shiny metal for the Hairy Ones. Then others would take their places, and others after them.

He dozed. Hardly had he begun to rest, it seemed, when he heard the harsh voice of a Hairy One ordering them up. The voice drew nearer. He heard the snap of a whip and the unwilling stir of bare feet. He saw his friends struggling to rise; some could not. He watched in growing despair.

Of a sudden his smoldering defiance burst through. He did not rise, even when he saw his captor moving upon him. This white-skinned man had hair on the backs of his hands, under his long nose, and on his chin and cheeks like the fur of an animal, so thick that his narrowed eyes seemed to glint behind vines, and his mouth was like the den of a beaver overhung with roots. These Hairy Ones also imprisoned their bodies in heavy clothing. There was an odor about them that nauseated a Navajo. Although no stronger than drying hides and other camp odors, the smell was strange and discernible this moment, despite the bad air in the tunnel.

He tensed but kept his face inscrutable as the Hairy One said: "Get up, Roberto."

"My name is Hosteen." His words came awkwardly in the alien tongue he was learning, the tongue he detested.

"On your feet. Remember, you are a slave and a heathen."

Hosteen, not rising, continued to stare at the muscular figure towering over him, the whip dangling like a long black snake.

"I am a Navajo. My name is Hosteen."

"Heathen! Your name is Roberto."

"Hosteen."

It struck him as he knew it would, quickly

and powerfully, as it had before when a slave lagged, the whip slashing his naked legs, now his arms and shoulders. He took each blow without expression, refusing to show pain before an enemy, while inside him he cried out. He heard the voice again: "If I punish you much more, you cannot work. Say your name is Roberto and get up."

"Hosteen," he breathed. "My name is Hosteen."

Again the rain of pain. Just when he was about to cry out, it ceased. He sank back. The arm-weary Hairy One was turning away to herd the others to their work.

Hosteen swayed up and fell into line, a grim awareness coming over him. Another beating like that and he would not rise to see another day. He must try to think. One must be brave, but not foolish brave.

Trailing back into the dimly lit tunnel, he chose a pick and began digging and filling the stout sacks. His hands bled. Dust filled his nose and throat and filmed his eyes. He coughed. All around him there was coughing. And before him, like a sweet dream, rose the wind-swept red rock country where he was born, far to the north, bright and high and clean. Would he ever see it again? He feared not.

A nearby clattering broke his musing. He

turned. A boy lay face down across the handle of his pick. Hosteen knelt and lifted the boy over on his back and touched his slack face, seeing the glazed eyes. He stood, eyes smarting tears, as the boy was hauled away by his heels.

Afterward, with the others, Hosteen strained at the lumpy sacks and fell to dragging and carrying them to the entrance of the tunnel, then down the mountain to the high-wheeled *carretas.* Here, for a few moments before he was shouted and lashed back up to the tunnel, he always rested his fascinated eyes on the "Mystery Dogs" inside the log corral. That name, which the Navajos had given these four-legged creatures because they were burden bearers and carried people on their backs, did not fit them somehow, for they were too beautiful and did not look like dogs.

He had seen them first when many Hairy Ones raided Hosteen's tribe and took only young captives, slaying the elders. On the long walk down the Río Grande to this stony mountain he had constantly observed the Mystery Dogs, which the Hairy Ones called *caballos* and which the Navajos were not allowed to go near. Astride their *caballos,* the Hairy Ones had come like gods and left in evil.

"Stay away," Hosteen had been warned. "Don't touch the *caballos. Caballos* eat heathens."

Terrified, he had obeyed. And yet, he asked himself many times, why did not the beautiful *caballos* also eat the Hairy Ones, since they were like the Navajos except for the paleness of their skins and the furry hair on their bodies? It was strange. It challenged his reasoning.

Hosteen also noticed that his captors handled these mystery creatures with great care on the trail, feeding them corn and staking them at night to eat the sparse grass, and leading them to water several times each day, and brushing their smooth skins, which glistened in the sun, and combing their glossy manes. And when the Hairy Ones wished to ride, they placed a thing of leather pieces sewn together on the creatures' heads and a straight thing in their mouths and controlled them by pulling on long leather reins attached to the straight thing. And on the creatures' backs the Hairy Ones placed a blanket and on top of that a horned thing of leather that made a seat. How lazy his captors were to ride! How puzzling it all was!

His mind whirled. Could it be that these beautiful beings were the Hairy Ones' secret medicine or power, more powerful than the medicine sticks his captors possessed that made noise and smoke and hurled tiny objects that killed Navajos? Indeed, everything the invaders did was strange and destructive.

Straining, his body streaming sweat, hacking for wind, Hosteen helped lift the last sack into a *carreta* and stepped back, his eyes fixing on the corral, searching for the *caballo* he had seen yesterday for the first time. His throat caught. There it was now, curiously watching among its fellow creatures, its wide nostrils flaring. He caught their pungent smell. He liked it.

He stared in awe, momentarily lost to his surroundings. This *caballo*'s skin was as red as the Navajo sun, and a broad streak as white as snow ran the length of the proud face. How beautiful! How swift! For he had seen the *caballos* run. His spirits lifted higher. If only he might possess such a wonderful creature, if only he dared touch one and not be eaten alive. Still, why would a being with eyes so intelligent and brave, so warm and gentle, devour a helpless Navajo boy and not the evil Hairy Ones? He yearned to know the truth.

As he stared, a Hairy One ordered the Navajos back to the tunnel. Hosteen lingered a moment longer. Instantly a whip lashed his shoulders. He turned and followed his tribesmen, conscious of an unlooked-for strength. Somehow the whip didn't hurt so much now. Had the red *caballo* — which he decided he would not think of again as an undignified dog of burden — working in its mysterious way made him braver? Perhaps he could ride the *caballo* to freedom. The moment the bold thought sprang to his mind he shrank from it, stiff with fear.

When he staggered into the sunlight again to start loading, there was a noisy commotion in the camp of the Hairy Ones, a rushing about. Looking off to the south, he saw a line of bobbing *carretas* and many four-footed creatures bearing packs, the braying ones with long ears that did not approach the beauty of the proud Mystery Dogs. Watching, Hosteen remembered. One moon ago he had seen such an arrival. Tonight, he knew, the Hairy Ones would drink much crazy water and shout and sing and fight among themselves until it was time for Grandfather the Sun to leave his robes and look upon the world.

Twice during the long afternoon Hosteen saw boys drop in their tracks and be dragged away. That evening, as he ate the watery corn gruel, which the Hairy Ones fed them like dogs, a somber realization crowded his mind. He could not endure much longer. He must try to escape. He must be brave. Better to die under the open sky, eaten by a beautiful red *caballo,* than here in the darkness of a foul cave.

Presently two guards entered to tie the slaves for the night, weaving and talking boisterously as they went from boy to boy, binding their wrists behind them and then their feet with leather thongs.

"Why tie them?" the first Hairy One asked, "when they are too weak to run away?" His laughter spilled. He gave an enormous belch and reeled against the wall.

"Because," said the other, drawing himself up stiffly, "our illustrious *commandante* so orders. It is our sacred duty to save these heathens from their savage ways."

"Their wrists are as thin as reeds."

"Tie them anyway."

"Save them, it shall be." Attempting to deliver a mocking salute, the first Hairy One lost balance and fell backward. His companion roared with laughter.

When the captor came to him, Hosteen smelled the sourness of crazy water like a further taint on the fetid air.

"Because of your heathen stubbornness

today," the guard said, "I will double-tie you tonight."

Hosteen was dismayed. He hadn't expected this.

After the guards left, taking the torches, the tunnel was still but for the coughing and an occasional low moan. Now and then, faintly, Hosteen caught shouts and snatches of song from the camp. *Tonight,* he thought. *If I do not escape tonight when the Hairy Ones are full of crazy water, I will not be alive when the supply carts come again in another moon.*

Twisting about, he felt along the wall behind him for a cutting rock. There was none. Struggling to his feet, he felt higher and to each side. There was none. Now he worked at his rawhide bonds, hoping to slip his wrists free. He could not. Instead, the rough leather seemed to bind him tighter, and in his squirming he knocked over his water gourd.

Next, he scooted forward and with hands and feet searched clumsily for a sharp rock on the tunnel floor, but it was deep in rubble and dust. He found nothing. Weakness overcame him. He lay there for a while. Worming back, he groped for his water gourd. It wasn't there. He had lost his bearings in the darkness. When morning came and he wasn't in his place, the guard would whip him again. He sagged against the wall to rest.

Something dug into his back. Something sharp.

He turned with new strength, feeling for the jagged edge of the rock, and began sawing his wrists back and forth.

A long time later his raw arms dropped free. He sank to the floor, spent. But in moments he was untying his ankles and jerking up and freeing the nearest slave.

"Listen to my words," Hosteen said, when they were all around him. "There is only the guard between us and freedom. I will take him. Then we will ride away on the *caballos.*"

"No . . . no!" He could feel their fear, their shrinking back. "The Mystery Dogs will eat us. You know what the Hairy Ones say."

"I have not seen this thing happen. Why do they not eat the Hairy Ones if they like human flesh?"

"We are afraid, Hosteen. We will walk."

"And the Hairy Ones will catch you on the *caballos.* Well, come. You will need your water gourds if you are going to walk."

As he slipped toward the mouth of the tunnel and saw the first dull glow of light, the voices of the camp sounded stronger. With the yelling and singing was a rapid, string-like music not unpleasant to his primitive ears.

He stopped. There was no one at the entrance. But he could not believe the Hairy Ones would leave the slaves unguarded. He moved to the opening, then froze at a whistling sound.

The guard lay flat on his back, snoring steadily, deeply. Crazy water smell was strong. Hosteen stiffened as the guard mumbled and stirred. Another moment and the snoring resumed, rising and falling. Hosteen relaxed.

Stepping back, he led his young tribesmen out and down the trail, past the noisy, torch-lit camp at the foot of the mountain, and onward to the clutter of *carretas* loaded the previous day. Just beyond rose the corral. From here a valley beckoned toward the north. He paused to draw in the sweet-smelling air.

"The Mystery Dogs will eat you," some-one said. "Come with us, Hosteen."

He did not quite understand himself. It was strange and compelling. He said: "I must find out about this thing. Go on."

He watched them hurry away, becoming smaller and smaller in the moonlight until their small figures dissolved. A sense of loneliness stabbed him. Would he live to see them again?

His heart leaped faster as he turned and approached the corral. The warm pungency of the *caballos* sent excitement racing through him. He had covered but a few steps when he heard snorts and a ruffle of hoofs. Although he had made no sound, the four-footed beings had discovered him. Did they fear him, a mere boy? Or were they hungry? He was both puzzled and frightened.

He had seen the low house near the corral where the Hairy Ones kept the leather things that went over the *caballos*' backs. Entering, he took one of the leather things and examined it closely. The attached straight thing, which he remembered went between the *caballos*' teeth, was as hard as rock.

Now, going outside, he called on all his courage and slipped between the bars of the gate and stood motionless. Would the *caballos* rush upon him with teeth bared?

To his relief they trotted to the far end of the corral and swung about, trampling and snorting. How beautiful under the golden light! For a moment his fear left him. One head stood out. The white-blazed face of the red *caballo.* Hosteen stared, entranced. Did he dare touch this most mysterious and powerful of all creatures? For to touch an enemy was the bravest feat of all.

He did not remember stepping forward, but he was, drifting, as silent as smoke. He was some ten steps away when they milled and trotted off. He froze. And an insight came to him: Was it his smell that made them turn away? Did they fear him? But why, when they were the powerful eaters of human flesh?

He became stone still for so long that the *caballos* seemed to lose interest in him; some strayed from the bunch. He began a slow drift again toward the blaze-faced *caballo,* pausing at longer intervals. The creature was blowing softly through its wide nostrils, watching him, more curious than afraid.

By now Hosteen was quite close. He extended his hand, although he never remembered lifting it, toward the quivering nose. He took another careful step, fascinated by the beauty he saw so near, the large eyes more luminous and soft in the moonlight. One more step and he would touch this fearsome Mystery Dog. He was trembling. He had no breath.

With a suspicious snort, the red *caballo* bolted away. And suddenly all of them were running around the corral.

Hosteen glanced in alarm toward the camp. Had the Hairy Ones heard? He listened. As the *caballos* quit circling, he picked up the unbroken strains of stringy music and the hum of voices.

Once more he stalked. Once more he stood close. Only this time, as he reached out a trembling hand, he murmured softly: "Oh, *caballo,* you are beautiful and strong. As red as Grandfather the Sun. As swift as the great wind. You are not a dog. Now I tell you this thing . . . I would rather you ate me here than die in the Hairy Ones' dark hole. If you must do this bad thing which the Hairy Ones say, do it now. I am afraid, but I am ready to die brave like a Navajo."

Little by little he stretched forth his hand. Would the dreaded moment come when he touched the nose? He felt dwarfed as he sensed the creature's enormous strength. Its pungency, strange yet warm, flowed over him, making him even weaker.

He felt the tip of his forefinger graze the nose; to his surprise it was sensitive and also warm. Now he touched the nose with his hand, while his mind spun. Why didn't the creature open its mouth and devour him? Still, he did not draw away, letting the creature breathe his Navajo smell. A shudder ran through him as he felt the lips move. But nothing happened. He felt no pain.

Emboldened, he stroked the white blaze while murmuring all the while. Breathless, he very gradually brought up the leather thing and held the straight, rock-like thing against the *caballo*'s mouth. It opened, and, when he glimpsed the great, even rows of teeth, his fear jumped again. But when he slid the straight thing against the teeth, they parted and did not bite, and quickly he drew the leather thing over the short ears as he had watched the Hairy Ones do.

He was bathed in cold sweat as he stood back, holding the reins. Would the *caballo* follow him out of the corral? Would it eat him when he attempted to ride? Or would it devour him now, when he turned his back? He did so, feeling the tingling up his spine, and pulled on the reins and marveled when the other followed him obediently. *I am not fooled,* Hosteen reminded himself. *The Mystery Dog acts friendly, but so did the evil Hairy Ones when they came to my people.*

When Hosteen let down the wooden bars to go out, it occurred to him that the Hairy Ones could not pursue his friends if the other *caballos* ran away, so he left the bars down.

At last he halted. He no longer heard the

camp or hoof sounds. He stood in a lake of moonlight. *Now,* he thought. *It will happen now.*

With dread, he drew the reins over the *caballo*'s arched neck and moved to its side. Grasping the long mane, he pulled himself to its back and waited, resigned — for the blinding crash to the earth, the thud of hoofs, the ripping of his thin flesh. He closed his eyes. He must be brave to the end.

A moment. More moments.

He opened his eyes, bewildered. It was strange, but he felt nothing. To his astonishment the *caballo* stood quietly. It seemed to wait.

Shifting about, Hosteen happened to touch his heels to the *caballo*'s flanks. And instantly he was aware of gliding movement beneath him, of being carried away as if on the wings of an eagle. A rhythmic drumming reached his ears. Faster and faster he was moving. He had the headlong sensation of the moon-drenched night rushing past. Cool wind teased his face. A sudden knowing came and deepened, absolute and true. He had found his power, and beauty as well. Above all, he was free again.

The Deadly Friends

I

It was the last year of the great slaughter when long-haired buffalo hunters swarmed the Texas plains and hide buyers hauled dried robes like hay on racked wagons and the doomed Indian saw his own destruction in the smoky sign of the Big Fifty Sharps. . . .

Here along the humping rise the wind whipped in face-burning gusts, in a violence carrying the far-off booming, and now the sick-sweet scent. Lieutenant Jonathan Emory ducked his head against it.

"That damned smell," he said.

Sergeant McQuinn's mouth cracked his sun-blackened face. "Strong enough, sir," he said patiently. "Wind's straight to us. Skinned buffalo meat don't keep long."

It was a dead, wasted smell, heavy and rank. *A stinking job,* Jonathan thought, *this herding a bunch of reservation Cheyennes on a hunt with eight bored troopers.* In five days from Fort Reno, traveling through shot-out country, they still had to see their first live buffalo. Ahead of them rode Privates Harrigan and Raidler, looking for meat.

McQuinn muttered — "Over there." — and Jonathan saw across the low-holed creek the scattered shapes of the buffalo carcasses, stiff and bloated. Sight of them nettled his nostrils, made him aware of the heat and the wind on his sensitive Eastern skin.

"Little Robe won't like this," the sergeant said in a worried tone. "Nor Howling Wolf. He's the Dog Soldier . . . the old man's nephew. Makes an Injun sore to see his commissary wiped out. It'll get worse when we meet hunters. Nothin' a buck hates worse. Way we're headed, we'll hit the Pease pretty quick, and the hide outfits'll be camped thick around the water holes. That's where the racket is."

He was a stringy, wiry man, with a burned-out expression in the squinting eyes under the sandy brows, and the sun had worked on his sharp features until he looked ten years older. There was an almost irritating unruffled competence about him, and suddenly the sourness of this ride rolled through the lieutenant.

“Sooner the buffalo’s gone the better,” he said curtly. “Can’t expect the tribes to cut out their foolishness till then. Maybe they’ll quit playing ’possum in the winter, raising hell when the grass turns green.”

There was a silence between them. McQuinn grunted and his red-rimmed eyes held a doubtful look and an old soldier’s patience, too.

Jonathan pressed his lips together, realizing how he’d sounded, an officer only two months at Fort Reno. But he had come West to fight Indians, he told himself, not nurse them like spoiled wards who kept repeating their sly horse stealing, their devilish raiding.

When the party stopped at the sluggish creek, he watched the Cheyennes water their bony ponies and pack horses. Cheyennes armed only with bows and arrows and lances and knives in strict observance of orders. A shiftless lot, he decided, fully capable of stealing your blanket from under you while you slept.

Afterward, Jonathan led them across the littered mesquite grass, into the belly-churning smell and the teeming hordes of fattening blowflies. White man and Indian reined up at the edge of the kill, showing the revulsion in their pinched-in faces, staring at the skinned mounds with the shaggy, massive heads. Within a hundred yards coyotes lazily gorged and ignored the horsemen.

"Somebody got a stand . . . look how they're bunched." It was the sergeant's matter-of-fact appraisal. But Jonathan's attention had caught on Little Robe's resentful eyes, on Howling Wolf's hard and reckless mouth. On both their leathery faces were tight shock and, Jonathan judged, a hate for all white men.

With the foulness almost choking him, Jonathan swung the gelding away and jerked his arm forward. They kept moving until the wind swept the fetid air clean. Coming out on a stretch of cedar brakes and sage, he saw the two troopers riding back. Dark blots rising and falling on the broken footing, hunched in their McClellan saddles.

Harrigan's red Irish face was slick with sweat as he rode up. "Buffalo, sir," he said, his salute ragged. "About two miles. Spooked off from the shootin' on the Pease."

He started to ride past, too hurriedly, and suspicion touched Jonathan. "You men go clear to the Pease, to the camps?"

"Buffalo's thinnin' out, sir. It was a long scout."

". . . and dry." Jonathan's voice was blunt. "Was the whiskey worth it?"

"Why, now . . . ," Harrigan began, and he rolled his bloodshot eyes. "Bein' a teetotalin' man, sir, I couldn't say. But from the looks on the faces of them that was drinkin' it, Hames still makes the same devil's belly-wash he did at Reno."

Jonathan felt the swift rush of something, a reaching back in his mind. "Y'mean Hames . . . the hunter . . . is out here?"

Harrigan nodded and slowly his round, sun-flamed faced took on a frowning look. "Somethin' else, Lieutenant. Ye've never seen a colder welcome this time of year. Tough outfit. They run off a bunch of Fort Sill Comanches two, three weeks back. Don't reckon Cheyennes'd be treated any kinder." He licked his blistered lips. "Never saw a hunter that liked Injuns around. It's hard on business."

Around them the Cheyennes restlessly swung their ponies. "One more thing, Harrigan," Jonathan said, remembering the Irishman's half-hearted salute. "We still observe military courtesies, even out here. Remember that." As the straggling detail moved out, he rode with his head slanted down, his mind running back.

There'd been no actual proof against

Hames, the shaggy hunter hired to supply meat for the garrison. Nothing except persistent reports of drunken Indians, surly and whooping among the teepees pitched on the flats, and troopers brawling in the barracks on pay day. But Jonathan knew, as the others did, and he had ordered Hames off the post with the commander's approval.

He remembered how Hames had shrugged his rocky shoulders. How his voice had jumped coarsely with wicked sarcasm. "This is big country, Gen'ral. Could be we'll meet somewhere. But next time you better have the whole damned cavalry with you!"

The threat was plain enough, but Jonathan had stored it far back in his mind as mere frontier bluster and bragging.

Looking down from the tapering slope, he could see buffalo bunched on the roughly rolling, cedar-studded land. Excitement grew in him and his eyes caught an odd change of color among the brown-black humps. He pulled his glance away as Little Robe muttered: "Wind no good."

"They can smell us," McQuinn spoke up.

Jonathan looked back and saw the animals stirring dust, lumbering off westward at a nodding gait. Too late, he knew, for the Cheyennes to ride in. He slid the Spencer repeater from the long saddle boot and dismounted. Leather squealed as the troopers got down.

"Back of the shoulder blade," McQuinn suggested in Jonathan's ear.

Belly flat, he felt the stock jump against his shoulder, smelled the acrid smoke. Carbines were cracking raggedly with his own and he saw three outside animals buckle in their short-legged trot, stagger, and go down kicking. He was lining up a hull when something crossed his vision. He pulled up, squinting. He'd heard old hunters. . . .

Little Robe's grunting voice broke in excitedly — "White buffalo!" — and suddenly Jonathan was lifting the Spencer again.

"No shoot!"

Jonathan raised up, driving his anger at the Cheyenne. "Dammit . . . you want meat to pack back!"

"Big medicine bull." The old Cheyenne's gray hair hung in skinny braids and there was alarm working in the sternly ridged face, in the seamy patchwork of sun-brought wrinkles. "No shoot . . . bad medicine. You kill white buffalo . . . all buffalo die. Maybe Indian die."

Jonathan snorted his disgust and swung

back. With a sense of lost time, he jerked up the carbine. He took a bead on the white blurred shape in the black, moving mass. He started to squeeze the trigger, hesitated, sighted again, then looked up.

A remote feeling, perhaps conscience, was breaking down his hunter's craving to shoot.

Strangely furious, he stood up, watching the buffalo running out of range. It came to him how he must look before his men, an officer swayed by an Indian's primitive superstition.

When he finally glanced around, Little Robe's black, burning eyes had a shine he'd never noticed before.

The Indian had moved in close. He stood rigid, one scrawny hand brushing the knife at his belt. The hand fell swiftly away, but Jonathan got it. In his pent-up anger, Little Robe would have struck him. Maybe knifed him.

Before Jonathan could speak, Howling Wolf sidled over. Beside the trail-worn Little Robe, he stood, tall and deep-chested, a fighting Dog Soldier with a broad, hooked nose and flaring cheek bones and a strong, wide mouth.

"Plenty buffalo now," Howling Wolf said, satisfied.

"They're headed back to the Pease," Jonathan said irritably, still watching Little Robe. And turning and staring at the three downed animals, he knew this wasn't enough. They would need many more before the hungry Cheyennes turned back, pack horses loaded with thin, sun-dried strips of meat.

McQuinn understood and summed it up concisely that night, with a veteran's thoroughness, as they chunked up the mesquite fire.

"If the wind hadn't shifted, we'd have enough meat. But it did and now the closest hunting is on the Pease. Dry as it is, you can figure a buffalo always knows where the water is. Smart hunters know that, too, and camp at the holes. The Cap Rock ain't far. I was through here in 'Seventy-One with the Sixth." The sergeant's pipe made a rasping, gurgling sound. "Old Kicking Bird made us hump our backs clear to Fort Richardson."

Stretched out, Jonathan felt the weariness sogging through to his bones. He could still feel the jolting motion of the heavy-footed gelding. He could still see the sweat and the brief flicker of resentment on Harrigan's whiskey-hungry face, the way Little Robe's hand had flicked.

Troopers' tired talk drifted with grunting Cheyenne. Half a dozen fires flared across the camp where Indians and white men had cooked their hump meat, the smoky, pleasant smell mingling with the carrying pungency of sage. A vast and lazy silence had settled down. Flat and rolling all day on the wind, the growl of the Big Fifties had raveled off with early darkness. It was a sound you got used to, Jonathan decided, and once it quit you missed it.

All at once, he pushed up. "Harrigan, how many men in Hames's camp?"

"Maybe twenty-five," a drowsy voice answered. "Rough count, sir."

Talk broke off and Jonathan, thinking of the run-off Comanches, got up and went to the picket line. In the streaky blackness, a trooper paced his rounds, and there was the pulling sound of horses cropping the short, dry grass. When the lieutenant came walking back, an Indian seemed to rise out of the ground at his boots. Jonathan froze.

"Ponies coming," he heard Little Robe's flat grunt.

"I don't hear anything."

"Me hear . . . plenty ponies." The Indian's tone was insistent, brushing defiance.

Jonathan stepped past him, feeling his annoyance. But now he heard it, the steady grumbling racket of trotting horses. It was close and he saw McQuinn rear up from his blanket. The Cheyennes were already up, sliding through the brush in the direction of their ponies. Harrigan growled: "Where'n hell's my carbine?"

From the blackness a hoarse voice shouted: "Hullo . . . the camp! We're comin' in!"

Jonathan felt his relief at the white man's voice. Brush cracked as horses moved to the sooty rim of the yellow light.

"Who's in charge here?"

Some of the lieutenant's ease left him, and he thought of the fires lighting the entire camp. "Hold up there!" he called, walking forward. A hammer snicked in the brush, the metallic click clear and sharp. From the edge of his eyes he saw McQuinn's shape.

It stirred Jonathan that he was being foolish, showing himself. Yet these were white men. He walked deliberately toward the drawn-up riders, toward the strong-chested man out front in dirty buckskins. Ten yards away Jonathan halted, with the outthrust light greasy on sweated horseflesh, on hard-angled faces, on Sharps rifles slung across saddles.

He was tight-lipped, straining to see. The big man shifted, showing the long bulge of his jaw under the flopped hat brim, the slashed cut of the bearded mouth, and Jonathan knew.

Tightness came across his chest. He kept staring at Hames. "Well," Jonathan heard himself saying, "what do you want?"

"You got Injuns here." Hames's voice rolled out in a suspicious growl. He shoved his glance at the camp and searched the long shadows.

"Under proper escort from Fort Reno," Jonathan replied with heat. Fury was wedging inside him — a blaming fury at his own wearied laxness for permitting armed hunters to ride into camp. Standing fully in the light, he saw Hames's broad head jerk in surprise. His eyes had a fixed and quickly narrowed look, a certain remembering.

"By God . . . ," Hames rumbled from deep in his throat. "Gen'ral, you picked a damn' poor place to show up."

"We came to hunt."

"Keep 'em away from the Pease."

"That's where the buffalo are."

Hames's voice bit back. "You won't hunt our country. Your Injuns'll whoop up the buffalo. Scare 'em off." He shook his shaggy head savagely. "No, by God!"

"I don't agree," Jonathan said coldly, "and I have my orders. We will hunt until the Cheyennes have enough meat to dry and pack back to Fort Reno. They will not approach your camp or make any war-like moves. I can promise that. I expect your people to do the same."

"Now don't go makin' no Army orders for me." A thin smile moved Hames's mouth. "Had my belly full of that at Reno. This was just wild Injun land when we moved in. We pulled the Kiowas' tail feathers first. We ran off the Comanches when they crowded in. We hunt where we take a notion. We camp where we please and to hell with what the Army says. . . . You take this bunch of gut-eaters and keep goin'."

Jonathan drove his voice at him. "Get out of camp!"

Deliberately Hames sat his horse, his slanted-down gaze mocking, challenging. At that moment he was a man thoroughly sure of himself. With a calculated slowness, he muttered — "Keep 'em away." — and abruptly spurred his horse around, the hunters bunching after him.

Jonathan stood quite still, feeling the hot burst of his anger. He was shaking when he heeled back and saw Little Robe, surprisingly close, step from the brush with a carbine swinging. He halted with his old warrior's eyes staring off where the beat of the hunters' horses was fading. He looked with a bright and bitter hate, and he seemed to grow taller in the half light. It was a hate pushing out into the sinewy face. It burned with a frozen intensity; it rippled in the eager way he gripped the short gun.

He turned and grunted: "We fight, huh?"

"This is no war party." Jonathan was aware of a solid weariness, disgust with Indian ways. "We're here to hunt and the Cheyennes will not go near the hunters' camp."

The hating face didn't change and Jonathan's voice lashed the troopers beginning to show themselves. "Harrigan! Get your carbine! From now on, keep it close!"

Harrigan shuffled over, his eyes sheepish. He reached for the carbine. Wistful, hungry, Little Robe handed it across. Now, Howling Wolf took a step, impatient, powerful, reckless. His knotted hands held a six-foot ash hunting lance.

"Hunters kill buffalo," he said, and jabbed the lance at the darkness. "Cheyennes fight."

Breathing hard, Jonathan tried to hold his voice level, to hide his contempt. "No fight," he snapped, and then he said the thing that loomed large in his mind. "Besides, you wouldn't stand a chance against the hunters' rifles. . . ."

He broke off, held by something. Slowly, like creeping back water, he was beginning to realize that these were proud people. Willing to fight, he knew, and willing to die. But savagely ignorant of tactics and the futility of trying to halt the crowding hunters spreading like a plague across the far reaches. His hotness rose in him, his scorn, as he swung on McQuinn.

"We'll make a meat camp tomorrow. Let 'em hunt and work off their cussedness."

II

Around noon, through the glasses, he sighted a knot of buffalo drifting lonesomely against the hot wind. In the distance wandered the Pease River, shallowed down to stagnant pools in the full summer's dryness. Finding only a bone-littered emptiness to the west, he had reluctantly turned north. All morning he had heard the booming. From up the river it grew louder, in full voice, swelling on the wind. The sound rose and fell, always to lift back in a low, muttering thunder. Scattered along the scrubby timber, he figured, lay Hames's hide quarters and, farther north, other outfits.

Caution drew on him and he told McQuinn: "This is close enough. Not many . . . four or five head . . . but enough to hunt." He squared around and flung his arm at the buffalo for Little Robe to see.

From the lip of a brushy hill, he watched the eager Cheyennes rushing across the grass-yellowed plain on their stringy ponies. Wildly Howling Wolf's whoop carried back and the buffalo spooked immediately. The Dog Soldier kneed a heavy-muscled paint pony alongside a fat, lumbering cow. His shoulders bunched powerfully, his thick arms jerked, and he thrust the cow behind the shoulder blades, in the lungs. The beast appeared unhurt and kept running. After a few short lunges, she pulled up brokenly, ponderously. Behind him the other Cheyennes were straining their bois d'arc bows, and it came to Jonathan, grudgingly, that this was sport.

His tightness was sliding away when he rode down the slope, with the troopers following. Several flattened, furred patches of buffalo, half the stampeded bunch, lay strung out on the flats. The Cheyennes had slowed down, their ponies spent and their rawhide quivers empty. Jonathan breathed easier, for he realized how deep running had been his concern to avoid a fight. The Indians had made their scant kills beyond rifle shot of the hide outfits on the river. In the first low hills behind him was the meat camp close to the gyp-water spring.

Squinting through the flickering heat

waves, he saw Little Robe check his pony. He waved once, frantically, and slowly his arm dropped. He was looking at the dark line of the river.

Suddenly Jonathan stood up in his stirrups. Far off, he noticed dust and bobbing humps and Howling Wolf closing in on the buffalo.

"The damn' fool's headed for the river," Jonathan said.

He knew he was too late as he kicked the gelding out. McQuinn's yell cut flatly behind him. As they rode, Jonathan saw smoke puff among the scrubby trees. Howling Wolf straightened. In the same motion, he seemed to grab and slide from the pony's bare back. He scattered dust as he hit, bounced, and rolled.

Little Robe got there first. When Jonathan came up and looked down, he knew the Dog Soldier was dead. The deep, naked chest was bloody and torn. At eight hundred yards, the lieutenant was thinking regretfully. He looked at Little Robe, expecting an outburst. The Cheyenne's face was like weathered sandstone, with the hate flinty and hot on the surface of the black eyes. Silently the old warrior pulled his stare from the dust-powdered shape on the thin grass and looked toward the river. It struck Jonathan that he was burning the location in his memory.

The white man's throat was dry. He felt an awkward urge to say something, although there was nothing you could put in words to a savage.

"We got a fight comin', Lieutenant," the sergeant said dryly. "We'd have it even if they weren't kin. His bein' a Cheyenne just makes it certain."

"Better take him back."

McQuinn barked and the troopers got down. They had the Indian's body face down across a saddle when the Cheyennes closed up. They took their silent, raging looks. There was a confused milling, and Jonathan's uneasiness kept pushing out. A brave with smallpox scars on his face started chanting. He swung his pony in a tight circle. It was a challenge, Jonathan realized, and his voice came sharply.

"Little Robe . . . get your men back!"

As he shouted, a shot sounded from the river. Jerking, he heard the flat thud of striking lead and the scream of the scar-faced Cheyenne's pony as it broke down. But Little Robe's howl was holding the Cheyennes.

Sergeant McQuinn's hands sawed on the reins. The question in his bloodshot eyes turned Jonathan sober. Because he hadn't known until now, as he held up, that he wasn't going with them.

"Go ahead," he said. "I'm going in to talk."

"You want the detail, sir?"

"You have your orders."

Briefly McQuinn worked it over in his calculations, chewing his parched lips, and his face told the lieutenant that he was foolish. McQuinn swung his head and pointed his horse around, plainly reluctant to go.

The coldness knotting inside him, Jonathan rode toward the river at a walk. Soon the drumming of the ponies and the troopers' horses pinched off. At once, it was all silence. It occurred to him that he was alone, perhaps very rash and lacking in field judgment. The sensible way out was to ride off with the others. He had been tempted to take the detail in with him. But he told himself this was a poor time to bring on a fight, out in the open, and McQuinn was needed to herd the disorderly Cheyennes back.

Wind whipped at him, rolling off the scorched plain, and the sun beat at the base of his raw neck. He had the surprising feeling of a growing anger, of an odd kind of recklessness. It drove him forward, hard-lipped, uncertain.

He saw the camp take cluttered shape and a coolness came on him. He raised an arm for the hunters to see. He could see the ragged cluster of tents, piles of dried black hides, fresh hides pegged out for drying, and the tracks where buyers' broad-wheeled wagons had broken down the short grass.

Men bulked in front of him, unafraid, unimpressed by an Army uniform. Harrigan's brief report was running across his mind as he stopped. He saw Hames's high-shouldered frame, the heavy Sharps easy in blunt hands. The smell of the place rose, rank and stifling. He singled Hames out with his glance.

"I want the man who killed the Cheyenne," Jonathan said.

Hard amusement crimpled Hames's mouth. "The Injun made a run at us. He was armed."

"You have remarkable vision at half a mile," Jonathan said grimly. "Howling Wolf carried only a lance. Granted that it looked like a rifle, no Indian is fool enough to jump armed hunters by himself. He was chasing buffalo. You could see that."

"White man's got a right to protect himself."

"I hold to that. Only these Cheyennes are

hunters. Without firearms. As long as they're in my command, I consider them wards of the Army. Due the Army's protection."

Hames shrugged and his voice whipped with contempt. "You ain't growed up yet, Gen'ral. Out here, the Army's say-so is just beller and bluff. You got a handful of troopers. I got a whole damned camp full of men. More out huntin'."

He flung an eager look around him and Jonathan's gaze traveled speculatively to the hunters and skinners. No ordinary hide outfit, he realized. No drought-hit Kansas settlers come south into Indian country for a quick stake, shooting and selling hides for the market, like many Jonathan had seen on his early patrols farther east. These men were close-mouthed, with a searching suspicion of all comers. Men like Hames, with something left behind them in the lawless frontier towns and on the lonesome cattle trails. He thought of his eight men, their short-ranged Spencers, and suddenly he was struggling with an inward coldness.

"I still want the man." He knew his voice sounded strained.

Hames's black glance beat out and his arrogance was a leaping, livid thing. "I'll show you what I think of the Army. I killed that Injun. Now you come an' get me!"

Jonathan's chin came up. "You don't give the Army any choice," he said, his mind slipping back to nine Spencers against twenty-odd Sharps, and the Cheyennes all but helpless and wild and completely undisciplined. "We'll be here, Gen'ral."

He tried not to show hurry as he wheeled and turned his back, the stiffness crawling along his spine and the fear like numbed fingers across his scalp. He kept going at a stiff, hard walk out of the following foulness. He kept straining for sounds, for sudden, violent movement breaking the dull blasts of hunters' guns up the Pease. He didn't look back until his horse climbed the low rise where Howling Wolf had fallen. He let his breath out. When he looked, the camp was quiet, too quiet. Later, from the hills, he saw a rider in the bright, yellow distance.

Hard-mouthed, he rode up to the seeping spring in the brushy ravine, where Cheyennes cut long mesquite sticks for drying racks. With squaws along, he thought, there would be wailing over the dead Dog Soldier on the brush scaffold beyond the camp. The proud, high-cheeked face would be painted and the dusty body wiped clean for the sweeping ride to the fat buffalo land of the Indian's dimming heaven.

"It was Hames," the lieutenant said bleakly when McQuinn faced him, raw relief on his burned features. "He admitted it, so he figures he's safe. We will have to go in and root him out. But not across the plain." His eyes swept the camp. "Best cover is down this ravine, then work up the river about dusk. There's a fairly clear field of fire approaching the camp from that end."

McQuinn's glance hung on the Cheyennes, swung back. "We'll need it," he said, and he raised a sandy brow and tilted his head at the furnace sky. "Be a nice night in Santone. The beer's cool and the women know when a soldier's lonesome."

Stiffly Jonathan sank down. His dread lay like a bitter core inside his tight belt. His muscles jerked from the letdown weariness and he felt the thick, crowding heat. His mind continued to turn on the Cheyennes, bitterly. Because of them, he had to commit the command. If not alone, still worse with Little Robe's plains rabble and their primitive weapons against forted-up hunters.

At 3:00 he pushed up and found Harrigan, sprawled in the thin shade. "Ride south a few miles," Jonathan told him. "Stay there. Come back in two hours and report directly to me."

Harrigan stared blankly, but Jonathan shook his head and walked to the spring, watching the Cheyennes cut and hang the meat strips, feeling the heat choke the dry hills.

About 5:00 Harrigan topped the rocky ridge behind the camp and jogged in. "Lonesome country, sir." He was yellow with dust, dull-eyed, and sluggish. His lips moved and Jonathan snapped — "That's all." — stepping away as McQuinn joined him.

Little Robe sat alone. In mourning, the lieutenant saw, stripped to the waist and the gray-streaked hair ragged and undone. He stood up and laid a level glance on the white men. His seamy fighter's face looked fixed, older.

"My scout reports many buffalo," Jonathan spoke fast, and he pointed south. "Take your young men and hunt. The soldiers will remain in camp until you return."

Unescorted hunting was counter to regulations and Jonathan saw that Little Robe knew it. Surprise built up in the muddy eyes, changing to bewilderment and suspicion. "Cheyennes' bellies full," he grunted.

But that wasn't the reason, Jonathan realized. It was the prospect of a revenge fight that held the Indian now, and the thought raked up a thrust of impatient anger.

"The soldiers' horses are tired," Jonathan said. "You kill more buffalo or your people are certain to go hungry this winter. Take your choice."

He had spoken the truth. Government rations of bacon and flour, sometimes rancid and wormy and seldom ample, had proved no substitute for buffalo meat. Still, Little Robe lingered.

Jonathan's voice whipped out tightly — "The scout saw the white buffalo, too." — and almost at once he saw the old Indian's face change. The reluctance was gone and a hard-bright and far-seeing look took its place. Little Robe's flat, bony chest rose and he looked briefly down the brushy ravine. With a grunt, he moved away and called to the hunters. When he held his bow and sat his bay pony, he lifted his eyes again on the ravine, on the rough ridge.

In a loose bunch, the Cheyennes straggled across the humped hill. A movement, Jonathan saw, plainly visibly from the river.

"A damned lie," he said. "But we can't chance having them around us when trouble starts."

"Never thought I'd hate to see an Injun ride off," McQuinn muttered thoughtfully.

"Cheyennes can fight when they take a notion."

"Against equally unorganized war parties . . . yes." Jonathan squinted at the sliding sun. "If we're going after Hames, we'd better start while we can see. Check the detail, Sergeant. Move out in thirty minutes."

Riding down the ravine, he could hear the men grumbling above the rubbing squeal of saddle leather. Here the heat closed in, sultry and oppressive. His breath came raggedly from his chest. Feeling ran far away from him, his mind settled on the scrub timber approaches to the hide camp. Gradually the hills began flattening out, dipping toward the river. Brush and rock shapes looked queer and dangerous under the long-slanted sun.

It happened suddenly, close ahead. Something bright flashed. Horses bulked dimly in the undergrowth. Then a gun blasted and a trooper's horse grunted and went down. The brush was churning with riders — long-haired white men. Jonathan felt the bite of their lead and bawled: "Fire!" Around him carbines rattled brokenly. He watched a hunter fall, watched Hames on a thick, black horse, weaving and turning.

Wheeling, Jonathan saw his men still in the saddle. He yelled: "On foot! Horse holders!"

He slid to the ground, with dust choking his throat. With the troopers milling and McQuinn shouting: "God dammit . . . take cover!" There was a steady booming running through the ravine, the gunshot echoes slapping.

Boldly Hames's men kept coming. Backing up, Jonathan felt the steady, forcing pressure against him. He turned and saw a trooper double up and Harrigan lumbering across and dragging the man back. Hunters, afoot now, slipped forward around the shadowed edge of the right slope. Jonathan knocked the lead man down. But he knew, darkly, they were pinching in the detail.

It started high-crying, a rushing and drumming and clattering off to his right, up high. It took a moment for him to sense the change. Dry-mouthed, he jerked and saw Indians low on their ponies' necks.

They piled down the rocky slope in a howling mass, defiant, savage. Not in an orderly skirmish line. But pressing and whooping — yet light cavalry with a battle plan. For the old Indian in front on the leaping bay pony angled off sharply, swinging against the hide crew's flank. Fire slacked on the command as bearded hunters turned. Lances and knives knocked men down.

All at once, the hunters gave way and Jonathan was shouting at the troopers. They roused up in a thin line, pushing forward, firing methodically. They were all mixed together in the thickening dust, in the smoky confusion.

Two horses sprang from the gray haze. Jonathan saw a hunter straining to break clear of the Cheyennes — caught a buckskin shape and Hames's bearded face. Jonathan was tilting his carbine, dimly aware of an Indian cutting in on his pony. The first man was close and the lieutenant heard his own bullet strike. He heard McQuinn's cracked voice calling: "Git back!"

And pivoting at the black wedge plunging toward him, he knew there wasn't time. He saw Hames swinging a pistol, saw the pony driving in from the side. As Jonathan dodged awkwardly, he saw a scrawny brown arm whipping at Hames and the knife coming down. Then the black horse's shoulder smashed him and the world went blackly spinning. He felt the shaking shock of the rocky ground across his shoulders.

It seemed a long time before he pushed up. Before his eyes focused, hazily at first, on troopers bunching the remaining hunters into a beaten, silent knot. Cheyennes drifted from the brush. Hames was a flattened-out shape and Little Robe stood over him. While Jonathan looked, the old Indian bent down. When he straightened, Jonathan saw the knife in his hand.

Harrigan and McQuinn came across, walking stiffly. "Three wounded, sir." His voice was hoarse. "Enough hide hunters left to fill the post guardhouse. Pretty fight, wasn't it, Lieutenant? Cavalry action, too." There was the ghost of a grin in his eyes as he glanced at Little Robe. "Funny, how the Cheyennes came up so fast. Just as I figured I'd never see Santone again."

Little Robe stood like brown stone. It came to Jonathan that Hames could have blamed the Indian hunting party for the wiped-out command. He faced the Cheyenne. "You didn't go on a hunt," he demanded. "You smelled a fight and you stayed close."

"No hunt," Little Robe said. But his eyes were bright, with a glimmer of defiance edging into the leathery face. Grunting, he shook his head, regretful and solemn. "Ponies tired."

"They didn't look it coming off the slope. The bite had gone from Jonathan's voice and he hesitated. "I'll remember this. Tomorrow we'll all look for buffalo. Have a big hunt."

"Sir" — Harrigan was clearing his throat — "ye won't have to go far. Plenty south of here. Includin' that medicine bull. Ye walked off before I could get it out. Didn't figure it mattered much."

Little Robe's mouth quivered, almost grinning, and Jonathan's jaw dropped. He felt himself flushing. He couldn't find the right words. But what could you say to a primitive Indian who led undisciplined plains rabble like something out of the tactics books?

Satan's Saddlemate

All that morning the feeling of waste had been growing in Owen Flewitt as they followed hard on the scuffed pony tracks. He could feel it now, welling up in protest, while he spoke the awkward words in the terrible stillness and the bareheaded troopers stared solemnly at the low-banked mound of powdery soil.

When at last he finished and stepped back, Sergeant Donahue fell in beside him. They moved without speaking past the still-smoking rubble of the cabin, only the blackened stone monument of the chimney standing in the naked clearing.

"Don't know how many times I've seen this lieutenant," Donahue said with quiet outrage when they came to the horses. "Maybe . . . if we'd got here an hour sooner. . . ." His iron voice broke off. Owen nodded and his mind ran back.

The scouting detail had found the three

shapes, pin-cushioned with arrows, at the edge of the thick brush. In open-mouthed shock. Owen looked down at the ragged, red-stiffened patches on the heads. The end had come mercifully sudden for the old man and the boy. But the sign said the gray-haired woman had fought with a desperateness, and Owen wondered how long the terror had lasted before death.

All this in one brief, frightful glance. Afterward, he had turned in his saddle and looked away, physically sick. This was his first scout and he asked himself if the stretching Texas land, so brassy with sun and cluttered with gnarled mesquite, was worth the price. Why did apparently sane men bring their families to Comanche country to live off the scorched soil?

Heat devils danced in the punishing light, causing Owen to half shutter his eyes against the savage glare. Cool, green country lay a thousand miles away at a Kentucky garrison, where a blue haze hung on shadowed evening hills.

"A foolish place to settle," he said. "Brackish water at best. Grass scarce."

"It was home, sir." The sergeant spoke politely, although disagreeing, yet holding his voice even-toned, flat. "They cleared the land and they built the cabin." He was a square frame of a man, thick through the chest, with gray eyes almost white against the rawhide face. A man hard to know turned uncompromising by years of service.

"But hardly worth the struggle."

"Guess they figgered their chances, sir."

There it was again, the stiff respect hiding the contempt. Donahue, straight-faced, rubbing in the *sir.* Resentment grew in Owen. He laid a bite into his voice: "Our orders are to patrol west to the Caprock. Tomorrow we join up with Captain Mills at Ruxton's ranch. The Comanches will be scattering now."

"Pardon, sir. But Comanches don't fight accordin' to the rules. They'll come at you when you're napping. They'll run when you think they'll fight. Nakonies did this . . . eight or ten bucks. Muguara's band."

"Muguara, the woman stealer?" Owen was reluctantly impressed. "And they didn't take the settler's wife?"

Donahue gave him the edge of his sun-flamed eyes, as if any officer should have known. "Too old, sir," he grunted, and went flat-footed toward the gathering troopers.

Owen was staring after him, his face hot, when a voice drawled in his ear: "You goin' on, Lieutenant?"

He jerked and a sour anger rolled through

him at his own jumpiness. Larabie, the civilian scout, had come up silently. It was a habit Owen could not get used to.

"Follow the tracks," he ordered. He heeled around, grumbled a command, and the detail swung to saddle.

They moved out in a spaced column of twos, flankers wide. At once the sun hammered into Owen's skin. Behind him came the mutter of dust-eating enlisted men. *They feel it, too,* he thought. *They know we're chasing red shadows again.*

At 1:00 Larabie halted. "Sign's bustin' up." He waved an arm and Owen saw the broken track pattern fanning out. He looked at Donahue.

Slack-shouldered, unconcerned, the sergeant shifted his gaze back and forth across the churned earth.

"An old trick," he decided. "They will come together soon. Ahead of us. No sense in a small party scatterin' unless it's to throw us off."

He squinted up at Larabie. The scout held the look. Owen wasn't sure how he knew, because it was gone like a grain of flying sand. But, briefly, he'd felt something behind the silence.

Then Larabie's jaws worked. "Reckon I know Injuns."

There was an outward mildness to Larabie, in the way he carefully shaped each word. A most unimpressive man and, like Owen, new to the command. His slouch hat was pulled low over high-boned, dark features. His flint-chip eyes looked at you with amusement, and the mouth was always half smiling.

"Keep moving," Owen snapped.

An hour later he led the detachment into a broken sea of rounded buttes and knuckled ridges. Far off against the brass-bright sky loomed a long-running shoulder, rocky and belted with stunted cedars.

"Caprock," said Donahue.

Dust made a grit in Owen's mouth. He sucked in the thin, dry air while the sluggish column rested. Wind blew in a hot heat and all at once he smelled wood smoke. Donahue had already caught it, stiffly erect and hand-shading his eyes. The smoke raveled up from the brush below.

Larabie shrugged it off. "Not much. Maybe a meat camp."

"Lieutenant, sir," said Donahue. "It's up to you, but the men keep remembering those people back at the cabin. And the sign seems to come together here."

Larabie had no comment and Owen worked it over in his mind. "We will feel them out," he heard himself saying, almost unwillingly. "Form fours."

They dipped down the ridge into the mesquite, into the blanketing heat and the crowding silence. Farther on, Owen's arm signal spread the detail. But he realized it was Donahue who actually pointed the command. The brush thinned and Owen saw the scattered teepees. An Indian rushed out, tall and naked. He wheeled at the hoof rumble, raised a high-pitched cry. Owen saw bucks running, and two squaws. An Indian whipped up a rifle, the shot blasting the stillness. At that the line racketed forward with carbines banging.

There was a short, close-in struggle around the teepees. Automatically Owen fired his pistol at the dusky, flitting shapes. Still, it was Donahue, swearing at the troopers, who led the dash beyond the clearing and cut off the handful of frantic Comanches from their picketed ponies. All but one warrior.

Watching Donahue jog back, Owen had the letdown uncertainty of something gone wrong, of not having really fought. True, he'd gone forward with the others. He'd fired at the dodging Comanches. But the skirmish had been completely lacking in what he'd expected out here. No bugles firing a man's blood. No beautifully precisioned charge against feathered horsemen on a rolling green battleground. He looked at the sprawled bronzed bodies on the littered camping ground. The sight brought him up roughly, with a certain harsh understanding. This was grim, eye-for-an-eye fighting. These were tough, sinewy foes, unforgiving and hard-dying. Nearby huddled both squaws, wailing now. Already troopers had set fire to the hide lodges.

Then he saw the girl walking from the thicket. She stood rock-still when a startled cavalryman swung on her with his carbine, and suddenly lowered it. Before Owen could ride across, Donahue was pivoting his horse.

The sergeant's mouth gaped down. "God, lieutenant! A white woman!"

Yellow hair, Owen saw, and blue eyes. She seemed held by a kind of numb disbelief. She drew her glance across him, looking beyond him in alarm. And suddenly she ran forward, ducked inside a smoking teepee. In a moment, she came out holding a wadded bundle of red calico. As she passed the squaws, the youngest lifted a scolding voice.

With a swinging defiance the girl faced her. They stood like that, tense and glaring, until the girl turned and walked deliberately to the horse holders. Owen followed and got down.

Shock ran over him. Up close, she was thinner than he'd first thought. The hair ragged, although surprisingly clean, and she was still a pretty girl. She had a full-bodied slimness even in the loose-hanging buckskin dress. But those terrible scars on her arms — fire scars, he guessed. In her face was the patience of something buried in her eyes.

"Lieutenant Hewitt . . . ," he began, and stopped. And before he realized it, he had swept off his hat. An uncalled-for gesture in this smoke drifting from burning lodges and the wind beginning to whip the sand across the clearing. "We'll be at Ruxton's ranch tomorrow. An escort will take you to Fort Belknap."

Her lips barely moved, silently thanking him. Her mouth trembled and he thought she was going to cry. Then her eyes went fixedly to the hat in his hand, as if she were seeing a courtesy almost forgotten.

"I can make out now," she said, her chin coming up. Her hands, capable and work-worn, held on to the pitiful dress.

He was turning away when it occurred to him that he hadn't asked her name. But he saw that she knew, and she said: "Emily . . . Emily Harris."

"If there's anything you want?"

She shook her head. Sergeant Donahue came tramping up. He gave her a brief, wondering appraisal, spoke with his cracked voice: "We've burned the heathens' houses, Lieutenant. What about the squaws?"

"Let them go."

Donahue didn't answer for a moment. Finally he grumbled — "Yes, sir." — his eyes telling Owen he was wrong and the resentful doggedness inside Owen said — "Damn you . . . follow orders." — and he spiked his glance back at Donahue.

"How far to Wagon Creek?"

" 'Bout three hours, sir."

"We will bivouac there."

Climbing the long slope, Owen looked back over his shoulder at the slim-legged Harris girl on a bareback Indian pony. Her yellow hair made a bright smear of color against troopers' blue shirts. A sudden drumming along the ground pulled him around. Suspicious, he watched the brush for movement.

Larabie's soft laugh rubbed at him.

"What's that?" Too late, Owen sensed it was a question only a green officer would ask.

"Why, blue quail."

Even Donahue smiled, although there was seldom any laughter in him, and Owen knew his own face was flushing. Amused, the scout threw up his head, gave a clear calling whistle. From deep in the underbrush, there came a sharp, answering blast. Moving on with the file, Owen caught a trooper's dry chuckle, quickly suppressed when the sergeant shouldered around.

Sunlight bit into the lieutenant's skin. The water in his canteen tasted hot, flat, and there was no end to the vague, shimmering distance. Nothing moved beyond the column in this furnace-fired country. He could feel his physical torture, the sapping soreness all through him. Donahue, always restless, kept shifting his gaze from the flinty earth to the mottled buttes.

"Sir," he said with a hint of apology. "The buck that got away was Muguara."

"What's one Indian?" Remembering the naked, tawny shape, Owen felt an indifferent concern. When the fight turned bad at once, the Comanche had to run to a pony. He'd raced off through the brush, weaving from side to side, while the carbines boomed futilely after him.

"Muguara's no ordinary Comanche. And remember when the white girl ran to the teepee? Well, Muguara came out of it when we charged the camp. You saw him. We all did." Donahue drew in a draught of dusty air and his voice sounded squeamish: "Sir, the white girl belonged to him."

Suddenly the impropriety of it roused Owen. "I hardly see. . . ."

The voice cut in, insisting. "Plenty reasons why Comanches take women an' kids. It's the damned ransom money for one thing. Settlers don't have much, but they can beat a Mexican family's ante. Another idea is to keep the warriors' ranks filled." He swallowed hard. "Hear that young squaw howl at her?"

"There seemed to be some argument over the dress."

"Just part of it. The squaw was jealous. Now, we've killed six Nakonies and we took Muguara's captive woman. He'll come after us with every buck he can muster."

Larabie had reined his gelding in closer. "I wouldn't count on that," he said mildly. "Muguara got his tail feathers pulled."

The light in Donahue's alert eyes was almost scornful. "You know Comanches better'n that."

"I don't claim to read an Injun's mind." Larabie shrugged his bony shoulders. "Least of all, Muguara." He put his horse to a trot and rode ahead.

They were moving at a walk with the sliding sun punishing their backs. Owen coughed against the thin alkali dust. It rolled in fine, kicked-up puffs, powdering his jacket, grinding into his nettled face. The sergeant hitched around, his jaws working.

"Whole country's squirmin' with sign. I don't like it."

Owen faced him impatiently, feeling his annoyance. "You insist on smelling a fight."

"Fresh tracks, sir, and this is a bad place to get caught."

"I have no intention of risking sixteen men beyond patrol duties," the lieutenant said, snapping the words and jogging his head at the dreary monotony around him. "Not for this. I'm inclined to believe that Larabie's right. Muguara was badly whipped. He can't mount another war party soon."

"Could be, sir." The square, solid man spat deliberately into the wind. "But first thing a dead warrior's relatives do is plan a revenge raid. And they get help all along. Comancheros and white outlaws worse than any Comanche. What kills Army men in this country is goin' by the book. Never the way it looks. It's always worse."

Sundown was a settler's flaming cabin flaring across the low horizon, and the wind murmured a dreaded whisper through the scattering brush. Beginning dusk lay like thin smoke on the up-and-down land as Owen led the dog-tired command to Wagon Creek for gyp water and a cold supper.

"Double pickets," he ordered.

Purple haze hung in the draws when he saw the Harris girl take up the calico bundle and go down the creek. She looked over her shoulder once before disappearing around a twist of the streambed. After a while she came back, a slim, soft blur moving in the long shadows. Now he noticed she wore the dress. For no accountable reason, unless she reminded him of something lost and distant, he found himself wondering how she would look in flowing taffeta at the fort officer's ball. It was, he decided, an absurd thought.

Stiff-legged, he walked to the edge of the camp before turning in. Pickets made vague shapes in the gloom. Horse smell flowed rankly on the faintly cooling wind. Donahue growled at a trooper, the solid rasp of the non-com's voice.

"Lieutenant."

Owen saw her outlined in the sooty half light. The feeling ran through him that she was lonesome. That she'd been watching him.

"Better not go far," he said. "Donahue

says Comanches like to crawl in close to a camp."

She stepped forward, a composed girl whose walk was light and quick. He could smell the clean dampness of her hair, and he guessed she'd washed it at the creek.

"A pretty night," she said. At that moment, as she looked up at the pale sky, she seemed completely absorbed, listening, breathing hard, feeling. He'd scarcely heard her voice, so lost in her throat, wondering and unafraid.

"You have folks?"

"Gone now. We had a place on the Brazos. The Comanches came . . . that was three months ago." She shivered and her shoulders rose and fell with a resignation that called up his instant regret at having asked her.

"You've had a rough time."

She did not answer and he stood with his head bent, his mind considering what she'd left unsaid. She couldn't be more than eighteen, he judged, but she was fully a woman with a hungry desire in her to live. Thin, big-eyed, and quiet, she'd survived as best she could on the outer edge of the frontier, where Stone Age savagery and the pushing white man clashed and the weak died without sympathy and the strong lived on without looking back.

And now she spoke without apology for whatever had been, with an inner, hard-wrung patience. "I lived like a squaw."

"No." He felt himself protesting. "I didn't ask that."

Deep-breathing, she went on in her direct way. "I lived in Muguara's teepee."

In desperateness, he tried to stop her, aware of his own shame for her. "We meet the other patrol tomorrow." He kept his voice stiffly matter-of-fact. "Of course, you won't stay on the frontier. No place for a woman."

"But I will."

He almost gasped, for there'd been no doubt in his mind. "You mean you'll go back to the Brazos?"

"I have land and there's cattle."

He took a step and realized that he stood very close, all the while still feeling the rapid run of his amazement.

"Have you ever seen Texas in the spring?" He was hearing a music singing in her, a swift rush of feeling long stored-up and held back during the hard-driven days in the camp. "After a rain when the flowers come up? They're everywhere then . . . so yellow and blue and violet."

Hardly knowing he did it, he took her

hand and he could sense the hidden life and the loneliness in her crying out as if she must be close to somebody. He stood quite still, hearing in tiny detail every sound in the tired camp, until she stepped away from him.

"I think," Owen said, "we'd better get back."

They walked in silence, around them the muttering undertone of men's drowsy voices. Soberly Owen watched her go to the shadows and sink down, apart from the others. He went, slow-footed, to his blankets, suddenly conscious of a complete isolation. It hit him, remembering how she'd talked, that she thought like Donahue about this bleak world, and he knew that he could never see it as others gloried in it. The thought drove a suspicion at him, square on. Had he gone soft? An Eastern garrison officer fit only for the parade ground?

It seemed only minutes until Donahue's rough voice was shattering the early morning stillness. Stiff to the bone, Owen pushed up and stamped the soreness from his legs. While the men formed in the gray light, grumbling as they slapped on saddle gear, Donahue tramped up and saluted.

"We can make Ruxton's by noon, sir."

Donahue's face was like so much brown-weathered stone, the barest flicker of contempt edging in and lowering away in an instant. Annoyance climbed in Owen, and afterward a riding depression, still heavy and close to brooding when he called a halt deep in the morning at the scum-covered water hole. Letting the reins go loose, he slouched in the saddle while the gelding drank. A horse pressed in and he saw the Harris girl. She was looking beyond the column, her face deepening with pleasure like something familiar drawing closer. He followed her eyes and saw the monotonous, heat-hammered emptiness, a land passed over by fire.

"That," he said critically, "is what we're fighting for."

Her gaze remained fixed on the bronzed distances for a moment. It was, he thought, as though she hadn't heard. But when she looked at him from the corner of her eye, the far-away look had gone. "I know," she said in a considering tone. "My father thought so at first." A tiny signal flame began to build up in the wide eyes. "But he stayed. He didn't run."

The pony raised his dripping muzzle. Her eyes were quick-bright. Then she jerked the reins, came erect, and rode off without looking at Owen and he had the bitter knowledge that she'd neatly put him in his place.

Across from him Donahue had dismounted, bowed over the scuffed ground in frowning concentration. He straightened up, muttered — "A war party watered here early this morning." — and climbed back to the saddle.

The morning wore itself out, dismal, sun-scorched. Owen slanted the detail down into a shallow valley flanked by wooded, mesquite-grassed hills. The sergeant took his careful, traveling look and pointed.

"Ruxton's straight ahead, sir." Correct enough, the voice, although Owen couldn't miss the meaning in the outflung gesture. *There it is. What you've been wanting. You're a soft young fool and I've brought you here.*

"Your timing is excellent, Donahue. It's high noon." Fighting back his rising resentment, he couldn't help adding sarcastically: "I hope Captain Mills is fortunate enough, like me, to have a sergeant who knows the land so well."

Donahue's head swung around, whipped back straight. An eagerness seemed to catch along the line behind Owen. Troopers spoke up, their voices far-carrying in the quietness. Irritation came up in Owen as he saw Donahue, always the old kill-joy watchdog, glare at the file and quickly silence it.

The ranch house made a solitary square of hewn logs and jutting rock chimney off from the tangle of pole corrals and outer sheds. Beyond the clearing, Owen saw the notched gap.

Donahue was shifting and squinting and slowing his horse to a walk. The washed-out eyes touched the ranch layout, roved to the thick, stubby timber cover.

"Quiet," he said. "Too damn' quiet."

Owen knew something was wrong when he checked his horse in front of the silent house. Corrals stood empty, the bars down. Nothing moved and there was a blanketing stillness everywhere. It was a silence crowding on silence. It produced a peculiar kicking sensation in Owen's stomach. He noticed the absence of the wind, so constant and strongly unvarying all morning on the higher reaches.

He looked at the house with a dread. "Better take a look," he said, hollow-voiced. He dismounted and drew his pistol, his boots scuffing the hard-packed yard. Donahue swung down at once.

The two of them stepped inside, into a room of wildest disorder. Owen saw the rough furniture overturned and smashed, broken dishes littering the dirt floor. He smelled the lingering acrid stench of powder smoke, the faint musk smell of unwashed bodies. Wind sogged from his lungs, and suddenly he stood stonestill, not wanting to go farther.

"Over there," Donahue murmured. Owen dropped his gaze and saw the booted foot projecting crookedly from the room. Caution took hold of him, his chest heaving and falling. He forced himself to take a step, and then he saw the dead man.

"Cal Ruxton," the sergeant breathed. He clumped to the kitchen. When he came back, his eyes had a furious look, cold and grim and somehow old.

Owen took his look, turned his head, and went outside, aware of a hanging stillness. "They didn't burn the cabin," he was saying, faintly surprised.

"They don't always, sir. This is fresh. Maybe an hour."

"Mills? He should be here, waiting."

Donahue nodded, and, watching him, Owen knew what was passing in his mind. This was no book maneuver. You didn't fight Indians by the clock.

"The captain," said Donahue, looking at the gap, "has run into something or he'd be here."

Owen was mounting when somebody

called: "There's dust, Sarge!" Owen whipped around, thinking of Mills. He saw horsemen fanning from the timber up the valley, sun shining on greasy bodies. They rode forward and now he saw Comanches in bold mass filing along the trail.

Something lashed at his insides and it came to him that the detail, small against the gathering horsemen, was dangerously exposed in the clearing. Decision pressed at him, insistent, demanding. He flung a backward glance across the clearing and saw the dark line of the woods and swung his arm. He heard his voice, choked in his throat, give the command: "Fall back!"

Wheeling his horse among the trees, he caught in one swinging motion the set solemnness of the Harris girl's uplifted face. It was lost in the confusion of jostling animals and clanking equipment and grunting men. The Comanches had heel-jabbed their wiry ponies into a drumming run, the racket rolling. A rushing tide of brown, lean bodies bent low, whooping and shrilling. Owen thought they would keep coming. As suddenly they pulled up beyond carbine range.

He had his quick hope then, an elation that Donahue smothered. "Not yet, but they will. A Comanche's got to rooster around, have his fun."

An Indian rode out on a racy-looking, paint-daubed white pony. The rider cut a lazy, taunting circle and waved his arm contemptuously. Hooting, challenging cries came from the mounted ranks.

"Muguara." Donahue scrubbed a dirty hand across his mouth. "He's invitin' us to join the party. Says we're afraid to fight. That we're a bunch of women."

"We got the cañon behind us." It was Larabie's appraising voice, up close, the words sinking in. "We can run for it."

The thought spun in Owen's mind. Let them have this god-lost land. Common sense to avoid a fight, he told himself, when you were outnumbered. He reined around and drove his voice at Larabie. "Come on. I want a look first." Crisply he told Donahue: "I'll wave you in. Withdraw by fours."

The gray eyes had sprung wide. Donahue started to speak, appeared to think better of it. With an effort he held his mouth firm, very correct. "Pardon, sir. We're in good position here. They'll have to come across that clearing."

Owen stared him down. "I believe I'm in command here."

That was all. Yet riding through the short-shadowed post oaks, Owen wished that the sergeant had come. It rankled his pride to know how much he'd grown to depend on the older man's judgment. Through a break in the timber, he saw a wagon road.

Larabie checked up and said: "She's wide open, Lieutenant."

There was a stillness here, a mystery. It bit into a man and made him jumpy and caused his eyes to search the shadows with distrust. Daylight slanted down, casting cobwebbed patches of silver. Owen found himself straining for sound.

"Not much time." Larabie's tone gave out a pushing impatience. "Better git out of here."

Owen kept watching the wooded cañon road, crowded with close-growing brush and the black, silent timber. Over the ridge lay safety of a sort. At least a chance.

"Hurry, Lieutenant." The scout's eyes were on Owen, bright as an animal's.

Owen started to lift his arm. And yet, at that final moment, it all seemed too easy. He was seeing Donahue's dissenting face and an inner voice was telling him that you couldn't avoid trouble by riding away. Still, he hesitated and angled a glance behind him. The troopers seemed a long way off. He was twisting around, the reluctance dragging in him, when he heard the clear, sharp quail whistle.

Larabie was half pulled away, facing the road. His jaws barely moved, stopped working. Something slammed into Owen, something acutely warning. Then Larabie was swinging his carbine, even as Owen's hand went to his holster. Unthinking, Owen jerked the pistol and wheeled the gelding with a frantic awareness of being late. Larabie's face loomed cold and dark and sardonic.

The shots sounded almost together. Owen heard Larabie's bullet strike first, but he didn't feel it. His horse grunted and shuddered. He smelled the blooming cloud of dirty-gray powder smoke. Larabie lurched and made a choking sound and fell from the saddle. Owen's horse was wobbling strangely, floundering under his knees. He felt himself falling as the animal broke down, saw the blurred earth pitching up at him.

He hit and rolled, still clinging to the pistol. He heaved for knocked-out wind and pushed up and looked at Larabie, feeling a sickness and an odd trace of wonder. He saw Comanches swarming out of the timber and down the wagon road, and he knew dismally that he'd played it all wrong as the little pieces suddenly fell into place in his mind. Larabie always half smiling, silently amused. Larabie missing the tracks at the Indian camp. Now the sly call springing the ambush.

He seemed caught in a shrieking world of brittle, hating whoops, of naked warriors violently dashing their scrubby ponies forward. He raised his pistol and fired. His bullet knocked an Indian loose from his pony. The others rode on, screaming defiance, and he knew they would ride him down. Carbines clattered brokenly behind him. At the same moment, two ponies ran riderless. The war party sheered off. Running back, Owen thought he heard a far-off firing.

Then he was among the kneeling troopers. He heard Donahue's bull-roaring voice overriding other sounds. "Stay down! Stay down!" He stood, spraddle-legged, by a dead horse. The Harris girl was crouched nearby, her face tight, strained.

Comanches raced bright-colored ponies across the clearing, swinging to the offside and firing as they flashed past. Dust boiled up and bullets sang through the trees. Owen felt a steady dribble of small branches on his hat. He fired at the flitting shapes, and there seemed no end to them. Faintly in his ears, like some growling voice struggling to be heard, distant gunfire swelled louder. He saw Commanches, beaten off in their first rush from the timber, piling in thicker than he'd ever thought possible.

Pressure built up from both sides as the Comanches in front slashed at the command. Owen drove his shots at them, seeing them wheel and charge in bunches. One knot rode savagely against a clump of troopers. Owen was in motion before he realized it, with Donahue lumbering beside him. At once they were caught in the confused core of a swaying fight. Together they met the pivoting point of the weaving, shouting warriors. Donahue's carbine was blasting methodically at the milling mass. Owen ducked and fired at an Indian slashing at him from a white horse. He saw the bronzed body reel and spin down, and felt rather than saw a hesitation among the remaining Comanches. There was an abrupt turning away, and then they were sliding off. Donahue stood rooted with boots planted like stanchions, a blunt trunk of a man whose hairy hands still worked the saddle gun.

"Damn you . . . get down!" Owen yelled. The sergeant's jaws sprang open, as if he hadn't been shouted at like that in years.

Almost defiantly he roared — "Dead looies don't help!" — and wheeled back into the smoke. Owen straightened, listening to the growling voice again from the ridge road. It had the ripping violence of measured carbine fire, abruptly close. He jerked and looked at the wagon trail. A Comanche galloped down it and whooped at the warriors in the timber. They started breaking up, fading slowly, die-hard fighters stubbornly, reluctantly giving ground. There was a slackening in front now, an uneasy lull as the shooting pinched off.

It took a while for Owen to get it. The Comanches were drawing back, pulling out. He was soaked in his sweat. He took a step and stumbled, the rampant after-drag of this day whipping at him. In a kind of haze, he saw the head of a troop coming down the cañon. Their carbines sought the war party's remnants, pinching them in. The gunfire dropped off, save for stray shots, and Owen saw Captain Mills spur his horse toward the dismounted detail. The captain paused at the road's edge, looked down curiously at Larabie's shape, and rode on.

Mills reined up, blew out his breath, and drooped himself over the saddle with a groan. He was a heavy-set man sapped by hard riding, his long, sun-punished face powdered with dust. He shook hands with Owen and tilted his head.

"Larabie?" he said, a question in his bloodshot eyes. "You get caught in the open?"

Owen dug his glance at Donahue, looked at Mills but didn't speak.

"Almost, sir," Donahue spoke up politely, and Owen thought: *Go on . . . tell him Larabie made me look like a fool.* "He tried to lead us into an ambush, Captain," the sergeant was saying. "But the lieutenant smelled him out."

"Ah," Mills said wearily, as if nothing further could surprise him. "Never know about a new man till you get him in a fight."

"It's a long story." Owen said. "He wanted the detail to take the cañon road. I rode out with him to look it over."

"Good thing you didn't go on." Tiredly Mills raised a silencing hand. "Not now, Lieutenant. You can put the details in your report." Mills's eyes searched the timber, where the thrusting Comanche charge had lapped highest and rolled back furiously.

Donahue pointed. "Muguara, sir. He's down over there."

Owen was looking around him, suddenly remembering the Harris girl and striding off. He didn't hear Sergeant Donahue's low-toned remark to the captain: "We got us a fightin' lieutenant, sir. A bit reckless with his own person, but he'll do."

Mills was grinning in spite of himself. He was too bone-weary to say anything then, for it had been a shrew of a day.

Owen saw her facing him, and he knew without knowing why that she had been watching him. He went over to her.

"Your home," he said with a trace of worry, "is it far from the post?"

"Half a day's ride."

"I was thinking," he said, feeling a vast awkwardness, a vast impatience, "there'll be times when a patrol will be going that way."

Her eyes, so wide and solemn in the thin, high-cheeked face, changed swiftly. They searched his face and he saw the soft gravity of her features lighten. She was faintly smiling when she spoke: "It is a rough country."

"Why," he said, "I guess a man can get used to it."

HOSTAGE TRAIL

Off northwest, dust scuffed low on the brown mesquite-dotted prairie. It kept growing rapidly and Captain Peter Hambrick Cornett, 6th Cavalry, watched with the bleak attention of one who had learned to expect the worst in this unpredictable land.

Sergeant Barney Rudd, his square, homely face apologetic, was saying: "About the quartermaster stuff we're totin', sir. Corporal Jensen says the uniforms were loaded on at the last minute."

"Uniforms?" Cornett, only mildly interested, still eyed the dust.

"Yes, sir. Seems Fort Richardson needed tin washtubs for officers' quarters. But Fort Sill got Richardson's tubs and Richardson got Sill's new C Troop blues. Now we're packin' the whole caboodle back so the C boys won't run around in their shirt tails."

"I see."

The distant amber cloud materialized into horsemen. Cornett narrowed his gaze, squinting, and afterward felt relieved when he recognized white men. Then he grew taut again as he saw sunlight glint on rifle barrels.

"Jensen says. . . ."

"Never mind," Cornett said wearily.

"One more thing, sir," Rudd went on, hurrying. "It's old Eagle Heart. He's got another message for you. Claims he's put the war trail behind forever. From now on he follows the White Father's road. He admits he don't exactly love the white man, but he will shake his hand. He's put away his lance and bow. He's gonna quit stealin' Texas horses. His heart is good. . . ."

"What does he want?" Cornett cut in, remembering that yesterday the Comanche had complained of moldy bacon rations.

"I was comin' to that, sir. Been around Injuns so long, reckon I talk the same way . . . in circles." Rudd pursed his cracked lips a moment. "Well, it seems as how he wants you to make him a scout."

"Anything to get out of farming, I guess." The knot of riders veered sharply, setting a course that soon would cut across the line of march, and Cornett added, almost as an afterthought: "Well, tell him he'll have to take that up with the agent at Fort Sill."

Cornett hitched about, throwing the column a stiff size-up. His Conestoga wagons were creaking toward Red River in single file, twenty yards apart, ready to be corralled on short notice. His hostage Quahada Comanches — disconsolate bucks, squaws, and children — rode skinny ponies and jammed the wagons. Cornett's handful of troopers hung on the flanks, sun-blistered faces canted down.

Ten men made a mighty thin escort through country often traveled by Comanche and Kiowa war parties helling out of the Nations, and Cornett would have questioned the prudence of his mission except that Major Braxton's two troops, on scouts, were to join up. Yet that could mean anywhere within fifty miles, Cornett realized, depending on Braxton's whims.

With a scowl for the heat-hammered space around him, he halted the column. Captain Cornett was fifty-eight years old, two inches over six feet, and he rode with a straight-backed erectness. Almost ten years ago, in the Civil War, he had been a brevet colonel, serving well but without fame. Long ago he had understood that his career would be marked by steady application to duty rather than the flamboyant dash that shot some officers to the top. Men like Braxton, who fancied buckskin jackets and bright bandannas and frequently wrote of his own exploits for the Eastern press. So Cornett had patiently accepted his routine lot, a lean, gray-mustached man who took such dirty details as this without complaint — and who still longed for the green Ohio hills of his boyhood.

Now the riders came on in a fashion that warned him. They reined up several rods away, rifles across pommels. Dust settled. Then Cornett, walking his mount toward them, noticed some sat their horses awkwardly, like galled townsmen. Ranch hands filled out the bunch.

One man, tall and thick through the shoulders, came forward. Under his dust-covered hat, bright zealot's eyes peered out over a thicket of brown beard. His uncompromising glance ran over the column.

"Who's in charge here?"

Cornett flushed beneath his heavy tan, but answered evenly enough. "I am. Captain Cornett. Sixth Cavalry."

"My name's Damron," he said, as if Cornett should know. "Where you headed?"

"Up from Fort Richardson to Fort Sill."

Damron's direct eyes locked again on the wagons. He squared one big-knuckled hand on his hip, and Cornett had a premonition of what was coming. "Reckon you ain't heard, Cap'n. Heathen Comanches raided around Lost Spring day before yesterday. They stole plenty horses . . . shot up some folks. Feeling's runnin' high."

Cornett winced visibly. "I regret to hear that, Mister Damron."

"I see you got some heathens along."

"These people weren't involved in your raid," the captain said distinctly. "They're hostages, captured some months ago on McClellan Creek."

"Comanches, just the same. Heathens."

Cornett's mouth thinned. "As I told you. . . ."

"Maybe you don't get it," Damron interrupted, his voice brittle. "We're plumb wore out with Injun raids. We aim to stop 'em. And the Army's no help . . . never around when there's trouble."

"This is a vast country to patrol, Mister Damron."

"Makes no difference." Damron cocked his head, indicating the horsemen. "Citizens been forced to do their own fightin'. Townfolks . . . farmers . . . cowmen. A heap more where they come from. We're organized. We can throw a hundred mounted men in the field. And we got ourselves a law for heathen

Comanches and Kioways . . . we shoot on sight. Now you understand plain English? Or don't damyankees get nothin' straight?"

There was a thick silence, then Cornett answered very quietly: "I trust you understand my position as I do yours. I have my orders. Of course, we have no intention of stopping in the vicinity of Lost Spring and stirring up the citizens. We'll push right through. . . ."

"No, Cap'n," snapped Damron with an old bitterness. "You don't go through here."

Cornett became aware that he was biting his mustache. As he considered Damron's inflexible face, a cold anger grew in him. Yet, even now, he could understand why these people ached to fight. He was conscious of detailed sounds. The creak of saddle leather as a man shifted nervously, a horse's snuffle. Somebody coughed.

It was then that he discovered Rudd in the edge of his vision. He didn't recall seeing the sergeant ease up, but he had. He loomed two paces back to Cornett's right, steady as stone.

"We might detour," Cornett heard himself replying, striving for reason. "But the country's too rough east of here. West, it's dry as bone."

"You don't go no place, looks to me. Unless. . . ." Damron let his meaning dangle.

Cornett's chin tilted. "Unless what, Mister Damron?"

"Just this. I'm a reasonable man. Hand over your Comanche bucks and we let you take the rest on."

A disgust filled Cornett. "If I don't?"

"We take 'em anyway. That's how it is. The way of the ungodly shall perish. I told you we're wore out."

"You'd attack United States cavalry?"

"Don't want to unless you force us. But I never expected to see the day when cavalry protected scurvy savages." Damron's burning eyes roved to the wagon train. "You look pretty scant to me. Don't reckon you could hold us off long."

"That," said Cornett, rising in his stirrups, "is an outcome you'd better not count on."

Damron leaned forward expectantly. "So you'll come ahead? Risk it?"

The riders stirred. One seemed to detach himself unwillingly. He bumped as he jogged. He was a slightly built man dressed in a baggy black suit, now gray with dust. His pointed, sun-reddened face showed the havoc of unaccustomed riding, and the heavy rifle looked cumbersome in his pale storekeeper's hands.

"Now wait a minute," he began, giving

them both his uncertain stare. "Damron, let's not rush into anything."

Damron tossed him his acrid scorn. "Volunteered to fight, didn't you, Appleby?"

"I suggest we give him time to consider."

"Time! We've palavered too long now."

"Give him till morning," Appleby insisted. "If he doesn't surrender the bucks by then, I give my solemn word the town boys will help you take them."

Damron seemed to weigh it this way and that. At last he said grudgingly, facing Cornett: "Like I said, I'm a reasonable man. Mornin' it is. And you'll see. We want them bucks. We aim to hang every man." With that, he broke his horse away.

Erect, Captain Cornett watched them go. Some distance on, where the land rose to low, broken buttes, he saw several riders drop out. By that he knew Damron was taking no chances of permitting the column to evade him. Cornett thought of dispatching a messenger to Fort Richardson, but decided the distance was too great. He thought of Major Braxton off after Indians he'd likely never encounter and realized he could never locate Braxton's command in time.

A surge of futile anger had its way in him. He allowed it to flare, and then said — "Corral for camp, Sergeant." — and rode thoughtfully back.

Sundown clothed the land in bold, crimson strokes. Purple shadows splashed the distant buttes where Damron's men watched. A breeze stirred, faintly cooling this parched emptiness. Twilight settled down. Around the mess fires, burning as yellow spires, the Comanches nursed their silent hatred of the white man. Horses stamped. Troopers grumbled, the men making blurred shapes in the dusk.

Captain Cornett, outside his tent, caught all these sights and murmurs and found them familiar, fitting a pattern he'd long lived by. When an orderly brought hardtack, bacon, and coffee, he went inside and took his lonely supper under the sallow glow of candlelight. Afterward, he stretched his stiff legs, feeling looseness come to his muscles. It was good not to move. Still in his camp chair, he lighted his stubby pipe and thoughtfully considered the course before him.

It had not changed, he knew. Once again appraising Damron's threat, he figured the man would attack. It was eye for an eye with Damron, the way of the frontier, no matter the guilt where Comanches were concerned. Thus, Cornett could either run or advance. Either way he risked trouble.

Of a sudden he felt all the swarming pressure come solidly against him. For a while he bent to it. Then he straightened and a doggedness took hold. He had another pipe and thought of his wife, waiting for him at Fort Sill, of his one soldier son somewhere in the barren Dakotas. At that, he got up and fumbled in his gear for a map.

He was going over it when Sergeant Rudd entered for evening orders and saluted.

"You know this country, Sergeant?"

"Pretty well, sir."

"Good. We're going to use our imaginations a bit. We can't bull our way out. Not strong enough for that. Besides, I want to avoid a fight."

Rudd's shaggy eyebrows shot up. "We're not turning tail?"

"Not exactly. Now listen. I want these mess fires kept low and steady tonight. Not too high, mind you. Just enough so a man can see from the buttes." Cornett checked himself with a pull at his mustache. "It will be dirty work, but grease every damned wagon axle. Also, I want blankets covering all wheel rims."

Rudd's gray eyes, almost white against his weathered skin, blinked rapidly. The captain found himself studying the man closely, with an unspoken liking. Rudd, who would finish his Army days no higher than he now stood, was the kind of non-com who put backbone into a command. He knew Indians; he knew all the dodges of flagging troopers.

Movement at the tent door drew Cornett's eyes away. Rudd wheeled, then gave the captain an uncomfortable, wearying look. "It's Eagle Heart, sir. Guess he wants something."

Annoyance touched Cornett, but he said patiently: "Tell him to step in."

Rudd muttered and old Eagle Heart came noiselessly into the orange light. He was short and scrawny and naked from the waist up, with long, uncut hair and eyes that resembled polished beads embedded in the broad copper face. He showed a wrinkled, puckered expression, not unlike that of a recruit who had just downed a bitter dose of quinine.

He grunted, blending Comanche and Spanish, now and then thumping his chest. Cornett sensed an unmistakable defiance as the Comanche ceased speaking and stood back.

Rudd's face was very straight. "Eagle Heart thinks we don't savvy this scout business. Says maybe we figure he's afraid like a woman. He says if we'll mount him up like a pony soldier, he'll fight all the *Tejanos* tomorrow by himself. Out there on the prairie."

Cornett stared, controlling his own smile, his face fixed, inscrutable. He had learned one important rule in dealing with Indians: never step on their dignity. "Explain," he said quietly, "that we know he's a mighty warrior. Therefore, it isn't necessary for him to prove how strong his heart is. Secondly, the pony soldiers are not at war with the *Tejanos.* Thank him for offering his services."

It was something to watch Rudd. He began speaking slowly and gesturing, his square hands surprisingly graceful and sure. He pointed at Eagle Heart and made the sign for brave, his left forearm flat in front of his chest, his right fist striking downward past the other clenched hand.

Eagle Heart listened raptly. He seemed to grow taller and Cornett noted his fighter's pride. Then, as Rudd finished and dropped his hands, a glimmer of disappointment entered the tobacco-colored face. Eagle Heart pinned a bewildered look upon Cornett.

Without any warning, he started hopping from side to side, swiftly weaving and ducking, aiming his hands like a rifle. As quickly, he straightened and spoke again to Rudd.

In a moment he vanished from the tent.

"Guess I savvied that," Cornett observed dryly. "He was demonstrating how wrong I was in turning him down, what a great warrior he is."

Sergeant Rudd scrubbed his chin. "That's part of it, sir. Only he put it in a different way. Says if we won't make him a pony soldier, then all he can do is show us how to dodge bullets like Comanches. He thinks we ought to adopt the same tactics, instead of standin' still, as he says, to be shot down like buffalo calves."

"He might have something at that. Well. . . ." Dismissing it, Cornett returned to his map. But the sergeant's tone made him glance up.

"Eagle Heart just don't understand. You see, sir, he knows these Texans want his hair. I told him at mess. He can't figure out why, when we need men, we treat him like a woman. Won't let him fight."

Startled surprise made Cornett's normally level voice climb. "Have you forgotten they're hostages, being held in order to draw the other wild bands back to the reservation? Are you suggesting that I enlist them? It's ridiculous and dangerous. Why, only two months ago Eagle Heart was fighting Colonel Mackenzie on McClellan Creek. We might just as well wave red flags in front of these wrathy Texans."

"I see your point, sir, but the Army uses Tonkawa scouts."

"Against Indians, yes. Kiowas and Comanches are their hereditary enemies."

"I reckon, though," said Rudd, carefully selecting his words, "you could take Eagle Heart's word if he gave it."

"Trust a Comanche?" Cornett's snort ended the whole impossible thing. "Sergeant, I'm afraid you've served out West a little too long. It's clouding your judgment."

At 11:00 P.M. Captain Cornett quit his tent. He'd slept two hours, his campaigner's ingrained sense of timing rousing him at the proper time.

There wasn't much moon and the night lay, sooty and formless, save where the fires still burned low. Cornett's frustration, which had assailed him earlier, was gone. He had a plan now. He would follow it as best he could, as he had always, doggedly to the end.

Sergeant Rudd's raw voice reached him from among the wagons. Cornett stepped across, seeing troopers grouped around a wheel.

"Sergeant Rudd."

He emerged out of the gloom, trailing horse and sweat smell. "We're windin' things up, sir."

"Good. We'll break camp now. Move south about two miles, then west. I plan to circle Lost Spring and come out north. Better get Eagle Heart's people stirring."

Hardly had Cornett finished when Rudd was striding for the wagons. There followed some anxious moments as a half-wild team, harness dragging, tore loose from a drowsy teamster.

Before Cornett could take half a dozen bolting steps, a square shape shot across the campground. The team hauled up abruptly in a jangle of metal and leather. Then Cornett saw Rudd bringing them back, his thick arms hanging on the bits. His iron voice sledged through the murky light. "Dammit, Brady! Ye're handlin' mules . . . not hawrses!"

There seemed no end to the hooking up, the milling and saddling, the dejected Indians shuffling like indistinct wraiths. Rudd hurried everybody. He seemed everywhere at once. Confusion ended and order came. Finally they were stringing out, the white-topped wagons weaving. For another interval, the sounds of the train in motion seemed overly loud to Cornett. But soon the noises settled into a creaking rhythm. They traveled as quietly as lumbering Conestogas could upon blanket-wrapped rims. Yet Cornett felt vaguely uneasy. It was almost too easy.

Past midnight, Captain Cornett sighted the firefly lights of Lost Spring blinking off to his right. He continued north, more by sense, by feel, wondering what new decision the morning might bring. A chill got into him; he buttoned up his blouse. Twice he ordered Rudd back and the sergeant's hoarse urging carried to him distinctly: "Close up! Close up!"

An hour later Rudd came up. He said: "Jensen heard horses runnin'. Seemed close. He took a look. Couldn't find a thing."

Cornett's jaws clamped together. "Keep them closed up."

Around 3:00 A.M. Cornett halted the wagons. They rested briefly and went on. At 4:00 the captain, biting an unlighted pipe, saw the first streak of gray crack through the eastern blackness. He knew a dread, then, and there fell a weight across his shoulders. He stepped the column out faster. Once more Rudd prodded the laggards.

By degrees the blurred land came into

outline. The light broadened. It was, thought Cornett, like a blanket being ripped off the naked wagons. Now, with full daylight upon them, he stopped the column and reined his horse. Rudd sided him, his look a question mark.

They were riding past the first wagons when Cornett said: "You take the point. I'm going back."

As Rudd turned, an Indian stepped out. It was Eagle Heart and he went straight to the sergeant. In the fresh light the Comanche's face appeared even more squeezed and shriveled, the skin stretched like ancient parchment. He grunted from his chest; his hands cut swift, fluid signs. There was a bright eagerness in the muddy eyes.

Rudd muttered in return and swung to leave, almost ducking.

Cornett, annoyed, said roughly: "Now what is it?"

"Why, nothing much, sir."

For once, Cornett's patience snapped. "What the hell does he want?"

"Sir," said Rudd, unwilling, "seems Eagle Heart had a dream. About a big fight with the *Tejanos.*" Rudd swallowed, reluctant to go on. "He wants to ride with you, sir."

It happened too quickly for Cornett to voice his exasperation. A horse rushed up from the rear. And a certain cold knowing told Cornett, even before the trooper got out the words: "Riders, Captain! Coming fast!"

Cornett accepted it without show, except for the knotted angling of his jaws. He said quietly to Rudd: "Corral the wagons at once. You stay here in charge. If they fire . . . you fire. Understand?" He was already moving before Rudd could reply.

Cantering south with Corporal Jensen and four privates, Captain Cornett saw one solid wedge of horsemen driving toward him a thousand yards away. The sight fired a thrust of anger through him, and quickly a black despair.

The distance closed rapidly. A great drumming rolled over the prairie. After two hundred yards Cornett slowed to a steady trot. Farther on, Cornett could distinguish Damron's burly figure in advance of the sea of faces.

Then Cornett barked a command. The troopers drew carbines and Cornett folded back the holster flap of the .44 Dragoon revolver he wore butt forward. It was one of the worst moments of his career, certainly the most senseless. He had only one thought as he took his position and held up, and that was of the luckless men with him and the all but helpless wagons.

Damron boiled up at hard gallop. He raised his rifle and halted his men in close, making his gelding swerve. Appleby, the townsman, presented a bedraggled shape alongside him.

"Cap'n," called Damron, "you just about got away, but our night scouts spotted you!"

"My intention, Mister Damron."

"You make it hard, Cap'n. I'm all wore out with you."

"I warn you once more," said Cornett, his severe voice distinct for them all to hear. "There are women and children in the wagons."

"You warn us when you give us no choice!" Damron's eyes blazed.

"You give me none. I'm also warning you that Major Braxton will join us at any moment."

"We don't bluff." Damron slapped his rifle stock for emphasis, and his stare got glittery. "We're goin' in after them heathen bucks."

Behind him the mass of riders nudged forward.

Captain Cornett, who saw how it was going to be, said quietly — "Then you'll have to buy them." — and drew his revolver.

Damron looked into the pointed muzzle,

his mouth dropping open. In the next instant he caught himself and clenched his rifle.

"Don't!" Cornett ordered. Something stayed Damron's hands, and Cornett said: "Drop that rifle."

Decision wrestled in Damron's unyielding face. His eyes ranged around in a pleading look.

"If one man makes a move, you're dead," Cornett said. Still, he tensed for it to happen. He wondered why Damron's men did not act, then was aware of the troopers spaced to his flanks with carbines ready. Cornett said coldly: "You have three counts to drop your weapon, Mister Damron. One. . . ."

A struggle was going on inside Damron. His neck muscles stood out; he moistened his lips.

"Two. . . ."

Suddenly Damron dropped the rifle. As he did, he turned his outrage upon Appleby. His voice choked. "Damn you! You stand there. . . ."

But Appleby wasn't noticing. He was gazing off toward the wagons. He said nervously — "Heap of dust back there." — and heaved around at Damron. "Thought you said. . . ."

Cornett discovered that he was sweating. Yet he dared not hope. It was too impossible. But he heard Corporal Jensen's impossible voice, close to a shout. "Looks like Major Braxton, sir . . . ! He's forming to attack!"

For a long moment Cornett could not believe. It was incredible. He took a quick look and a tide of blessed relief swamped him. Good old Braxton!

"There it is," he told Damron. "Just as I warned you."

Damron looked grim, not budging, but he was watching, too.

It was Appleby who broke the tension. "You boys can fight the whole U.S. cavalry if you want to," he said in a sighing, give-out way. "I'm heading for Lost Spring." He seemed glad to go as he turned back.

Several townsmen swapped uncertain glances. In sudden unison they followed Appleby. Their movement became a magnet, drawing more horsemen. At length, only a small, stubborn knot of riders remained. They watched Damron.

"If I were you," Cornett said quietly behind his revolver, "I'd send them home before Braxton attacks."

Damron's will seemed to rise and fall. He glared once, then let out his breath in resignation. “I’m a reasonable man. I know when I’m stumped.”

He spurred his horse away. The others swung slowly after him.

Sergeant Rudd rode out to meet the detail, and Cornett, feeling younger than he had in years, said cheerfully: “Well, old Braxton did it. Ride back and present him my respects.”

But Rudd, who always followed orders to the letter, still lingered. Cornett let it pass for the moment and turned his grateful attention to the wagons, seeking Braxton. A man sat his horse in front of the drawn-up troopers.

Cornett stopped suddenly, his eyes wide. Somehow the line didn’t look right. Sort of ragged. He flung around to Rudd.

“Sir,” said Sergeant Rudd, his homely features a penitent red. “It looked bad for you. Remember the uniforms? Well. . . .”

Captain Cornett jerked in front with an exploding comprehension. He saw his own few men with carbines. But the others, the copper-faced, long-haired men in blue, carried sticks and singletrees from the wagons. And just beyond on his skinny pony sat old Eagle Heart, all but lost in his blouse. He pointed now. His hands moved swiftly, knotting.

"Sir," said Sergeant Rudd. "It's for you."

"What in damnation?" asked Cornett, but there wasn't any bite in his tone, only a wonder.

"Why, sir, he made the sign for brave. He means you."

Half a day's march south of Red River, two overtired troops approached the plodding wagon train. At their head rode Major Braxton, debonair in fringed buckskin jacket, yellow bandanna, and rakish hat. He waved boyishly and joined Captain Cornett.

"Sorry you weren't with us, Pete," greeted Braxton, shaking hands. "We flushed some horse-stealing Kiowas. Had a lively run till they slipped us. Any trouble coming up?"

"Civilians delayed us near Lost Spring. Wanted our hostages. But nobody hurt."

Braxton smiled sympathetically. "More dull routine, eh?"

"In a way," said Captain Cornett, breathing deeply. "I guess you could call it that when you consider not a shot was fired."

COMANCHE SON

He sighted dusty movement again when the slipping sun seemed lodged above the low summits of the rocky Wichitas. Through glass-bright layers of shimmering August heat the trailing horsemen looked dwarfed on the sea of yellow prairie.

A spare and unhurried man, he reined the big steel dust bay around and pulled a Spencer from his saddle boot below his leg, raised the sights, and sent a futile bullet flying at them. They halted as he expected, beyond carbine range, and he rode on, thinking how, in the beginning, four instead of three had jumped him on the Cimarron. Knowing them well by now, he sensed an added wolfish patience, a clenched hanging on for the gold that he carried after selling his herd in Caldwell.

He forded the summer-shallow creek, his mind edged with excitement at being so near the end of his journey. He passed Fort

Sill's orderly cluster of gray limestone buildings erected around a central square. He pressed forward through powder-dry grass and came to a huddle of sun-punished adobe buildings on the endless prairie.

He dismounted slowly, his deliberate movements covering a welling eagerness as he looked around, for a moment affected by the bleakness of this remote outpost of paternalism in the loneliness of Indian country. Smoke smell lay on the hot wind. Teepees rose on the nearby dusty flats. Camp dogs barked. Ponies grazed. He went in, then, long steps quickening, stirring the music of jingling spur rowels.

And presently he stood in a dim, still room and he was saying — "I'm Ben Wrattan . . . I've come for my boy." — which was all he could get out, so swiftly did the thickness fill his dry throat and the smothered feeling seize his chest.

Levi Sawyer looked more Iowa farmer than Indian agent. His enormous hands, lump-knuckled, hung like hammers on the sturdy handles of his arms. He had a plowman's stocky frame and his heavy mouth, wide and straight and firm, gave him a certain stern look. But beneath the craggy brows Ben saw the mildest, clearest, friendliest gray eyes of his memory.

After the first cordial greeting, the shape of welcome rounding Sawyer's face retreated. A frown formed.

"He's here?" Ben demanded.

Sawyer had the habit of looking up and working his lips, as if he drew the nub of a thing through his mind, back and forth, reflecting, examining, and sought a higher help before replying.

"Tehan," he said, speaking carefully, "the lad you read about in the Kansas newspapers, is still here. True. He's been attending our agency school since April, when the Quahadas brought him in."

"I sent word . . . came as fast as I could," Ben said, eyeing Sawyer for assurance. "Everything tallies. Your description of the boy, where the Indians said they stole him on the Brazos, the year and the time of year. He has to be my son!"

Sympathy stood in Sawyer's eyes. "It is always the same when Texas people come here looking for their loved ones. So positive, so hopeful. I cannot be so until doubt no longer exists."

"Let me see him," Ben said, and, when the agent moved uneasily, in silence, Ben stabbed him with a look of raw suspicion.

Sawyer said: "I only want to remind you that most captive children have endured terrible experiences. Many hardships. Much of what they remember is confused. Gunshots, yells, fire, horses running. Sometimes I feel they do not wish to recall what happened to their parents or kin."

"There's little for the boy to recollect. He was born in 'Sixty-two, after I left for the war. He was stolen in 'Sixty-Five, before I got home. Taken as he played in the yard." Ben was bitter.

"And . . . the boy's mother?" Sawyer asked, hesitating.

"She lived through the raid and she's still hoping. I've been as far as the Apache agencies in New Mexico and Arizona. My wife's told me so much about the boy, I feel I'll know him. I know I will!"

"There is another thing," Sawyer said, neither sharing nor discouraging Ben's enthusiasm. "It is true, Comanches can be very cruel, judged by our standards. Yet, when they adopt a captive, they love him like a Comanche."

Ben's temper flared. "If they loved him, why'd they give him up?"

"I withheld their rations until they did. There are few buffaloes to hunt this year."

"What's this got to do with my boy?"

Sawyer's eyes were wise, gentle with understanding. "The lad was treated with kindness by a Comanche called Two Strikes. Spoiled, in fact. Never a hand laid on him. All that will make it harder for him to become a white boy again."

Ben's voice turned harsh. "My boy wouldn't want to stay with a brute Comanche! Is something wrong? He hurt . . . crippled? This been too much for his mind?"

"His health is excellent," Sawyer said, quick to reply. "His mind is bright. His marks are high in school."

"In heaven's name what is it, then?"

"I will go get the lad," Sawyer said, in a forbearance that worried Ben.

Sawyer went out and the room fell still again, close with heat. Ben never moved his eyes from the doorway. What if the boy wasn't his? What was Sawyer holding back? After a while, Ben heard steps and voices. His blood was pounding as he got to his feet.

Just then a slim boy walked in, quietly followed by Sawyer, and paused with the sensitive wariness of a half-grown antelope. Sawyer had dressed him in shoes, gray britches, blue cotton shirt, and a nice dark coat. Ben stared, turned mute by a sense of unreality, seeing the proud, unsmiling face, its trace of suspicion, a face tanned dark as an Indian's, not a muscle moving — a

Comanche's wide-open look of country without end, of hot winds and curly grasses and rainy-weather lakes. But the eyes were a deep blue, and the hair, freshly cut, was pale yellow, like that of the big-eyed woman who waited on the Brazos.

Ben's gaze became a tearing thing. A feeling was beating high in his chest, but he forced himself to be calm. "Howdy, boy," he said, and waited.

For a little run of time the far-seeing eyes just stared, and then Ben saw the sizing-up arrogance. There was no answer. Ben flinched inwardly. "There should be a scar down the left leg," he said, all hint of command missing.

Sawyer said: "Show him, lad."

There was a pause while the boy, motionless, chin lifted, threw his insolence at the white man. A Comanche insolence, Ben decided darkly. To his surprise, however, the boy obeyed, and, when Ben looked down, he wanted to cry out. For it was there, dimly white but unmistakable, the long slash of puckered skin where Ben's firstborn had fallen upon the double-edged axe, as Margaret Ann had first described in her letters and then in person, afterward.

Ben threw a gleam of triumph at the silent Sawyer, and, his face wreathed in a broad smile, he dropped to his knees. "Son, your name is Jim Travis Wrattan. I'm Ben Wrattan . . . your father. Your mother is living. Her name is Margaret Ann. I'm going to take you home to her."

Ben was reaching as he finished and he pulled the brown face against his bearded one. That interval held, while the thickness climbed in Ben's throat until a sudden understanding crackled inside him. Why, the boy was like wood in his arms! Ben got up and stood back, asking silently: *What have they done to him?*

"My name . . . is Tehan," the boy said, a chopped-off, pushed-out Indian pride to his tone that Ben hated. "My white father dead . . . white mother dead. . . ."

"That's not true," Ben snarled.

"My people tell me . . . the Quahadas."

"Don't call them your people! Listen, they wounded your mother and killed your grandfather. They'd've killed her if Rangers hadn't been hot after 'em!" Ben was fighting for clarity, for persuasion, trying to pierce the unblinking copper expression. "Comanches did that . . . they stole you."

The boy was unchanged, scornful. "Kiowas make raid . . . Quahadas buy me. Two Strikes tell me." He slapped his chest. "Two Strikes great warrior . . . great horse thief."

"He lied! Comanches did it! They even told Mister Sawyer here they took you!" Ben stopped, realizing it was no use now. He spoke with a quiet desperation. "Boy, don't you remember the cabin under the pecan trees? The cool spring . . . the plum thicket?" He gained in eloquence. He called up every animal and incident he could remember from his wife's letters during the war. At mention of a spotted puppy the Indian look in the stern features seemed to lessen, just barely, then to return, set like flint.

"My white people dead," the boy said, almost in monotone. "I am Quahada now." He slipped into the cavernous new coat. A twist of his shoulders said the garment was nothing; it was white man.

Ben lowered his voice. "If I wasn't your father, would I know about the scar."

"He see marks," came the immediate skepticism, the boy pointing at Sawyer, accusing. "He tell you. All white men lie." His right hand, in fluid, graceful motion, cut the taunting sign of the forked tongue. "Liars . . . cowards. Like women. My people . . . the Quahadas . . . tell me. So it is true."

Ben looked away in resignation, sick at heart, sending his helplessness across the room to Sawyer. "Might as well take him back, can't drive these heathen notions out of his head."

Sawyer, expressionless, gestured to leave. Ben didn't look up until the boy reached the doorway. One moment he presented a slim, defiant shape there, lost in the oversize white man's clothes. The next he was gone, silently, like mesquite smoke. Like a Comanche.

"Won't he run off?" Ben asked in alarm.

"Agency employees are outside," Sawyer said calmly. "Yes, he's tried. Twice soldiers caught him trying to steal a horse from the stone corral at the fort. Another time we found him walking back to Quahada country." Sawyer turned his face upward, in his reflective way, and Ben, still shaken, was not prepared when the agent said simply: "I think you and the lad should leave tomorrow."

Ben couldn't say just now.

"There's a definite family resemblance," Sawyer said, smiling for the first time. "I noticed that at once. In spirit as well. The boy is strong-willed, like his father. I have no doubts."

"But he thinks. . . ."

"He is only a boy, brought up on proud Indian ways. Loyal to the Quahadas. Suspicious of whites. A little frightened, I think, at seeing the strange white man who claims to be his father. Just as you are troubled over his heathen notions, as you call them."

"How can I make him understand?"

"If you mean more evidence, you have shown more than enough. The need, I think, is of the spirit, of the heart. Be patient. Give him time."

"Time," Ben said bitterly, "when he hates all white men!"

Sawyer seemed to be thinking ahead. "A mail escort will be going south tomorrow headed for Fort Richardson."

As eight troopers, escorting a mule-drawn Army ambulance, drew up at the agency in the bright sunlight, Ben and the boy came out on the porch with Sawyer.

The agent's eyes swept to the well-muscled bay stallion, standing quietly, fox ears cocked. "What a fine animal! Must be sixteen hands high. Such a head, neck, and shoulders. Yes, and the short back and strong loin."

"He can pick 'em up and lay 'em down," Ben said. "Steel dust blood. He'll weigh close to twelve-hundred pounds. Bought him in Kansas to build up my saddle stock."

Several Indians had drifted up, watching

handsome horseflesh as only Comanches do, worshipping, craving, and Ben saw the boy give a start of recognition.

"Quahadas," Sawyer explained. "Camped here to draw rations."

Ben shook hands and motioned the boy toward a blue-roan pony, purchased that morning from the fort sutler. They started to their mounts.

Without warning the boy broke free, running westward, before Ben could grab him. Ben started after him, burdened by his high-heeled boots and heavy Texas-style spurs. He had gone but a few rods when he felt a rowel rake across an instep. His feet tangled and he was pitched into the dust. As he hit and rolled, he heard laughter from the cavalrymen and the Comanches, and the latter stung worst of all.

He knew his face was crimson as he sprang up furiously and paced to his horse, swung up, and spurred off at a run. Coming alongside, Ben saw the boy glance back and angle away, surprisingly fleet in the heavy brogans. Ben's mount, as if tailing a cow, cut with the motion, jumping out, and Ben reached down a scooping arm and lifted the squirming figure to the saddle. They started back in that fashion, the captive fighting like a wildcat.

"Boy," said Ben when he halted, "you will ride your pony, else I will tie you to the saddle."

Drawing painful kicks on the shins, he hauled the boy closer, rump tilted. Ben's flattened hand rose and fell, whapping, and unexpectedly the struggling ceased. Ben saw the tense mouth hinge down and a startled look spring the blue eyes wider.

"Two Strikes didn't whip me," the boy protested, with an eye on the watching Quahadas.

"He should have!" Ben barked. "Make you respect your elders. And that wasn't any whipping. You got spanked." As quickly, he was relenting. He let the boy down. "Now it's a pretty day. Mount up, Jim Travis."

"Tehan." The reply was tinged with insolence. Nevertheless, the boy went over and untied the pony's reins, and stepped around to the right side, the Indian side.

"Not that way!" Ben yelled. "He'll throw you sky-high."

True, as Levi Sawyer might have said, the pony shied and brushed against the hitching rack, and back, thereby making the mounting somewhat less difficult. But even as Ben saw his warning ignored, he wasn't expecting the cat-like swiftness of the boy's leap into the saddle.

Ben ate his chagrin in silence as the escort formed. At the last moment Sawyer held them up while he found a straw hat for the boy, then they rode off with the mail escort.

"The pony is yours," he said after a bit, laying no stress on his generosity. "Also the new saddle."

The blond head jerked, off guard, and, for a moment, Ben caught the small gleam of pleasure, rubbed out as the boy stiffened. "No *bueno* for hunting. White man's saddle will make his back sore. No horse for Quahadas."

"Maybe so," Ben said, without affront. "But I've never seen a horse that Quahadas wouldn't steal."

"Only the brave steal horses."

"Brave," Ben acknowledged, "if you are Comanche. If you're a white man, it is cowardly and you get hanged when caught."

"Me . . . ," said the boy, curling his lip, slapping his chest, "I am Quahada Comanche. No white man." And he spat into the brown prairie grass.

Red River lay southward. The day wore on slowly, into late afternoon.

It was then that Ben, looking back again, made out the familiar knot of toiling horsemen, and a feeling tapped, telling him they had never been far behind. Thereafter, they held a measured distance, varying little, biding, dogging, always there.

"You look back," the scornful voice broke in. "You afraid of white men?"

"I fought them once and there will be another fight soon. They want the gold I carry."

"So the coward pony soldiers will not help us?"

"They are going to Fort Richardson. On south. Tomorrow you and I will take another way . . . southwest . . . to our home on the Brazos."

The boy became thoughtful. "When the bad white men come, I will know how brave you are."

"Or how lucky. There are three of them."

"You will need strong medicine . . . look!" There was an excited westward pointing. "Quahadas."

It took some eye-burning and squinting for Ben to locate them, riding about parallel with the escort, using the low sun as a shield between them and the troopers. At that long distance it was hard to tell how many.

"Think they're coming for you, boy? Well, I'll fight them!"

He needed no spoken reply, for the blue glare alone told him what to expect.

Toward evening they forded the low, rust-colored river and made camp in a grove of whispering cottonwoods. The boy sat apart and stared his disdain at the pony soldiers performing the camp duties of squaws. During supper he wolfed down bacon and hard bread like a Comanche, using his fingers, wiping them on his new cotton shirt. Ben flinched at the Indian-camp manners and made a mental reminder for the future. Afterward, he saw the lad spread his blanket and turn his back in scorn on the circle of white men.

Light faded to purple darkness. Ben, having leather-hobbled his animals, made a restless turn of the camp and felt the damp breath of the river against his face and inside his soggy clothing. He marked the river bluffs, skylighted dimly, dark, low humps. And thus watching, scouting his gaze far left and right, he spotted something, high up. Sure as shooting, a small fire burned over there.

Indians or whites? *As if it makes any difference,* he thought, and turned back bitterly.

He came awake more on old instincts than from any intruding sound, yet not knowing why. It was still night, still quiet. Through the shuffling cottonwood tops he could see stars dappling the great moon-pale sky, feel cool wind rising off the scented Texas prairie. Beyond, hobbled horses and mules cropped the short grass. He stayed up on one elbow, vaguely disturbed, then, hearing nothing wrong, he relaxed and automatically looked for the boy. For a breath he went rigid and next he was up, springing, striding across the empty bed for the saddle stock.

Discovering the pony gave him a flash of relief, but the stallion was gone. As he paused, he heard the unevenness of a crow-hopping horse in the fooling darkness. He was off with the sound, his stocking feet noiseless. A moving clump appeared, a horse snorted. He lengthened stride and there he found them. The stallion, the small shape bent down, working at the leather hobbles, now jerking up.

"Boy!"

Ben grabbed and caught the arm-swinging figure and felt a rain of kicks and fists.

A picket ran up, carbine ready. "What's this?"

"Loose hobble," Ben said, not thinking, ashamed to admit what had happened, quieting the struggling boy by main force. "My son ran out and caught the stud. It's all right."

The walk back took the spark from Ben's anger, and he held himself carefully when he spoke. "There will be no more night-hawkin'. This tryin' to sneak off to Quahada country. You savvy that, boy?" he said, hoping for an indication of obedience.

"My name . . . is Tehan."

Ben longed to shake him. Slowly an impulse deepened. Why not put him on his honor? "Will you give me your word you won't run off again?" A silence took hold, a Comanche's scornful silence, Ben realized with a dull defeat. "Boy, you're plumb contrary. I'll have to tie you up for the rest of the night."

He looped his lariat around the skinny waist, tensed for a fight. Perversely the boy sat like a post. Ben made a knot, lay down with the other end wrapped around his right wrist, and tried to think what he had done wrong since the first meeting in Sawyer's office. He thought of a captive deer he had seen as a boy in the settlements, its graceful neck broken when it leaped high for freedom and struck the rail fencing. Was it right to pen a wild thing against its will?

Morning seemed to bring a change in the boy's manner, the night's humiliation forgotten, the arrogance gone. *Has a lesson been learned?* Ben wondered, as he finished saddling.

He saw the boy measure him a calculating look — and slip to the right side of the pony. It went walleyed and Ben shouted: "The other side!" He was surprised and not surprised. Contrariness. But, again, Ben hadn't counted on the boy's lithe quickness. In close, one hand clutching mane, he was already swinging into the saddle.

It was a pretty piece of riding, Comanche style. Ben read as much in the troopers' amused expressions, and a grudging pride lifted inside him, a feeling he smothered on intercepting the sidelong look of triumph behind the blue eyes.

Around noon they left the escort. For the first time, Ben allowed himself to consider that they were no longer followed. All through the morning he had sighted no pursuit. Had the white men and Quahadas figured he and the boy intended to go on with the troopers? Ben led off southwest, into a sun-blasted vastness of buffalo and grama grasses that rolled in massive folds across the deep country.

The boy looked miserable and sympathy crept over Ben. When he spoke, he received only a mechanical nod or a grunt or a single word, low-spoken. Between them now, he recognized a gap that kin blood might never close. The gap between Comanche and Texan, and that was a painful plenty. He gave up making talk. Meanwhile, the puzzle behind him increased. There was no sign. Neither had there been on the Cimarron until almost too late. Except there, he had picked off the lead rider and the fleet steel dust horse had taken him out of danger. Today the light pony, not conditioned for hard riding, was lagging. Its jaded trot set the pace.

It was far into the afternoon when they entered choppy country, patched with gnarled mesquite.

Ben dragged out the Spencer, scowled at the hiding ridges and rode ahead, the boy trailing. They crossed the dry bed of a small creek. Not many rods on, Ben drew rein, every sense keyed high. He turned in the saddle. "Boy, you hear anything?" There was no answer and Ben was about to go ahead, when the boy made a throaty noise. Something ran quickly across his face. "Horses . . . on rocks. . . ."

Now Ben heard it. Horses running. The ring of metal shoes on stone. Close ahead. He waved the boy back. The pony switched tiredly around, balking, and Ben used his quirt. They went hard until Ben, alongside, motioned up the twisting creekbed. As they turned, he looked back and saw the three white men. Onward, he pulled up in a willow clump and heard the clattering pursuit pause. A bitter knowledge came. No reckless rush. They'd use caution this time. He knew them. Despite that, he had let himself be circled while the pony lagged. So he figured there was time left him. He rode to thicker cover, his decision building as he dismounted and faced around. "Boy, you stay with the horses. . . ."

He saw the slim face, already flushed with excitement, go tense. The questioning eyes fastened on Ben's lariat.

Ben shook his head. "No more of that. Listen, boy. When the shooting starts, you get on my horse. Be careful to mount him on the white man's side. If you see the white men coming, ride fast. Circle around. Find the pony soldiers. Be ready . . . watch sharp. . . . It's either that. . . ." Ben left it unspoken, unfinished. "You savvy, boy?" he said thickly, rougher than he intended, and saw the jerky nod. Ben kept looking at him, marking the features on his memory. Kin or not, could you cage a wild thing? Without another word he handed the stallion's reins to the boy and swung back, thinking they had come this far and still neither knew the other. Each a stranger, blindfolded.

He found concealment in a stand of willows. In the long-running stillness, he missed having the alert boy beside him, and, as the uneasy silence hung on, he found his mind split between them and concern for the boy.

It was too quiet.

When the first shot slammed, he was caught looking downcreek. He jerked at the crack of sound, flattening, in surprise. A patch of powder smoke rose above the wooded ridge across the creek. He placed a bullet below it and crawled deeper into the willows. As yet, there was no stir along the creek. And now the rifleman commenced a rapid shooting. Ben held his fire. After a time, he decided the marksmanship was more bothersome than dangerous. Did it mean he was being circled again?

He spotted them, then, spaced like infantry skirmishers, bent over, advancing through the scrawny mesquite that studded the slopes rising above the creek channel. He became quite still. The rifle on the ridge crashed again, searching the willows. He ignored it.

Possibly they were too confident, made bold by superior numbers and the covering fire. Ben let them come on until he could see the non-descript faces clearly. Both seemed to locate him at the same instant, in etched astonishment. Ben facing them instead of turned toward the ridge, unsuspecting.

His first bullet knocked the foremost man to the ground. The other, dodging, made a snap shot, a panicky shot, and fell. He jerked up, hurt, shocked eyes bulging fear, and went scrabbling back into the mesquite, pulling one leg after him.

Ben lowered the short gun, aware of an extraordinary stillness. His ears were ringing. He tasted powder smoke. He waited and presently heard boots slamming down the ridge, and after a while he picked up the shuffle of horses going off north. Those sounds faded. He reloaded the tubular magazine in the butt stock of the carbine with fat, copper-cased cartridges, and glanced up. The man lay where he had fallen.

Ben got to his feet, a gray revulsion striking through him. He walked heavily, in dread. It seemed longer to the pony than he remembered. It was there, tied. He had expected that and moved on. Nowhere did he see or hear the steel dust horse, and again he was not surprised. Yet, when he walked ahead and stopped, everything rose up to hurt him. The worn-out, searching years, even the finding.

He was standing still, indecisively, when he sensed he was not alone.

"Look . . . quick . . . look." It was a young voice shrill with alarm.

Ben wheeled to see a coppery shape stepping from behind a mesquite, very near. The Indian's bullet was so close Ben felt the rifle's breath hot on his face just before he fired and the Indian fell.

Ben was no longer interested in the Indian. He was jerking to the sound of horses running down the slope. He saw them through an opening in the mesquite, coming like the wind. Several Quahadas, led by an Indian on a paint horse. Somewhere the steel dust horse was trumpeting.

Ben got ready. At that moment, the boy materialized between him and the Quahadas. Ben checked himself, afraid to fire, expecting the Comanches to scoop up the boy. Instead, they swept past him for the creekbank willows. In there, all Ben saw, moving dimly, whickering, making the branches shake, was the picketed stallion.

Ben could shoot now. One man fell forward abruptly and held onto the neck of his pony. The rest milled in confusion at the firing behind them, whirled, and, hanging low on their horses, dashed to the creekbed and down it as Ben continued to shoot. Something told him they wouldn't come back, for the horse-stealing party was already a failure. One warrior lay here and another was wounded.

Ben eyed the fallen Comanche before he spoke. "Two Strikes?"

"He got away," the boy said, shaking his head. "He was on the paint."

"Why didn't you take the horse, boy?" Ben asked curiously, his bewilderment growing. "The way was open . . . clear to Quahada country. Else go with them? You . . . just a boy . . . a mighty horse stealer?"

The blue eyes avoided his. "Quahadas wanted the big horse . . . not me. You saw them."

"Leastwise they didn't kill you."

"They have thrown me away." The boy seemed more puzzled than angry.

Ben watched him, considering. A thought caught, flashed. "But you warned me before they made their rush. You didn't know they wanted the big horse. Why, boy . . . why?"

Despair and maybe the old arrogance — Ben awaited both. Neither came. The blue eyes fixed him straight and there was the beginning of an expression he couldn't define unless it was pride. Comanche pride.

"You gave me the big horse," the boy said in an awed tone that was new to Ben. He came in a step, his eyes enlarging. "You went back. You fought brave . . . so I could get away. My white father is very brave. My heart is glad."

Ben saw the dark face change, saw it twist, crumbling, as the boy ran toward him.

PRICE OF THE BRIDE

Since early daylight Tom Bard had driven under a hot and yellow sun across dipping flatlands of matted buffalo grass. Across a broad and gently rounded hill country beginning to show the intruding upthrust of homesteaders' windmills and the square shapes of sod houses. When he came to the Mustang road, he turned the team along the narrow ruts before he pulled up. Then, for the first time this morning, he looked steadily at Star Woman.

"I been thinking what we'll need," he said, his voice low and patient. "Rordan carries good calico. You'll need a dress."

She sat quietly on the wagon seat. She sat at the far side, away from him. As she turned and her blue-black braids moved, he felt the shock of something, a sudden awkwardness. It ran through him that she looked very young in her belted doeskin skirt and beaded blouse. He watched the sober face. A high-boned Indian face, the cheeks faintly hollowed in, smoky-eyed, full-mouthed — and it held nothing for him.

She said — "I am not a white woman." — and he noticed the faintest flicker in the deep eyes. "But I will wear it."

"All right," he said.

He faced around, realizing there was nothing more to be said. He was tight-lipped when he lifted the reins, his gaze caught on dust streamers down the road rolled up by an oncoming wagon. He let the team foot out and stir again the rumble of the spring wagon. And suddenly he was thinking of the cameo he'd bought in town. He'd given it to her after delivering the ponies to Hard Rope, and they'd been married at Darlington Agency, where she had gone to the white man's boarding school and learned her stiff, halting English. But she hadn't worn it, and somehow he knew she never would. It was her way, her silent, Indian way, of closing him out while she went through with the bargain made by her father.

Approaching the wagon, Tom felt a quick twinge of pity. It was a nester's sorry outfit, with a hunch-shouldered man in a ragged shirt driving the sore-backed team, with his sun-wrinkled wife beside him. Tom saw bedding, chairs, and an old trunk piled inside. Kids peered out from the rolled-up canvas, their pinched faces curious, sprung-eyed. Toward the tailgate Tom could hear chickens squawking in a coop, and behind the wagon a boy on a lumbering plow horse trailed two cows.

Tom pulled off the road to let them pass. "You're headed the wrong way," he said, grinning. "Mustang's west of here."

The nester shrugged. "Came through there," he announced flatly. "We're pullin' out." His watery eyes traveled almost resentfully to Star Woman. "Hard enough without Injuns burnin' and hellin'. Me an' Ma sold out for next to nothin', but Mort Sain didn't get much."

Tom stiffened and looked at Star Woman. Her face was like so much stone, but he thought he saw an interest there as she listened to the brittle, bitter talk. For it was Sain, the Mustang merchant and Indian trader, who had offered more ponies for Star Woman than had Tom. Yet, Hard Rope, a lover of much horseflesh, had refused Sain.

"Sain no good for Star Woman," Hard Rope had told Tom afterward with an emphatic wave of his stringy-muscled arm. "Purty soon him get tired of Indian wife. She no good any more. But you . . . you want Star Woman for keeps."

But it cut Tom that he was so painfully awkward with her, unable to break past the taciturn wall of her mind, of her feelings. That in her eyes he was only a broad-knuckled white man, rough and not talking much, his driving interest being the bunch of lank Texas steers he grazed on the grass-lands leased from the agency. A slow-talking man, not easy and smooth like Mort Sain.

Jaws working, the nester grumbled at the team, and Tom watched them go. "I can't figure it," he told the Indian girl. "Your people have settled down. No trouble since Big Horse's northern Cheyennes broke away."

Her eyes were hard-bright. "Cheyennes too poor to fight now," she said.

Wordlessly Tom swung the team back. Traveling the scarred trace of the prairie road, he was aware of a dread building up in him of the trip ahead. He felt it at once when they drove along Mustang's gusty, powdery Main Street. Curious heads turned, watching them, and he understood the abrupt hush when he stopped in front of Rordan's General Mercantile. He jumped down, tied the team, and stepped back to offer his hand.

Somebody muttered and Star Woman

hesitated, the round, black eyes uncertain, divided between him and the watchers on the boardwalk. Down the street, Tom heard voices, high and sharp.

Half defiantly he said — "It's all right." — but they both knew Indians weren't welcome in Mustang. That also stood for a white man's Cheyenne wife.

Men were staring as she stepped down and Tom wheeled, his eyes fully covering them until the gawking quit. At that moment a woman came out of Rordan's in a rustle of long skirts. Her eyes picked at Star Woman with a tilted, critical glance before she walked rapidly away. Tom saw it and understood and he felt his face go tight. He took a step and Star Woman fell in behind him. All at once he wanted her alongside him, like a white woman. But she trailed him like a squaw, into the musty, cluttered store and its strong smell of new leather and stacked goods.

George Rordan shuffled up along the counter. His short hulk ran heavily to tallow and he wheezed when he moved. He squinted over steel-rimmed glasses resting on a long slash of a nose.

"What'll it be, Tom?" Rordan asked. His glance touched Star Woman, hung there in brief and knowing speculation, slid away.

"Reckon that's a foolish question when a man's just married."

Rordan tried to smile, but it was a frowning, broken grin. As Tom gave his order, it flashed across his mind that neither was there a welcome here.

Rordan started checking off the list. "Got it all but the wire. It's comin' by freight day after tomorrow."

Outside, there was a shout from down the street. Boots beat along the boardwalk, the sound of men moving restlessly.

"They'll stir it up yet," Tom heard Rordan's wheezing complaint. "Dode Parsons got burned out last night. And he's not the first. There's been others. You can see 'em leaving every day. Let this go on and there won't be enough trade to feed a jaybird."

"Burned out?" Tom stared at him.

"Yeah," Rordan grunted, his voice high and angry. "Cheyennes, they claim. Young bucks." His eyes lifted uneasily to her. Then he turned back to the loaded shelves.

"Calico, too," Tom said. "She'll pick it out."

Star Woman stood very stiffly and she watched Rordan with a straight-faced intentness while he unfurled a bolt of bright red cloth. Tom saw the ghost of a held-in desire in her eyes.

"Go on," Tom urged her. "Pick what you want. . . ." He broke off, for she hadn't moved. She stood rooted, the hunger gone from her face.

"No," she said, and Tom saw her quick, hard pride.

"Forget it," he told Rordan, who looked uncomfortable.

"I'll have your stuff packed in the wagon when you're ready," Rordan said dryly.

There was a kind of rough pride stirring in Tom, a pride because of her, as he walked out with the soft scuffing of her moccasins a whisper behind him. They stepped out among bunching ranchers, townsmen, and nesters. Tom hung back, watching the crowd gathering in the street, now watching a square and chunky man wheel and look.

Mort Sain's shrewd, black eyes jumped in surprise. For a moment, Tom saw realization crimp the broad face, saw the quick heave of the flaring chest. Then Sain coolly rolled his shoulders and came forward. There was a small swagger to him.

"I won't congratulate you," he said in a level voice. "I don't believe in saying things I don't mean."

"Didn't ask for it," Tom snapped. For this was part of his dread, this seeing Sain so soon, and he glanced at Star Woman. Her face was without expression, with the full mouth firm. Yet her eyes covered Sain with complete attention.

Looking at Star Woman, Sain said: "I wouldn't hang around . . . there's trouble out there." And he cocked his head toward the street.

Tom looked him in the eye. "We'll leave when we're ready."

Sain shrugged and turned away deliberately as a man's shout drove across the milling sounds. Tom saw a quarrelsome, lank-bodied man pacing out in front of the half-circled men. It was Dode Parsons from over on Dead Soldier Creek.

"Guess I been around long enough to know a Cheyenne's whoop," Parsons was growling in his harsh, positive way. "Wasn't daylight yet when they rode up and fired my haystack. But I could hear the devils yellin', and the light was strong enough to see it was Injuns."

He was red-faced, features blunt and thick, and he punched out his anger now with vigorous swings of his unusually long, powerful arms. "Time we showed the Cheyennes we're here to stay. You men got your rights. It's your land . . . quit runnin'! We'll ride out to Hard Rope's camp and burn it down!"

Tom heard the following shuffle of boots, an uneasy tread traveling the broad spread of the fine-dusted street. Awareness climbed in him, a leaping alarm. He could feel Star Woman brushed against him by the shifting crowd. Her face showed an Indian's patience, an Indian's outer impassiveness.

"I dunno," a man Tom recognized as Frank Boyd spoke up cautiously. "Remember when Big Horse busted loose? He rode right through our bunch . . . emptied some saddles, too. No sense going off half-cocked. I say let's wait for the troops."

"Troops, hell!" Parsons threw back his head, and Tom saw the fury working along the jaw. "Wait for what . . . so they can palaver around?"

"Dode's right," somebody joined in.

Fear rolled through Tom, a skin-cold shudder and a flash of feeling. Anger choked his throat, moving him, because he knew that Parsons was going ahead and nobody here would stop him. Tom found himself pushing to the rim of the crowd. Roughly he shouldered a man aside, only dimly aware of his complaint. And like something primitive, he heard Parson's cry: "Come on!"

Tom was lurching out in the street. He heard himself call in a strange voice —

"Parsons!" — and saw Dode Parsons spin on his boot heels. The black brush of Parsons's bearded mouth cracked open.

"You hold up," Tom said, and he sensed the deliberate turning and shifting of the closely ranked crowd, the savage attention focused on him. He felt alone and caution took hold of him.

"If I was you," Parsons said with a rush of anger, "I'd stay out of this."

He half turned to move down street, but Tom didn't budge. Parsons halted and made a quick wheeling motion. His eyes swung to the crowd's edge, to Mort Sain, a solid bulk observing all this. A rock-shouldered man neither urging nor stopping the bunching men. Pressure began to pile up. It was a steady pressure on Parsons, and he hesitated and Tom saw his puzzled look.

All at once, Parsons tore his glance from Sain. "Dammit," he grunted at Tom, "get outta the way."

"I don't mind a posse," Tom said. "But you seem mighty anxious to take it out on somebody . . . anybody. Hard Rope's settled down. His young men are trying to farm."

"You always was friendly to Cheyennes." Parsons's voice was heavy with suspicion, his face full of contempt. "Your place close to the reservation ain't been touched . . . and you got yourself a real blanket now."

There was a violent wildness thrusting through Tom. Parsons stood ten feet away. He was standing with booted feet braced wide when Tom moved. Parsons's long arms came up in a fighter's stance. But before he got them fully up, Tom smashed him in the belly. The blow drove a surprised grunt out of the man. Parsons back-stepped and around them Tom heard the high-pitched shouting, only half saw the wolfish glitter in the dark faces ringing him.

Of a sudden Parsons lowered his shoulders and charged into Tom, butting savagely with his head. Tom felt the pain flooding across his face, tasted the warm, salty blood. The tall man closed in, swinging. Off balance, Tom ducked and pinned down the thick arms and hung on until his head cleared. Parsons tore loose and lunged back — towering, powerful, impatient. He swung and missed, his rapid breathing sawing in Tom's ears. Then Tom drove a fist through the wildly punching arms that knocked off Parsons's hat.

The shaggy head snapped up. But when Tom rushed in, Parsons clenched with a grunting desperation. They were milling in a tangle of stamping boots, of churned-up dust, and the close, rancid smell of sweat. Abruptly Tom felt the hard body change. He slid away as the blunt wedge of Parsons's ramming knee ripped past and missed his stomach.

They were at the crowd's edge and Tom spun and hit him solidly across the face, across the deep chest. The harsh face slanted around, stricken eyes digging toward Sain in a plain appeal for help. Tom was measuring him when he felt a foot thrust quickly between his boots. He was down in the dust, with Parsons piling on top of him, clawing, hammering. Tom broke and rolled away and came up on his knees, the thought firing through him that it had been Sain's foot.

In a bobbing, bleary haze, Tom saw Parsons lurching after him, right arm cocked like a sledge. His boots beat a quick tattoo, and, as he piled in, overanxious, Tom weaved away and he heard the bite of the air moving past his ear. He shouldered up, catching the nester as he heeled back too late. Tom threw a fist at the lean, belted belly. Parsons wilted like a stuck steer. His arms slacked down and he fell in a lazy sprawl.

Tom's glance cut at the crowd, at Sain there, staring. When Tom looked back at Parsons, he was straining to his knees. In a step, Tom was over him. With a hard-handed roughness, he grabbed Parsons by the neck and along the crotch. Grunting, he heaved the man up and, with a rocking motion, threw him at Sain's wide, short shape.

The onlookers bent away and Sain dodged quickly. Parsons's looping body crashed on the boardwalk. He rolled and lay on his back.

Tom's breathing was a ragged rumble tearing his chest, and suddenly he felt the cramping weariness. He wiped blood from his puffed mouth. He swayed, with the numbness in his hanging arms, and he saw Sain step forward and take his eyes off Parsons.

"You just made the wrong turn," Sain grunted. "You busted up Parsons bad."

Tom ran a grimy hand across his still-bleeding mouth. "He tried to get me any way he could. He had help, too."

Men grumbled, not understanding, and Tom knew that, in the scrambling, dust-fogged struggle, nobody had seen Sain stick out his boot. "Plays hell with the posse," a man with a Yankee twang cut in.

"No, it don't," Sain bit back. "There'll be a posse and I'll lead it."

Tom stared at him wearily, feeling the old, helpless anger.

Sain settled his shoulders, his face poker-game straight with the flat look of a man used to hiding his shrewd thoughts. "We'll ride out to Parsons's claim and take a look," he said in a loud voice. "If Hard Rope's involved" — Sam shrugged — "well, that's up to Fort Reno to look into."

It was sogging through Tom's tired mind what Sain had done. With a few words, he had turned this to his advantage. He had taken over the stirred-up crowd and — the realization flared resentfully in Tom — Sain was looking righteously into Star Woman's eyes.

"You coming?" Sain said roughly, mocking.

"Fifty men's enough to read sign," Tom told him, and he made a path with his shoulders, looking for Star Woman. She came forward, her eyes seeking his face. Her hands rose and fell and she spoke, but it was lost in the scuffle of Rordan's heavy boots. "Your order's in the wagon," the fat man said with a ponderous wheeze.

Rordan wallowed behind them to the wagon. When Tom untied the team, climbed aboard, and looked down, the merchant stood uncertainly at the front wheel. Along the street, horses wheeled from hitch racks and men hurried to the Star Feed & Livery for more mounts. Two men had Dode

Parsons's loose shape by the shoulders. Sain's driving call sang across the racketing noise. Rordan placed his attention on the assembling riders while he spoke.

"Let the wire go, Tom. Come back in a week or two. Give things time to simmer down. These folks ain't bad, but fellows like Parsons rile 'em up."

Tom couldn't hide the surprise from his voice. "Why, much obliged, George. But I need the wire."

"You don't need it that bad."

Rordan looked up and Tom knew his own face was stubborn. Slowly Rordan backed off, shaking his white head, as Tom lifted the lines.

With Mustang falling behind, he felt a physical letdown crawling all through him, a steady hurt throbbing along his tight, bruised muscles. But dark and hard in the core of his mind was an understanding. George Rordan had merely touched upon it, talked around it briefly. For Tom realized that he had made his choice. He was a squawman now, and he had sided in with a bony-faced old Indian with ropy black hair living out the fag-end years on a squeezed-in piece of country the swarming white men called a reservation. And the home-hungry settlers, worn out farms in half a dozen states behind them, could see nothing but the cheap, unbroken land.

Stiff and sore on the rattling wagon seat, Tom fell silent. When they topped the first long, fingering ridge beyond town, Star Woman appraised him critically. "He cut you up," she said, her eyes roving his face.

He sifted the words, decided they held only the concern that any woman might feel for a beat-up man. "He did," Tom said with a cracked smile, "but they carried him off."

He handed the reins to her and slacked back. Afterward, he noticed the distant shape of the homestead that Frank Boyd had settled on. As the wagon ground along, he found himself watching the round points of her shoulders, the small brown hands. Crossing a rough-bottomed swale, the front wheels bucked and dropped and Tom groaned. She turned with a fast, sliding expression in the wide eyes.

"You hurt bad?"

Something touched him, held him. But the high-cheeked face switched swiftly, straight and fixed again. Gruffly Tom said — "I'm all right." — and felt the ease leave him.

They angled downgrade to the shallow ford of White Buffalo Creek, where gangling cottonwoods stood in stubborn rank. When they had splashed across and climbed upon the flattening prairie and felt the wind again, Tom took his look. The stretching emptiness never failed to move him and it stirred him now. He saw the timbered hill, his one-room sod house and the single pole corral, and, beyond, the curving line of the creek twisting in the beginning of a low-cupped valley. Squinting, he could see smoke raveling up from Hard Rope's camp among the crowding trees. On the wind there came a faint drumming, and, turning, Tom saw a tawny band of antelope breaking free to the west. He was sagged down, one arm loose on the wagon seat, when Star Woman spoke.

"Mort Sain did a good thing," she said, tones of her voice thoughtful, "taking the white men the other way."

Tom's hand tightened on the wood until the raw knuckles stood out like red knobs. He wanted to tell her about Sain's unseen interference. But he faced straight ahead, thinking there were some things you didn't tell a Cheyenne girl still smitten by a trader's soft talk. It was his own pride, too, Tom knew — a man's foolish weakness.

Star Woman noticed the bare-backed pony first. The dismounted, bony Indian in greasy buckskin leggings holding the rawhide reins and soberly watching as the wagon jangled up in front of the house. Hard Rope's coffee-colored eyes were quick, and Tom realized that he was reading the sign of Parsons's fist marks on his face.

"Big fight," Tom said, unhitching. "No guns . . . just fists. A settler named Parsons. You've seen him with Sain." Tom paused and regarded Hard Rope a moment. "The white men claim Cheyennes are raiding homesteads. They got a bunch of men out scouting. Maybe they'll come to your camp."

"Maybe," the old Indian grunted, unimpressed. He swung his braided head, his open flannel shirt showing his lean chest.

"Your bucks," Tom persisted gravely. "They say your young men are doing it."

"Me hear." Hard Rope waved a gnarled hand. "Take young men on long rides, go see."

"Better keep your people on the reservation." Tom wondered if Hard Rope really understood. "You got plenty of hills west of White Buffalo Creek. Good time for antelope."

"Purty soon all antelope gone like buffalo." There was a momentary wistfulness in the wizened face. Then Hard Rope straddled the pony, his bowed legs slapping. "Let white man come."

It occurred to Tom that the Cheyenne wouldn't run. Star Woman continued to stare after her father. *Homesick,* Tom thought. *She wants to go home.*

Long after supper, Tom sat in the sod house doorway, listening to the brush of Star Woman's moccasins while his glance hung on the purpling valley as the lavender evening shadows closed down. The dull soreness of the fight still gripped him, and he went inside for water. In the yellow light of the coal-oil lamp, he saw the cameo on the wooden packing crate he'd shaped into a rough dresser for her. Its finely cut lady's figure pale and pink, rimmed with a thin gold band, the tiny, rounded piece lay where she had left it the first day he'd brought her here — unwanted, untouched. Looking around, he saw her at the door, and it raked into him that he was completely shut out from her. He could see that in the way she stood bent forward, in the way she stared off down the blackening valley, yearning, hankering.

Tom pressed his mouth together hard, took a slow step. She would never say she wanted to leave. But she would show it clearly — in a single gesture, a far-away look, a long-running silence, like now. When the light was gone from the room, and the night's first coyote bark lifted thinly and they lay apart, he saw in his mind the shape of the thing. With dread and certainty, he knew he ought to send her back to her people. . . .

At first gray daylight, Tom was riding west. Deep in the morning he found the Texas steers, still gaunt from their long-striding walk up the Chisholm Trail, drifted beyond the leased graze. He worked the rolling country, chasing them back. The timber was throwing black shadows when he crossed the White Buffalo on his way home.

When he got back, he looked around and caught the sliding motion of the black horse and the wide, thick rider. Immediately he knew, without having to look again, and he was thinking of Mort Sain's shrewd talk when he rode up to the house. Star Woman faced him from the door.

"Sain stop here?" Tom asked bluntly.

She nodded, but her eyes told him nothing.

"He bother you?" Tom couldn't curb his running anger, and he knew his voice was rough.

There was the barest hesitation before she said quickly: "He didn't come in." Almost too fast, Tom thought. "We talked. He said white people still stirred up."

"That all?"

He had his unspoken answer as her lips firmed, as suspicion touched him. She stared at him, round-eyed, anger and hurt mingling in her face. More had been said, he realized, but she'd never tell him. He let it go, his voice dry, weary. "I'll be going in tomorrow for the wire. Our stock's drifting clear across country. You stay here," he told her finally, thinking of Parsons and Sain and the half-wild crowd.

They ate in silence, the thought drumming at Tom that no man had the right to hold a woman who didn't want to stay. But once Tom broke the bargain, would she go to Sain?

He brought the team out in the early, sun-bright light. Deliberately he fought back the desire to look back. Rejected it as foolish for a man who already knew what he had to do and, more foolishly, kept delaying. Foolish, maybe, like the worn Colt he'd belted on.

An hour from Mustang he saw the black smudge rising above a ridge. He studied it with only a half interest, his thoughts back at the house. He lost the smoke following the dipping wagon trail, but picked it up again when he pulled up on the ridge. From here on the spread-out prairie he could see the Boyd homestead, the broad flat of the hay meadow this side of the bending creek — and the still-smoking haystack, and the blackened square of the barn.

Figures moved around the house and Tom angled sharply down the slope. He didn't notice the rifle until the woman wheeled at the wagon's running rumble. She was a young-old woman, very thin and very brave. Three yellow-haired children stuck close to her.

"Nothin' you can do," she said before he could speak. "Al, Frank's brother, was shot in the chest. I'm Frank's wife . . . we're all right." Her voice barely broke and the ragged sound of it hit Tom. "Frank took him in the buggy to Mustang. Couldn't all of us go. Somebody'll be coming soon. Frank was gonna tell the neighbors."

"I'll wait," Tom said, remembering Frank Boyd as the settler who'd argued with Parsons. "Get a look at the riders?"

"Frank and Al ran out. That's when it happened." She shuddered. "Frank said he saw Indians. Guess so, because you could hear 'em whoop. Right after that we heard some more shots off down there."

She pointed toward the reservation and Tom nodded gravely. He waited until he saw three horsemen ford the creek and race across the yellowing grass, until the Boyd woman's drawn face showed its recognizing relief. Driving off, Tom knew that it was coming fast now. Another burnout was bad enough, but a wounded white man would fire Mustang to an aroused savageness.

He was rolling up dust down the last hill when the realization struck him. Somehow, it seemed too pat, too set. All the burnings had followed the same pattern — Indian-looking horsemen always partly hidden by the darkness, the telltale whoops as they rode off.

Tom looked up as a man rushed across the street carrying a rifle. And at the street's end, riders' dust rose around the Star barn entrance. George Rordan stood in front of his wide store, taking in the scene. He turned and Tom caught his surprise.

"Came for my wire," Tom said.

"You picked a hell of a time," Rordan said with heat. "They're going after Hard Rope. It was Frank Boyd's place this time, and they shot Frank's brother. Maybe he'll pull through."

Tom split his gaze between Rordan and the posse, and at that moment he made up his mind. "I'll still take the wire, George," he stated.

Rordan gave him a critical look and muttered to a watching boy, who turned reluctantly. Two rolls of wire had banged upon the wagon bed when Tom saw the horsemen swing away from the barn. They rode solidly, deliberately, saddle guns racked in long holsters. Mort Sain's rocky frame bulked in front. The big man's head tilted up as he took in the wagon.

Tom's throat was dry. "I'll give the boy a hand," he said.

"Sain'll be waiting for you," Rordan predicted.

Tom stepped inside, and, when the boy turned back with another roll, Tom kept moving to the rear of the store. Letting himself out in the alley, he heard the choppy noise of horses. Then he was running for the Star's back feed lot. He climbed the board corral and jumped down, the feeling of time heavy upon him. How long would Sain wait at the wagon?

In the barn Tom's eyes ran along the shadowed, empty stalls. Empty except for the undersize dun gelding no posse man wanted. But he knew it had to be the gelding, and he saddled up.

A tight band of fear laced his stomach as he rode out the back gate, rode past the shack houses behind Main Street, the high-voiced growl of the crowd keen in his ears. At the town's edge, he began a half circle and worked around to the Mustang road. But when he glanced back, barely showing himself from the grassy hill's rim, the posse was already a ball of dust on the road only half a mile away.

Tom raked the gelding hard and felt the stringy frame lurch. It was a ten-mile ride across up-and-down country, he remembered, and a posse headed for Hard Rope's camp had to pass the ranch house. When he left the Mustang road, he saw the riders as a dark, forceful clump. They seemed to come on faster now, because the hills had flattened out, exposing him.

White Buffalo Creek was a jagged line of black timber before Tom twisted and looked again. His heart slugged its drumbeat in his chest, for the horsemen were rapidly closing in. Across the creek the gelding floundered, in a stumbling run, and the little horse made a grunting, scrambling racket as Tom headed him toward the empty yard.

Calling hoarsely for Star Woman, he glanced backward. He slid down and saw her running from the house, holding his Winchester saddle gun.

"Get on!" he told her, and he saw that she knew by the way her eyes shifted toward the creek. “Tell Hard Rope to pull out anywhere!” It seemed like a long time as he watched her climb up. It came to him that he’d have to say more.

“You stay with him,” Tom said in a flat, dead voice. “You don’t have to come back. Tell Hard Rope to keep the horses.”

He saw the heavy shock of astonishment climbing in the slim face, in the deep, round eyes. He saw something that he’d never seen there before, something swift and searching, now bewildered. And then he slapped the dun across the flanks and Star Woman was gone.

Tom turned deliberately, with a dryness in his throat, with an oddly detached coldness. He stood spraddle-legged, doggedly, in a kind of daze. The riders had cleared the creek bottom. He saw Sain’s thick arm whip up and the posse driving forward in that solid, wedging mass. Slanting sun glinted on rifle barrels, on sweaty horsehide.

Tom felt his loneness, his dread, and he drew in his breath. As they topped the low rise below the house in the thickening timber, he slipped out the Colt. Most of these men were townsmen, he saw bleakly, moving with caution pulled tight on their jaw-hard faces. He noticed Frank Boyd, thin-lipped and stiff beside Sain, a shotgun in his rough hands.

Sain rode ahead, swaggering a little as his heavy body rolled in the saddle. His gaze raked up from Tom's pistol, traveled suspiciously to the house and the empty corral, and back. "Figured you'd be here," he said arrogantly. "Where's the Injun girl?"

"You mean my wife?" Tom felt his muscles grow rigid.

Sain's tone was sarcastic. "Yeah . . . the pony woman."

Rashness burned all through Tom, yet he knew that every word meant time — time for Hard Rope to rush his people from the camp. But Sain whipped his harsh voice at the posse. "We're losin' time. She's told Hard Rope by now."

"Go down there," Tom said coldly, "and some of you won't come back. He's got the women and kids out now. He'll cover them with every man in camp."

"We're going," Sain announced, "right over you." He edged his horse out, but pulled up as the posse line hesitated. "Damn you," Sain bellowed furiously, "gonna let him bluff you?"

Frank Boyd's sun-blackened face twisted, rigid, drawn. "Been one white man shot. Show some sense, Bard."

"Funny thing" — Tom heard his own

pinched refusal — "but Cheyennes don't raid in the dark. They say a brave killed before sunup don't go to the hunting ground." He could feel the keen edge of the cramping tension, the squeal of leather under shifting bodies.

"Frank" — Sain heaved around, playing his shrewd glance on Boyd — "you're yellow if you back down . . . after they shot at Al!"

Tom saw the quick flame of the blood flushing up Boyd's knotted neck, across the rigid face. Boyd's eyes flashed. He straightened. "Let's get it over with," he grunted finally. Around him men muttered. Boyd shoved the shotgun at Tom and Tom held the pistol on him. They were framed like that, glaring and unbending, when the movement of Sain's horse split the pressure.

Tom followed him from the rim of his eyes. Sain reined up in the shadow of the timber. "You're a damned fool," he said thickly. "Star Woman won't stick with you. She told me . . . you saw me ride off."

Sain let the words drop like a weight, and Tom felt the impact, like a shaking sickness. He was facing a ringed-in world of closing horsemen. He licked dry lips. He caught the wildness in Boyd's flinty eyes. Sain was bringing up his rifle, unhurried and sure.

"Go on, Boyd." Sain's prodding voice.

But Boyd seemed frozen, his eyes fixed beyond Sain. And Tom's thought, like a flash, went to Sain. With a feeling of lateness, Tom pivoted desperately toward the big man.

There was a single slash of gunfire from the timber. A puff of crawling smoke. Horses clumping there. Sain jerked and he was swaying awkwardly. His rifle spun down. With a violent and straining concentration, he clawed for the saddle horn. For a few seconds he held on. But the wide hands loosened, almost lazily, and he fell ponderously as a horse moved from the covering trees.

Tom saw Hard Rope walking his pony forward. Behind him rode bearded Dobe Parsons and two shaggy-haired white men, paint smearing their faces. Behind them Star Woman slanted the carbine. It took a moment for Tom to understand that she'd really come back. Hard Rope raised a bony, signaling hand, his rifle in the crook of his arm.

Hearing Boyd's angry grunt, Tom wheeled. He saw the hard mouth working, remembering. Boyd was whipping up the shotgun when Tom lunged. He felt the numbing pain clear to his shoulder socket when his arm smashed against the barrel, felt the shotgun tear from Boyd's hands.

"White men dress up like Cheyennes. Burn down houses." There was a stillness, broken only by Boyd's outraged breathing, and Tom realized Hard Rope was speaking. "But Cheyennes catch 'em last night."

Now Tom remembered the old Indian's long rides beyond the reservation, and the shots the Boyd woman had heard. As Tom stared, Hard Rope casually let his rifle tilt on Parsons, sullen and bent shouldered.

"I don't believe it," Boyd spoke up.

"Look at that paint," Tom cut in. "And Hard Rope stayed. He didn't have to take the risk. But he wouldn't run."

"You better speak up, Parsons." Boyd's face had changed all at once, with a bitter-eyed realization.

"Yeah. . . ." Parsons took in the packed riders, hope glimmering through the streaked paint. Then Hard Rope's rifle twitched slightly, hung there, and Tom saw the defiance wash out of Parsons's flat eyes, followed by the shine of fear.

"I told Sain we were pushin' our luck." Suddenly Parsons's voice was high, nearly shrill. "But he was land crazy. He had to have those homesteads cheap." He glanced nervously at Hard Rope. "Now get me away from this damned heathen!"

"Maybe," grunted the old chief, making a strangling, throaty sound, "you better stay Cheyenne. White man got many long ropes."

Wildly Parsons kneed his horse away, and the posse closed him in. Boyd looked sheepish when Tom handed up the shotgun. "You'll need help building back that barn," Tom said. "I'm close."

Sober-faced, Tom watched the posse load Sain's body across his fidgety horse, watched them trot off. They seemed eager to go.

"You got plenty bullets? Hard Rope's gun empty."

Tom's jaw dropped open and he faced around. "Plenty," he said slowly, "but you fooled Parsons, and you just needed one bullet for Sain."

Hard Rope gave him a sliding, muddy-eyed look, like a man who'd said too much. Now Tom noticed the worn-out dun gelding, reins dragging, and a reluctance tore into him. Slow-footed, he walked stiffly to the house. Inside, he caught the quick movement of Star Woman's brown hands as she stood with her back to him.

"It still stands," Tom said awkwardly. "You came back, but you don't have to stay here. I'll help you get your things."

She kept turned away, with her back rigid, and he had the strange awareness of not understanding.

"Sain told me to leave you," she said in a strained voice. "He said he'd kill you if I stayed. I wouldn't go . . . I am the one who shot him."

"But Hard Rope had a gun. It looked. . . ." It rolled over him and, like a stab, he understood the Cheyenne's pulled-in expression, and he felt himself stirring. Yet. . . .

She faced him and he saw something pink at her throat. Her hand slid to the cameo, fingers possessively pinching around it. He saw her upturned, high-boned face, tightly drawn. There was the same searching look he'd caught before she rode off, trying to tell him she wasn't going back.

THE RAVAGED PLAIN

I

Westward as far as Tom Reed could see, the short-grassed Texas prairie swayed away like a restless green sea, more vast than he had ever imagined back home in Missouri, and the May wind carried the sweet scents of wildflowers. But around him he was aware of a strange stillness and an even stranger emptiness, as if all life had vanished. Where were the buffalo?

It was time he sighted game, on this second day out from Fort Griffin, following the meandering wagon trail that led to Rath City, the hide hunters' town on the Double Mountain Fork of the Brazos.

Impatience moved him. He clapped his heels and the reddish bay gelding, seeming to awaken from a deep drowse, fell into a jarring, listless trot.

Before noon Tom rode upon a swell of land. He saw no game and the country hadn't changed. Yet something was different. A glistening white down covered the prairie. Riding on, he saw bones and curved-horn heads bleaching on both sides of the road. Not the scattered buffalo skeletons first noticed yesterday. Instead, a great snowfall of bones, everywhere, that wearied the eyes.

He was suddenly appalled at the waste, and all at once the empty vastness of the prairie rushed over him and he felt alone.

He passed a low ridge and came to a glistening branch. After watering his horse, he knelt and drank his fill. All morning he had ignored his hunger. Now, giving in, he opened the little pack of beef and cornbread, only to stare in dismay at the scant supply left. Unless he found a hunter's camp by tomorrow, or shot himself a buffalo, he would be without food. Catching the appetizing odors, he was tempted to wolf every bit.

Instead, rationing himself, he drew his Bowie knife and carefully cut a small piece of meat and broke off a corner of bread and sat down under a mesquite, considering his mount while he ate lunch.

Tom called him Red. The old bag of bones had cost him one month's wages at a farmer's place on Red River, yet was as necessary as the knife and Tom's wide-brimmed hat and red shirt and oversize cowboy boots, likewise earned along the way.

But he was proudest of the long-barreled Dance revolver snug in the holster at his belt. Some punkins of a handgun, the storekeeper had assured him. Converted to use metallic cartridges. You betcha. Tom agreed the single-action weapon looked its part. Rawhide bound the broken wooden handle, and the sight was battered. Afterward, he learned it shot eight inches to the left at thirty paces. Even so, it gave a man a comfortable feeling.

Thinking he might locate a hunter's camp or buffalo, Tom started up the ridge, the heavy revolver wobbling on his skinny hip, his feet lost in the boots, a slight swagger in his walk. His high, clomping steps took him through a stand of prickly pear to the top.

There he looked off, hand-shading his eyes. To the west he could see more of the ash-like pallor, northwest the same, and south more littered emptiness. He heard not a sound except the purring southwest wind.

Discouraged, he looked eastward. Something caught his eye. He strained forward to see. Whatever, it was lost in the pitching land. Something dark and low. Like buffalo, he imagined, a beginning excitement in him.

Some time passed. He sat on a rock to watch. And again, much closer, on the spine of a ridge chain, he saw the stir of movement. Then his shoulders sagged. Not buffalo. Just riders strung out. A few minutes went by. Some of the horses were pulling long poles, and some of the riders looked like women and children. As he looked his throat contracted and the strength left him.

Those were Indians riding steadily toward him.

His impulse was to run. But if he did, they would see him outlined against the sky, and old Red couldn't run fast enough to take him out of danger. Tom flattened out behind the rock and swept off his hat. His hand was trembling as he drew the revolver.

Straight on, the Indians came. And then, at the base of the ridge, the cavalcade turned.

Tom let out a sigh of relief as the Indians began passing below him. He could see the warriors plainly, their coppery, glittering faces like eagles. All seemed to be looking far off, as if searching for something, even the solemn children. Tom heard no voices. Only the drumming ruffle of hoofs through the short grass and the rustling of drawn poles on which were tied the Indians' possessions.

Like a shadow over the prairie the little band passed, gone so soon that Tom almost doubted that he had seen Indians at all.

He mounted and followed the road, feeling a new caution. Other than fresh wagon tracks angling in from the northeast, he saw no signs of life during the afternoon.

When the eye of a fire and the white blurs of two parked wagons appeared through the evening haze, he heeled Red into a trot. Appetizing food smells scented the cool wind. Near camp he reined up and called.

A tall man rose beside the fire. "Tie up over there," he said.

Sauntering forward, Tom saw the man eye him curiously, then lower his head as if to hide an expression. "Had your supper, boy?"

Tom forced down his eagerness. "Not yet. But I got grub."

"Better save it." He gestured in invitation toward the fire.

Two men sat there, eating. Each nodded. Not enough hands for a hunting outfit, Tom decided.

"Good evening, young man. Sit down. Alex will get you a plate."

The speaker wore a derby hat. He regarded Tom through eyeglasses that rested near the tip of his narrow nose. A close, brown beard, flecked with gray, covered his face like curly moss. His precise voice, which gave the impression that he was used to being obeyed, nevertheless conveyed a natural courtesy. But it was the eyes that drew Tom's attention. An unusual warmth shone in their brown depths.

Tom sat on a wooden box. Alex, bandy-legged, stooped, handed him a heaped tin plate, knife and fork, and set a steaming tin cup of coffee on the edge of the box.

While Tom attacked the generous helpings of beans, salt pork, and biscuits, he saw the three eyeing him and his get-up, and not without some amusement. Still, no one asked his name or reason for riding alone. He liked that. No doubt they figured he was a man or he wouldn't be here. When Tom emptied his plate, Alex loaded it again.

At last, Tom finished. He sat back, feeling a fresh confidence. He shifted the heavy holster for comfort, let his left hand slide across the Bowie's handle, pushed his hat back a notch, and looked around,

"Meet anybody on the trail today?" the tall man asked.

"Just Indians. I gave 'em the slip. But I was ready" — Tom tapped the handgun — "if they tried any monkeyshines."

A smile flitted across the leathery features.

"Man sure wants to be ready when he's outnumbered that way."

Tom nodded to that, impressed. Everything about the lank, brown-skinned man suggested wind and sun and far places: the wrinkles crinkling the corners of his light-blue eyes, which looked white against his stubbled cheeks and the straight, Indian-black hair that hung shoulder length beneath his slouch hat.

"Injuns?" he reflected. "All bucks?"

"Women and kids, too," Tom said.

"Means they're lookin' for meat. Which way'd they go?"

"West." Tom corrected himself. "No . . . it was northwest."

"You're certain?"

"They went northwest from the road," Tom said, cocking one eye. "I figure it runs about due west."

"It does." The man's faint amusement vanished and he turned to the others, a frown ridging between his eyes. "Perfessor, looks like they're headed for Kiowa Peak. If there's any buffalo left, that's the place. If I's a hungry Injun, that's where I'd ride."

"Which is precisely where we must go, Jack," came the enthusiastic reply.

"Point is, they won't know what we're tryin' to do. We'll be just another bunch of white men come to crowd in on their last huntin' ground."

"I'm willing to take the chance."

Now the prairie night enveloped the camp and a keener coolness turned Tom's thoughts to the coat in his saddle pack. Also it was time to go.

"I'm obliged to you for the supper," he said, and rose.

"Stay the night, young man," the professor said. "You may sleep under the big wagon."

Next morning Tom did not linger after breakfast. The professor looked preoccupied as Tom spoke his thanks. Tom was leading Red out to mount when he saw the professor coming toward him in short, jerky strides.

"Young man . . . what's your name?" he demanded, pointing a detaining finger at him.

"Buck . . . Buck Woods," Tom mumbled, caught off guard.

"Buck Woods," the professor mused, and pulled on his chin. "Reminds me when I ran off from home. Let's see . . . believe I was Chris Boyd. Terror of the West. . . . Remember I got as far as the Ohio." The firm but understanding gaze seemed to bore inside Tom, to tear down his silence. "I mean your real name, son."

What did a name matter when he was riding on? "It's Tom Reed."

"And where is your home?"

Where from didn't matter out West, either. "Saint Louis," Tom said, and started to mount.

"How would you like to work for me for a few days, Tom?"

Feeling rippled through Tom. "Hunting buffalo?"

"In a way. I'm Professor Gideon Trumbull. I represent a group of Eastern zoological societies. That's Jack Dean over there. The noted hunter and guide. And that's Alex Roth. . . . We're here to save the noble bison from extermination, if we're not too late." He waved Dean across.

Tom's interest ebbed. As Dean reached them, Trumbull said: "We're short of help. Hunters and skinners have all left the range because there's nothing to hunt."

"If that's so," Tom said, in a countering voice, "then how can you save any buffalo?"

"Mister Dean, here, knows where a small band may be. Up around Kiowa Peak. Northwest. Which is why we need your help, Tom. A strong boy to wrestle some calves."

In a flash, Tom saw through everything:

the good meals, the friendly talk, and what had seemed like an interest in him. All the professor wanted was a boy to do men's chores. Tom had had his fill of that.

"I came to hunt," he said, letting them see his scorn, and climbed to the saddle. He looked down into Jack Dean's wind-burned face.

"It's like the perfessor told you," Dean said. "There's nothin' to hunt."

"Is around Rath City."

"Everybody's pulled out."

"You're saying that to keep me here." Tom swung Red out, in case Dean tried to snatch the reins.

Dean didn't move. "You won't like what you find. But I reckon you got to see for yourself. Just be on the look-out. Remember the real buff'lo runners have quit the range."

That morning Tom rode through the littered dreariness of more shot-out country. Once he spied white dots scattered on a green slope. Leaving the trail, he saw the dots were the rump patches of buff-colored animals with pronged horns. Antelope! He'd shoot one for his supper.

Hardly had the thought stirred when the graceful creatures took alarm and bounded away, phantom-like, shrinking to miniature in a few moments, their speed astonishing.

In disgust, Tom returned to the trail. Without warning, a terrible stench swept over him. A stench so strong he had to hold his nose. He bowed his head against it. Nostrils pinched, lips squeezed, he rode ahead, and noted recent signs of slaughter. Vultures sailing the sky. Wolves lurking boldly off the trail. Buffalo bones thickly scattered. Black, woolly hair still clinging to the curved-horn heads.

He rode on, sickened.

As the afternoon wore away, Tom kept thinking of Rath City and how far it was and whether he would find the town deserted. He was certain of only one thing: he'd need meat before he got there.

When he saw a jack rabbit sitting, he tied old Red and stalked forward, revolver drawn. The rabbit bobbed away and sat. Holding the Dance with both hands, Tom fired. Dust spurted to the rabbit's left. Before Tom could fire again, the rabbit scurried off and sat.

Tom circled around, crouched, aiming a little to the rabbit's right. At the sound of the gun it fell, kicking, and Tom ran over with a shout. Exulting, he went across the plain, in and out of a dry wash, and came through the stand of mesquite where Red was tied.

That was when he saw the two riders eyeing his horse and the good second-hand stock saddle. Each wore the same greasy-bearded look. Each displayed a row of butcher knives stuck inside his belt. One man grinned at Tom now, showing stained, broken teeth, and said: "Heard the shootin'. Figured some poor soul needed help, didn't we, Brack?"

"Yeah, Smiley."

"Our camp's just over the ridge," Smiley said, his quick, black eyes hanging on Tom's revolver.

"You're buffalo hunters?" Tom asked.

Smiley's hesitation was momentary, but Tom caught it. Smiley's face gathered in a sloppy grin. "Anything with a hide on it."

Tom's elation made his voice flute up, for he'd found real buffalo hunters. "Could you use another man? I learn real fast."

Smiley, gaunt and slope-shouldered, craned a look at his impassive partner. "Hear that, Brack? Nubbins wants to hire on."

"Yeah, Smiley."

"Depends," said Smiley, hanging out his lower lip. "Just depends." And, as if weighing Tom's merits: "We'll see." Once more his black eyes flicked across Tom, the grin slid into place, and he said: " 'Bout supper-time. Come on."

Tom wasn't expecting the clutter of wagons, horses, and mules, and the score of men slouching near the cooking fires. But close in he saw the wagons were rickety, their covers ragged and patched, the animals bony and hard-used, the shaggy men as dirty as Smiley and Brack. Four wagons had frames like hay wagons; on them lay hides lapped with ropes.

Before dark Tom went to a hide wagon. He'd seen buffalo robes, but never a fresh hide. He touched a hide, peering and feeling. He stepped back in surprise. The hides were small and grayish. They were wolf hides, coyote hides.

At supper Tom cooked the rabbit on a mesquite stick. He offered Smiley a piece. Before Tom knew it, Smiley was helping himself to more rabbit, eating wolfishly. The rest of the crew dipped stew from two big black pots. There was no bread.

Smiley swiped a sleeve across his mouth. "Nubbins says he came West to hunt buff'lo." There was a roar of laughter. "Trouble is, nubbins don't know the buff'lo's wiped out." The crew, hunkered down, eating off tin plates, suddenly reminded Tom of a circle of hungry wolves.

"Not all of 'em," Tom replied, stung to anger.

"Is that so?"

"I know where there's plenty buffalo," Tom went on, brag creeping into his voice. "A whole herd."

"A herd? Just where, nubbins?" Smiley didn't believe him.

"Don't call me nubbins."

"All right. Where?"

"Around Kiowa Peak . . . that's where. Jack Dean said so. He's going there." A wrongness brushed him the moment he finished. He wished deeply he hadn't told them. A hush fell. They were all watching him.

"Dean? Him?" Smiley's scoffing was gone. "How big a herd?"

". . . It was a joke." Tom tried to smile, couldn't. "That's all it was." He saw Smiley's intent gaze, the angles of his greasy face hardening under the whisker thicket, the black eyes glittery. At once the eyes changed.

"A joke." Smiley grinned. "That's a good 'un, all right."

Tom's uneasiness lifted. He took Red away from the wagons, picketed the old gelding, made his blanket bed, and lay down. There wasn't going to be any job, and he was glad. He didn't like this camp. He listened to the camp sounds a while. *Is there really a buffalo herd around Kiowa Peak?* he wondered. Yet he kept seeing the earnest faces of Professor Trumbull and Jack Dean swimming through his drowsiness, and that quiet little man, Alex.

He opened his eyes to star glitter hearing Red's restless movements. Tom turned on his side. The camp was black silent. He was about to fall asleep, when he heard the footfall. He drew the Dance, his body rigid. Now he saw the looming figure, almost unreal in the muddy light.

Tom cocked the hammer. At the audible click the gaunt shape froze. After a long moment, it faded into the murk.

Smiley, Tom knew, breathing again.

He lay back, a violent drumming in his chest. A cold fear sprang him upright. Quietly he saddled and, taking his bedding, led Red into the night.

Daylight found him on a rise, chilled, hungry, watching the camp break up, wanting the lead wagon to turn eastward on the trail to the settlements. A sinking came over him as, instead, it pulled northwest and the others followed, the drivers whipping the teams.

Tom's guilt was unforgiving. He bowed

his head. By talking big, he had given away the location of the last buffalo herd in Texas, for all he knew maybe the last buffalo in America. There wouldn't be any more.

Was there time to hurry back and tell his friends? They were his friends. He knew that now.

He got up then.

II

The sun's bloody eye glared straight overhead before Tom saw the covers of the two wagons bulging on the trail. Jack Dean rode horseback in front. Next came Professor Trumbull, driving the heavy wagon, followed by Alex Roth in the cook wagon.

"What's the matter, boy?" Dean called. "You look peaked."

It was all Tom could do to meet the questioning eyes. He began to tell, stumbling in his haste, omitting no details, not sparing himself.

"So you spilled the beans?" Dean pressed his lips together. But when he spoke again, he sounded as relieved as he was harsh. "A wonder you're alive, and with everything you have not stolen. That bunch . . . they're wolfers."

"Wolfers?" Now Tom remembered the grayish hides on the wagons.

"Lowest, dirtiest, thievingest no-account breed on the plains. Poison buff'lo carcasses, they do. Wolves an' coyotes eat the poisoned meat. Die in agony. Wolfers take their skins." He spat. "I'd better tell the perfessor."

"I'll tell him," Tom said.

A frown puckered Trumbull's placid features while he listened. Although he said nothing for a moment, Tom could see his quickening concern. "But you did come back, Tom," he said, nodding. "Jack, what can we do?"

"Cut across country. It's our only chance."

"With wagons?"

"This trail's not much better. Our mules are grain-fed. They're fast steppers."

And so it was decided. Dean turned off the trail and struck northwest. Tom swung in beside him, expecting the hunter to order him back to the wagons. Dean ignored him.

To Tom it seemed that the bone litter was heavier than ever, for he was never out of sight of débris, which crusted the May prairie like some kind of pestilence as the country about him climbed and dipped, and then fell to occasional washes flashing earthy reds, yellows, and browns.

Around midafternoon Tom saw Dean check his horse and hunch forward, a sure sign of trouble ahead. Catching up, Tom found the steep sides of a shallow stream some fifty yards across. There was no way around.

Using picks and shovels, the four of them gouged and dug and tugged rocks aside until a rough passage slanted to the bottom. Then Dean and Roth and Tom strained on ropes tied to the wagon, holding it back from a headlong slide that would smash the frame and cripple the four mules. Trumbull shook the reins and the skittish mules started downward.

Tom saw the wagon top begin to sway, joints creaking, the mules nervous, head-tossing, jangling harness and chains. He heard a loud crunch as a front wheel struck rock. Dean yelled in warning the same instant that Tom saw the wagon skidding sideways, the canvas top about to topple.

Tom jerked with all his power, boot heels dug in. Little by little, he saw the wagon righting itself, heard the wheels settling. But the mules were acting up. They lunged. Dean and Roth yelled. Tom, holding fast to the rope, felt himself being dragged through brush and over rocks.

The sky was spinning, whirling faster. Pain shivered up through his legs and back. His hands burned, but still he hung on. Dimly he heard the bouncing crash of wagon rims and tortured wood. After that, the sky grew black and he didn't know where he was.

Far away, a voice was calling him. When it sounded near, he opened his eyes and Professor Trumbull's neat, bearded face, drawn in worry, came into focus above him.

"You all right, young man? That was quite a thumping you took."

Tom, swaying to his feet, felt the rope fall away from him. With a vast relief, he saw the wagon intact and the tail-switching mules standing nervously.

"Our calf wagon had a big bump, but nothing broke," Trumbull said.

Next time Dean led the mules down and the light cook wagon reached the bottom without mishap. It took another half hour to cross the sandy stream, cut a notch in the far bank, and fight the mules to the top.

"Leastwise," Dean said, when the last wagon stood on high ground, "we're goin' as the crow flies."

"As the crow hops, you mean," hacked Roth, who rarely spoke.

Dean continued northwest, across rolling swells of prairie, scaled white and odorous like the country through which they had passed. The sun was well down the western wall of the sky when Dean stopped suddenly and motioned to Tom, who had dropped back to let old Red lag with the tired teams. Professor Trumbull halted.

Dean was staring down into a draw as Tom rode up. The hunter held up his hand for silence and pointed, and Tom saw a single buffalo. It was grazing away from them.

"An old bull," Dean said sympathetically. "Wind's from him to us, so he can't smell us. Notice how edgy he is. He's lost his courage. He's come here where he won't have to rustle too hard for feed an' water."

Fascinated, in the grip of awe, Tom watched the huge, dark beast, observing the massive head, forequarters, and hump, the black chin mop brushing the grass as he grazed. The old bull seemed pathetic in his isolation. *All alone,* Tom couldn't help thinking, *where there used to be millions.*

"Take a good look, boy," Dean said. "May be the only buff'lo you ever see."

Tom had seen enough bones these few days to understand. Yet he was also puzzled. "Why'd the hunters kill so many of them?"

"Money," said Dean, "though it was never easy money. A man took chances, too . . . Injuns, blizzards, sandstorms, thieves. An' there was the stink, the flies, bedbugs, fleas, an' graybacks. Why, at one time they say better'n fifteen-hundred men hunted buff'lo out of Fort Griffin." A little of that old excitement laced Dean's voice. "A good hide used to bring as high as three dollars and fifty cents. Tongues sold for fifty cents. Buyers shipped the hides back East for robes an' leather. Tongues went to fancy hotels, where they got white cloths on the tables an' a man has to take off his hat 'fore he sits down to his vittles."

"Couldn't the government stop it?"

Dean snorted. "Why, the government wants the buff'lo wiped out 'cause the government can't handle the Injun. Buff'lo's the Injun's commissary. Kill off the buff'lo, tame the Injun. Make way for the rancher an' the sodbuster. If the Injuns you saw don't find meat, they'll have to go back to the reservation or they'll starve."

Dean glanced at the sliding sun, yet seemed reluctant to go. He considered the bull again. "Wolves'll surely get him before long. I ought to shoot him, but I won't do it. I want that old fellow to live as long as he can."

He rode on, and, as the creaking wagons drew near, the old bull threw up his shaggy head and lumbered off. The last Tom saw of him, he was plodding warily down the draw.

As they went on, the whitening litter thickened. They came upon a wide stretch where the profusion of bones made Tom think of drifted snow. Red's hoofs ticked on the scatterings. Behind, the quick-footed mules stepped gingerly through the bleaching mass, and there was the steady crunching of wagon rims on bones.

"Bone-pickin' is the business now," Dean said, his tone disdainful. "In Fort Worth they pay six to eight dollars a ton. All you can haul in. Seems buff'lo bones make good fertilizer." He pointed to a swale particularly thick with bones, where the glistening skeletons seemed to lie in a pattern. "Somebody got a stand over there. That's when a runner makes a big kill. It's not sport. It's just plain slaughter."

Dean did not halt until darkness purpled the prairie. Tom helped him water the mules and saddle stock from barrels on the wagons and afterward picket them for grazing.

"I've been thinking about tomorrow," the professor said at supper. "How many calves shall we need?"

"Seven or eight heifers," Dean said. "Two or three bull calves."

A hopefulness that was almost boyish shaped itself in Professor Trumbull's face. "How I should like to be able to take back a full-grown cow or bull," he said.

"Perfessor," Dean objected, shaking his

head, "you can't drive buff'lo like cattle. An' if you roped a big bull, you'd sure wished you hadn't."

"I'm assuming, of course, there are bison in the vicinity of Kiowa Peak."

"We'll know tomorrow. May not be any at all."

Tom crawled under the calf wagon, rolled up in his blanket. He had no more than fallen asleep, it seemed, when he felt a touch on his shoulder and heard Dean's clear voice: "Let's hit the grit."

They traveled on the rest of the night, feeling their way, with halts that were shorter and shorter, and, when daylight rushed in, peeling away the soft prairie darkness, Tom saw nothing had changed. The monotonous whiteness extended in all directions, as empty as yesterday. Not one buffalo. Not one old lonesome bull. His disappointment deepened.

Around 10:00 Dean halted, fed all stock a measure of shelled corn, rested briefly, and pushed hard ahead.

Several times Tom dismounted and walked beside the old gelding, which was tiring now, head hanging, as Dean continued the fast pace. Even the hardy mules were slowing down. Morning burned away into afternoon, the grass smells coming stronger to

Tom as the sun struck hotter and the springtime wind whipped his face.

Hopefully he watched the northwest while riding alongside the calf wagon. A flash of color met his eye, lost as the footing under him dipped. When Red took him to the next rise, he spotted it clearly. A shaft of reddish brown. A solitary butte or peak, standing out like a castle's broken battlement, strange in the white glaze of afternoon heat.

Dean rode back. "There she is . . . Kiowa Peak. Grass is always good. There's a big spring on yonder side of the peak. Real Injun hang-out. That's why runners steered clear of it."

"See any bison yet?" Trumbull asked, standing in the wagon to see better.

"Nope. If we don't *pronto,* the buff'lo's gone, perfessor." He rode off.

But by now Tom knew that distances on the plains were often deceiving, so the peak was miles away and there could be buffalo, he told himself. An hour or more went by. He kept his eyes sweeping the prairie. Now and then, playfully, it changed from its sparkling green face to coverlets of yellow or white or purple, wherever wildflowers flourished.

And finally a thought jarred him: *There wasn't any bone litter now.* He swung around in the saddle. Only far back, miles back, did he see the awful splotches. Did that mean buffalo were around here?

At least they were getting out of the waste. Still, when Tom looked off at the peak, looming larger, glowering there, filling his eyes with its savage remoteness, no buffalo darkened the heaving floor of the prairie.

A distant boom shook the glazy stillness off there by the landmark peak. Another. Another. An erratic popping reached Tom. And Jack Dean was racing back from far in front, and Tom knew, dismally, what it meant before Dean yelled: "Wolfers! They beat us!"

Tom hung back.

Trumbull listened to the firing for a space, his face coming alight. "But, Jack! That means we've found bison . . . they're out there . . . alive!"

"We can't stop that many wolfers."

"Perhaps we can parley with them." Trumbull sounded eager.

Dean threw him an astonished look and galloped toward a humping ridge. Trumbull whipped the mules forward. Roth brought the cook wagon rattling and pan-chattering after him.

As Tom topped the ridge, the scene spread out before him like facing pages in a book:

the eroded hulk of the crumbling peak on his right, and shaggy buffalo beyond to his left — many bunches that, other than milling and bellowing and hooking slain buffalo, seemed oddly undisturbed while crouching figures poured lead into them from several hundred yards away.

"They've got a stand." Dean bit off the words, bitter, knowing. "Pickin' off the outside animals first, so they can wipe out the lot. Everything's right. Wind's to the wolfers. Day's lazy hot."

He spurred his horse, veering when he could ride straight to the peak. Tom questioned why until he saw the peak come between the wolfers and themselves hiding their approach. Behind him, as he heeled old Red into a half-hearted run, he could hear the creaking and rumbling of the wagons.

New movement scuffed the land to the right of the peak, back beyond where water streaked a thicket-lined gully. Not more wolfers, but Indians. Women and children scurrying to take down hide lodges, bucks mounting up.

Tom saw Dean jerking to a halt, saw the hope on his face that sight of the Indians might scare off the wolfers. But there weren't many bucks; in moments, the whole band was fleeing on horseback as well as afoot.

Dean rode ahead, slower this time, a short way past the peak, between it and the gully, and stopped to observe the milling plain. "They're shootin' calves, too!" he shouted when Trumbull and Roth drove up.

No one said a word; they just watched the slaughter. The white blooms of the wolfers' powder smoke. The bewildered, milling animals lurching and falling; the prairie dotted with dark, unmoving mounds. Tom could see his own helplessness taut in the others' faces.

"Must be a way we can stop this," Trumbull said, though his voice lacked conviction. "There must be. I'm going right out there."

"Butt in, you'll get shot for sure," Dean said, humping his shoulders. "Heap of money out there, scarce as hides are."

A recklessness soared through Tom, a wildness, an unbearable feeling. After traveling so far and so hard and finding buffalo, it wasn't right to be denied saving a few little calves.

He blurted it out. "Can't we scare the buffalo away!"

"If you don't mind, young man," snapped Trumbull, shaking a forefinger, "Mister

Dean and I shall decide." As he finished, he squinted at Tom, a rapid blinking behind his spectacles. "But, you know, I rather like the idea." He turned his head. "Jack?"

Dean seemed ready to rule that down as well. A powerful scowl plowed through his brows. An inwardness grew in his eyes. He jerked, glancing at the gully, over at the milling buffalo, and then back again.

"Perfessor," he said, "those Injuns just missed a good bet. All you fellows grab a rope. You an' Alex can straddle mules."

When the mule riders were ready, Dean entered the gully on a worn buffalo trail that skirted the narrow stream. Trumbull and Roth, unaccustomed to riding, bumped along bareback on their brown mules. Above, in the distance, Tom could hear the methodical booming of the wolfers' rifles. A spring gushed from the face of a rock wall. There the trail climbed out.

Dean looked back. "When we get up there, spread out. We're gonna stampede the buff'lo. Wave your hats. Whoop like Injuns. An' stay low." He sent his horse up the deep cut in a grunting rush.

On top, Tom found himself spaced out between Dean and Trumbull. Dean whooped and Tom jumped Red into a stiff-legged run, bent low in the saddle, screeching and waving his hat.

For a count or so, the buffalo seemed too startled to run. Straight ahead of Tom stood a massive bull, head lowered as if to charge. Tom kept yelling and waving.

With a sudden start, the bull whirled away, and, like a dark, brown wave, the buffalo broke in the opposite direction, bunching up, crowding and bumping, faster, faster.

Tom heard a beginning rumble and felt the earth trembling under Red. The shooting ceased all at once.

Through the fog of dust boiling over the onrushing herd, Tom made out the dim figures of the wolfers running for their picketed horses. Some of them wouldn't make it. That was all Tom glimpsed over the sea of bobbing brown creatures, for in front of him scampered tawny little calves, left behind as their savage mothers fled in fright.

Tom, obeying an impulse, cut off three of them as a rider came up. He heard the hiss of a rope and saw Jack Dean cast a loop that settled over the neck of the nearest calf. Not very far away from him the professor and Roth were cutting out more calves.

Real, live buffalo, it came to Tom. He took down his rope.

Gun Loose

A shout climbed raggedly on the steady wind. Logan Brazle heard it as a great voice straining across the green prairie, as a far-off call drawing on his hunger for distant places. Looking down the drawn-up line of riders and white-topped wagons, Logan guessed the fiddle-footed urge was a rooted part of him.

Long ago he'd glimpsed it first in Old Asa, his father, who had yearned even while he worked the black-soiled Missouri farm. Old Asa would halt suddenly, lifting his sinewy hands from the plow handles, and stare westward with a look of dreaming in his hawk's eyes for something never found, that yet was always there beyond the smoky skyline.

The cry faded momentarily, then cut through the restless racket of harness and stamping teams and excited talk as other men yelled it along: "Ten minutes!"

Logan looked at Barney Miles, a thick-chested young man on a fast dun horse, reckless blue eyes on the cavalry troopers posted at intervals to hold back the settlers until noon. This was late April, 1889, and before them lay more than fifty miles of raw, unbroken Oklahoma reservation land being opened to the homesteader's plow.

Turning icily, Logan let his glance stray to Matthew Douthitt, the sun wrinkles of sixty-odd seasons on his weathered face. The Douthitt girl, Jessie, placidly mended a shirt as she sat on the wagon seat while they waited. They had come down from Kansas in a loaded wagon pulled by a poor team, leaving behind them a drought-ruined farm.

"Remember what I tell you young fellows," stated Douthitt in an old man's positive way. "Wheat's the thing for this new country. Got my seed in the wagon." He fished a huge silver watch from his pocket. "Eight minutes now. Get ready, Jessie."

"Been ready since daylight," she said, smiling faintly as if to humor him.

But she put down the shirt and Logan noticed how calmly she moved. She had a patience the others didn't have. He'd seen that last night. There was the open-handed friendliness here of people moving into strange land, and Logan and Miles had shot the prairie chickens and divided them at the next camp with Douthitt, who had obliged with an invitation to supper.

Logan had a clear impression of her then as the lights of hundreds of campfires sprang up and the stars seemed close enough for a man on a tall horse to grab. She was not plain as he'd first thought. She was straight and slender without thinness, her face full and gently rounded, her eyes wide-spaced. When she stepped close to the fire, Logan saw the bronze lights touching her mass of dark hair that she had carelessly pinned off her neck. He admired her and, at the same time, he was almost afraid of her, because she reminded him of things he had left behind. She would not, he decided without knowing why, follow on the heels of a drifting man. He sensed this while he saw her readiness for laughter and her capacity for temper.

"You don't look like a farmer," she said. Her eyes took him in without appraisal. Still gazing at her over his coffee cup, he sensed her interest.

"I'd make a poor farmer," he laughed, and the rebellion inside him was a fast-running current, swift as the wind. "I've been about any place a horse follows a cow and I'm still travelin'. We'll stake our claims . . . move on to Utah when a latecomer's price is right."

He thought her eyes, quickly on his face, considered him unseemly, although she said reasonably: "This is good land."

"It is," he agreed, and regret edged his voice. "Was open range country." Thinking of the Douthitts' bony team and overloaded wagon, he said: "I rode over most of it for cow outfits. Fine bottom land southwest of here on Turkey Creek."

"Father is going straight south."

"Trouble is," Logan protested mildly, feeling his rider's contempt for a farmer's footed judgment, "most folks will rush in there first. Easier to get to. You'll be up against long-winded horses and wagons stripped light. People everywhere."

Her lips moved and she weighed his words for a moment, suddenly thoughtful. "My father," she said, "says many of these men on fast horses are rainbow-chasers. They will run past the best land without seeing it, and then they'll go kiting off somewhere else."

She was looking at him with a straight-eyed directness as she spoke, although not condemning him, and he felt a faint annoyance. He finished his coffee and handed her the cup.

There was a constant passing from the

nearby camps. Out of this traffic Logan noticed three riders stop and deliberately walk their horses within the outer rim of the Douthitt fire. They stared steadily at Matthew Douthitt, and, when he felt their presence and turned to look, they drifted away. His eyes followed them, and all at once he stood up.

"What is it?" Jessie asked.

"Nothing," Douthitt said quickly, but he continued to gaze after the riders and his eyes were troubled.

A man came striding into camp. He was slab-bodied in his black coat, as thin at the waist as he was at the chest. His voice, surprisingly strong, boomed: "Howdy, folks." He bowed and tipped his high hat to Jessie, and passed out cards all around.

"Friends," he said impressively, "I'm Harrison J. Carmire. Specialist in land title litigation, with offices at the new town of Dalton. If you have any contests, look me up. If you want to sell out, see me first."

He was gone then, with another bow for Jessie and a nod for the men.

"Something to remember, eh, Logan?" drawled Miles, waving his card and Logan nodded.

"Five minutes."

It was Douthitt's land-hungry voice,

Logan realized, rousing him from his dreaming. Barney Miles had dismounted to tighten his saddle cinches. There was a jostling now, an uneasy pushing forward among the home-seekers. A racy-looking team reared. The driver, hauling powerfully on the reins, flat-cursed the animals to a trembling nervousness. Shouting for room, another man tried to wedge his mules between two wagons. He was yowled back. When a woman drove her buggy across the line, a trooper barred the way and waved her back.

Logan could feel the mounting pressure like a hand pressing against his back. All these men were armed, as he and Miles were. Last night's neighborly talk was gone, because they were thinking of the free land. And then he noticed the three horsemen. Led by a man in a pulled-down black hat, they rode single file past Douthitt's wagon and drew up in front of the Kansan's team.

Recognition worked across Douthitt's rugged old face. "Get back!" he ordered angrily, and stood up in his wagon. "I'm in front here!"

The black-hatted rider shouldered around. "You can't stake this!" he argued. His mouth formed a twisting line in his sun-toughened face, and his eyes, like two buried mesquite coals, roved with contempt over the stringy bay team. "Your horse judgment's still bad!" he said, calling out the words loudly.

"Traxell . . . pull back there!" Douthitt shouted. His arm whipped out and he lashed the loose rein ends futilely at the riders. Fear whitened Jessie Douthitt's face. She tugged at her father's arm, but he kept striking and falling short with the lines.

There was more here than mere argument over a position in the line, Logan knew, something flaring up from the past. The man called Traxell continued to hold his place, plainly mocking Douthitt, daring him.

Logan was not aware of his own movement at first. He had watched the thing start slowly, and was taken aback by the suddenness of it. Now he was jumping his horse forward. He drove his voice at Traxell — "Get back where you belong!" — and saw the quarrelsome eyes roll in surprise.

Two of the men had the same long-boned features, the same wild temper showing in the matched, sharp, dark eyes. Traxell loomed thicker and taller, though, than his companions. The man closest to him had a crooked shoulder, which gave him a twisted look. The third man, much younger, seemed held by an inner reluctance he was afraid to show.

In a sweeping glance, Traxell read Logan's gelding and worn saddle rigging. "Won't be drifter country long now," he said, putting a sharp edge of scorn on the words.

Softly a bugle's notes came drifting up the line. At once a trooper raised his carbine and fired. Traxell wheeled his horse at the signal, and Logan, head lifted, heard a world of voices shouting. Single horses, trained for this moment, broke running with their riders whooping; wagons lurched and rolled. Glancing through the clouding dust for an instant, Logan saw Douthitt whipping his team, and caught Jessie's face. She waved and Logan waved back, and, pivoting his horse away, he felt a small twist of regret.

In his ears was the bumping of clumsy wagons and the quick-spinning rush of the lighter buggies. Ahead of him men on horseback fanned out across the prairie, rapidly leaving the others. As his own horse ran, the sounds gradually lessened and fell behind. He remembered it was ten miles to the creek, and angled southwest.

Logan caught up with Barney Miles on a rolling rise. Together they rode hard until the ranked line of dark timber showed, until they came to the creek and saw the spread-out bottom land like a waiting promise.

With a shout, Miles rolled off his pony and ran a few steps. He jerked a wooden stake from his belt. Grunting, he drove it into the soft earth with his boots. "Here's mine!" he yelled, and Logan saw the devil lights in his eyes.

"Good enough," Logan agreed. "I'll go down a way. Remember your corners. You'll have callers."

Riding downstream through uncropped grass that brushed his stirrups, Logan passed thick stands of jack oak and walnut, ash and cottonwood. He heard horses running far off, but there was a quietness here, and wood, water, and pasture — all a man needed for a start. Eyes half shuttered with thought, he gazed long at the greening richness of this place. It was new and yet old with the teeming strength of a thousand years bedded into the untouched soil. He had always carried the faraway places in his mind as an image of tall grass and clear water and a cool wind talking. He had a knowing then, and the surging unrest in him was stilled, as he got down and drove his stake. But when he straightened and looked at the horizon, he wondered how long it would be before he'd be drifting again.

Later he found his corner stones and came

back to the shade. At that moment a horseman rode out of the timber on a blocky farm animal, pots and pans clanking from the saddle. He held a shotgun across his arm.

"I saw you come in," the man said roughly. He was rail-thin, not framed for violence, and in trying to make his voice commanding, it sounded almost shrill. "This land's mine!"

"Plenty west of here."

The homesteader's chin came up, loose with nervousness. "I was here first!" he challenged, still attempting to force his bluff.

Logan saw the rashness and uncertainty, and the hunger in the jumpy eyes, like a sickness, and the thought raced through him that this man would kill for the land without really wanting to kill. Easy in his motion, Logan drew his pistol.

"Keep going," he said, hard-voiced. "Don't come back."

The man stared at Logan's gun. Carefully his eyes dropped to his shotgun, figuring the risk and rejecting it. "I guess," he said, already lifting the reins, "it's better over the hill." There was a naked relief on his face as he rode westward.

He was the first horseman to pass through the shallow valley. Twice others paused and speculated over the claim, noticed Logan, and passed on with the frustrated look of men who rode late. Much later, when wagons began covering the distance, drivers came by. But whenever a man pulled up his team, Logan waved him on, and by late afternoon wheel rims had cut ruts a foot deep where untracked grass had stood before.

And watching the wagons, Logan thought of Matthew Douthitt and the girl and knew their chances, gone here, had been even slimmer to the southeast. Then the unruly feeling, never far below the surface of his mind, came clawing up inside him. Beating it down, he mounted and went up the creek.

There was no sign of Miles and he rode on to the next claim. He saw the wagon first, a patch of white against the thinning light, and felt a quick astonishment at sight of the bony team grazing with Miles's hobbled gelding. As Logan came slowly into camp, Jessie Douthitt looked up from the fire. It was a thoroughly calm look, as if she'd been expecting him.

"I thought," he said, surprised at his pleasure, "you went south."

He could see the hint of something in her face, almost amusement. "We started that way."

Head up, and gripping a rifle, Douthitt stepped from behind the wagon. He lowered the gun and Logan saw his sudden embarrassment. "Sometimes a man changes his mind," Douthitt admitted, giving Jessie a sheepish look. "We staked our claim and here we'll stay. Fine land . . . wheat land." Frowning, he leaned the rifle against the wagon as Barney Miles stamped in from the creek with an armload of wood.

"Never hurt a neighbor's feelings by refusin' to eat a bite," laughed Miles, dropping the wood. "And never keep a lady waitin'."

"That fellow," Logan said, grinning, "could smell biscuits in a snowstorm." When he dismounted at Douthitt's invitation and tied his horse, the farmer faced him.

"You did me a good turn today." A gratefulness made his voice husky.

"Rough boys." Logan nodded, thinking this was no quarrel of his. Yet he felt his interest, while he wondered how so peaceful a man could draw so much trouble.

"You just postponed it a few days." Douthitt's tone was drawn in and pitched, Logan knew, so Jessie couldn't hear. "They'll catch up." There was a weariness in him as he said it.

Of a sudden Logan found himself trying to shut this thing out of his mind. It wasn't fear, he thought, for he'd had his share of brawls in the wild cow towns, and he was handy with a pistol. All simmered down, it was a realization that another man's fight could tie you to a place if you got involved. He reasoned that way, even as he considered that Douthitt was old and slow and awkward with the rifle. All he had was heart and pride.

"Big country," Logan said then, gently. "It'll take some lookin' to find you. You figure they'll try to claim-jump you?"

"The Traxells don't want land," Douthitt answered with disgust. "That's work. They'll head for the nearest town." His shoulders dropped. "Five years ago they stole a neighbor's horses. I testified against them and Sid Traxell swore he'd get even. The drought gave me good reason to move just before they got out of Leavenworth, but I didn't go far enough. Sid's the big one, the gamey one . . . you saw that today. Frank's just as bad. That busted shoulder makes him meaner, I guess. They did the stealin'. Jay's a kid old man Traxell took in years back and carries the name. He's not bad yet, but he hasn't got the chance of a snowball in hell with that crew."

"You can sell out."

The instant he spoke, Logan knew he'd said it wrong. Douthitt's head tilted, and Logan saw the flinty pride, unyielding, outraged.

"Not this!" Douthitt kicked the earth and his refusal had the ring of iron. "We're staying and I'll take my chances."

Jessie's call drew them to the fire and, watching her, Logan lost the roving feeling. She had, he realized, the disturbing habit of silently changing him. Scowling, he took the plate she handed him, not looking up.

Soon after dark a man's "Hello!" came from along the creek. The shout sent Douthitt striding to the wagon. He wheeled with the rifle slanting and searched the deep shadows for a full minute. Satisfied at last, he invited the caller in.

It was Carmire, the self-styled claim buyer and land attorney, riding a cold-jawed mule with the cramped agony of a man accustomed to town comforts. Long, bony legs half bent in the short stirrups, Carmire leaned wearily on the saddle horn.

"Friends," he announced with a tired wave of his hand, "this is a welcome sight." Groaning, he slid from the saddle. Dust covered his wrinkled black coat and he swayed when he stepped back to regard the animal. “A mule’s place is in front of a wagon,” he said bitterly. “Not under a man.”

“You alone?” Douthitt’s manner was casual, although he still held the rifle.

Carmire’s deep laugh pealed out. “All day, sir. Even the wagons passed me. A mule . . .” — he made a gesture of disgust — “is not a race horse.”

“You’ll need some supper.”

At that, Carmire brightened and bowed stiffly to Jessie, and tied the mule to a wagon wheel. Within seconds he was eating wolfishly, his voice a vibrant drum between mouthfuls.

“Coming in, I noticed likely land along the creek,” he observed. “The development company I represent is prepared to pay as high as three hundred dollars for the best claims, provided the property’s free of contest.”

Quickly Miles whipped his eager glance at Logan, who shook his head and said: “You’re low. This is the pick.”

He saw Jessie’s lips stir in the beginning of a protest, and then she suppressed herself. After a moment, her face was calm.

“You can raise the ante,” Miles suggested.

“All depends.” Carmire stared thoughtfully at his coffee cup. “The land isn’t improved.” His gaze, shrewd as a traveling horse trader's, sought Douthitt. "How about you, friend?"

"Douthitt's the name." The old man had been sitting and now he stood up, a solid man in whose blunt hands the rifle looked like a boy's stick. "Any one of these farms is worth five times that." He was making no effort to hide his scorn. "Three hundred dollars is a jackleg offer. Only a fool would take it. My homestead is not for sale at any price."

Logan felt a burning sensation fanning across his face. Douthitt's outburst, spoken with a fierce love for the land, had hit him like a swinging blow. It was, Logan knew, a passionate rebuke also meant for him. Jessie gave him a quick glance, looked away, and abruptly everything had gone wrong here. He sensed it in the lingering silence, in the way Douthitt continued to stare at the fire, ignoring Carmire.

Carmire coughed and got up. "Deal's never over till the last offer's made," he said in a tone eased off to mildness. "Look me up in Dalton after you file." Straddling the mule, he moaned a little as he settled in the saddle and heeled the animal forward.

An overwhelming restlessness came over Logan and he heaved to his feet. "We'd better go," he said, muttering his thanks, and walked to his horse.

Miles was a while unhobbling and riding over, and, as Logan waited in the saddle, Douthitt's tired voice murmured: "A man can't keep riding forever. When you come to a great land like this, take a long look. Get down and feel it under you. Grab a handful . . . taste it. Think of the poor country you've been in and the poorer country you'll see."

Nester's talk, Logan thought, scowling.

"We'll go in and file tomorrow," he said. "Carmire will step up his price, I believe." He paused a moment. "We could all go together."

Douthitt did not answer at once. Finally he said — "All right." — and Logan understood. Douthitt would never sell and any price was still a fool's give-away.

Riding off with Miles toward the black timber, Logan glanced back once. With firelight behind her, she looked slender and graceful and he remembered the startling prettiness of her face at the first camp. She stayed like that, a full-bodied woman outlined against the wedge of light, until Logan heard her father call.

An hour after daybreak they were stringing across the wild prairie, with Logan and

Miles in front. Douthitt had carefully checked his rifle loads before starting, and now he rode with the gun against his knee.

Miles noticed and swung his horse in close. "The old man's worried." When Logan told him, Miles hopefully patted his six-shooter. "Maybe things need regulatin'."

Logan shrugged. There was a kind of depression in him. He couldn't shake it, even when he thought of distant Utah like a vision. Always before it had been enough to think of wandering.

They approached a shallow creek, and, while Douthitt watered the team, Jessie pointed to a cloth-covered basket behind the wagon seat. "Dinner," she told Logan. "You'll both eat with us."

"Too many star boarders," he said, "will discourage the cook." He was studying her face, clear and tanned under the sunbonnet. Her smile faded as she watched Douthitt.

He raised his eyes to search the grass, which bent and rolled like green waves in the pungent wind. "By workin' hard," he said, his words slow, "a man could buy enough land to handle cattle."

Barney Miles cocked his head. "Thought you said this was wheat country, Mister Douthitt?"

"I did." He slid his eyes at Logan, briefly. "Just a notion all my own, I guess."

In the distance they could see other wagons long before Dalton reared its scattered shape and the red dust boiled up in low-hanging clouds.

Riding past the wagon yard, Logan saw the mass of people and horses and stalled wagons on the single street. This was the Land Office town, the core of all this vastness come to life, a city of tents and unpainted board buildings yellow with the brightness of new lumber. Men and women formed a restless line, headed from an open tent over which a sign read: *U.S. Land Office.*

Logan lifted his voice above the racket of hammers and the shouting excitement: "We'd better get in line."

With a jerk of his head, Douthitt drove his team in front of a half-finished store where carpenters swarmed. He got down and Jessie, her face flushed as she scanned the crowd, said: "I'll look in the stores till you get back."

Logan, who had tied up at a hitching rack, half turned in his tracks. Douthitt stared fixedly at the rifle left in the wagon, swung around, and studied the crowd with a frown.

Against his judgment, he said — "Don't

go far." — and walked impatiently to the end of the line.

He kept a tight-lipped silence while they worked forward in the line. He could not hide his plain worry, Logan saw, but neither did he speak of it. It was past noon when Douthitt reached the counter. After a minute, he turned with a look of pleasure and relief.

"All clear," he said. "Nobody else's filed yet." His attention went back to the street again. "I see a hardware store over there. Come by the wagon when you finish."

As the old man made a path through the crowd, Logan saw the dread streaking back and the head-swinging caution return once more. When Logan came to the line's end and gave his claim number, a clerk checked it on a map.

"All right," he said after a moment, and Logan paid his filing fee. He waited for Barney Miles and afterward they crossed to a saloon.

Miles halted at the edge of the plank walk. "There's Carmire's sign down the street," he suggested.

"Plenty of time for that," said Logan, walking on. Miles gave him a long puzzled look, shrugged, and followed. Not until he was elbowing through the packed saloon doorway and inside did Logan realize he was delaying. He went to the bar.

The moment he finished his drink the sensation of something wrong touched him. He had the awareness of being watched, cold on the back of his neck, and he turned and saw Sid Traxell watching him. Traxell stood only three places down the long bar. Frank flanked him like a crooked shadow, and behind him hovered young Jay, his face stiff and suppressed.

Miles said softly: "Guess they let anybody drink here."

Sid Traxell heard and he lifted his brooding eyes. At that motion, the men in between swung back and away.

There was this short gap separating them as Logan, feeling a crowding irritation, said: "No doubt you made the run?"

"Don't give a damn for that," Sid Traxell rapped out, his quick temper rising. "You see Douthitt?" The words burst from him with a stored-up bitterness.

"Why," answered Logan, shrugging his shoulders, "didn't have time to look behind me." His voice came out steady, but he was struggling with a sour anger and thinking: *This is not my fight. . . .*

"Come to think about it . . . maybe we did." Miles was drawling it out, and, when

Logan looked, he caught the mocking soberness. "Wasn't he that skinny peach-orchard gent with the eight hungry kids and the flea-bit mules? Said he was headed for where they got hills to break the wind."

Violence pushed its ugly mark across Sid Traxell's high, bony features. Straightening, he flicked a signal at Frank, who stepped wide. Young Jay stood frozen, the tight skin around his mouth strung white. Frank kept angling to the side with the unhurried step of a man taking position in a familiar game.

"Don't do that!" Logan called sharply. It came to him that he was the only one speaking in the room.

Frank Traxell raised an eyebrow. "No rule against walkin', is there?" But he stopped.

"We asked you something," Sid Traxell cut in maliciously. "Your pardner gave us funny talk. I don't like it."

"I'll tell you again . . . plainer. We haven't seen Douthitt since the run started."

The brooding expression didn't change, and from the corner of his vision Logan saw a man step inside the saloon and stop. There was a rubbing silence, broken by a bartender's abrupt challenge: "No trouble in here." He slanted a pistol across the bar. "These fixtures are fancy. All the way from Kansas City."

Without turning, Frank Traxell rubbed long, tough hands on his lanky thighs and waited. In a moment, Sid Traxell said — "Never mind." — and nodded him back.

Logan felt the ease spread through his body and knew it was over. With a glance at the Traxells, he moved slowly against the crowd drifting back to the bar, knowing he had come as close to a showdown as a man could and not draw a gun. He saw Harrison Carmire come forward, shrewd eyes bright and patronizing.

"You boys file?"

Logan nodded. "And no contests."

"You're talkin' to landholders," Barney Miles bragged with a laugh.

"Now," said Carmire in his booming manner, "I've been thinking about you." He frowned, speculating. "No improvements. . . ."

Suddenly impatient, Logan pushed his face closer to Carmire's. "Listen. You want the land, but you won't get it for three hundred. Make us an offer. We're leavin' town today."

Carmire's teeth clicked. "Five hundred?"

Miles whistled softly, but Logan said: "Six hundred."

"Five-fifty," parried Carmire. "Cash."

Logan said — "It's a deal." — and the

next moment realized he'd been hasty. Carmire's nod followed too fast and eager. "Come by the office for your money, boys."

"That's pretty good, Logan," Miles agreed. "A good stake."

Logan shook his head. "Not enough. I wasn't thinkin' hard enough about the money." He had almost said *the land,* and now he sensed a loss, like a man outsmarted. Only it really wasn't the money; it was the land. His mind was all mixed up with the Traxells and the Douthitts, and he could not drive out the thought of an old man, stubborn in his pride, and slow and awkward with a rifle. He said — "Let's go." — unprepared for the lack of interest he felt.

"Old man Douthitt," Carmire began loudly, "hasn't changed his mind by now, has he?"

Startled, Logan sucked in his breath, the feeling clamping cold on his neck again. Carmire's voice had carried above the murmuring talk like a drumbeat, and the realization stirred him, whipped him around. Sid Traxell was staring, the full meaning of what he'd heard strong in his acid smile.

But before the man could move, Logan shoved and punched Miles. They shouldered past Carmire, who called out in surprise:

"What's the rush, friend?"

Outside, Logan saw Jessie Douthitt far down the street, alone in the wagon. "Look in that hardware store first," Logan told Miles. "Sneak him out to the wagon yard."

Boots made their hard beat behind Logan just inside the saloon. With that pressure at his back, he lunged in among the people clogging the street. He soon lost himself in the crowd halfway across, and took his backward look.

The Traxells stood in a tight, menacing clump outside the saloon entrance. Their bleak glances traveled up and down the street. Frustration stirred Sid Traxell's lips. He motioned Frank to his right, and they angled up the boardwalk, sauntering, observing. Young Jay formed the rear guard, slow to follow.

Missing Douthitt on that side, Logan thought, they would swing across to the other. Working down it, they would see the wagon yard. Making a way with his shoulders, Logan came to the wagon. She looked up, her face pleasantly flushed by excitement and heat. He untied the team and climbed to the seat. She didn't speak until he took the reins.

"You're in a hurry," she said, surprised and somehow pleased.

"Traxells," Logan grunted, and backed the team.

Fear drove across her face, softly curved under the sunbonnet. "But . . . ?" Her lips were bloodless.

"Barney's bringin' Matthew around to the wagon yard. Better there."

Driving off at a trot, he swung in sharply and, skirting a tangle of buggies, wagons, and buckboards, drew up where they could watch the street.

"You . . . you're going back with us?"

"It's like I told you." He hadn't realized how hard-coming the telling would be, like an apology, and he said it fast: "We're selling out to Carmire. He met our price."

She nodded and he thought she had known for sure all along he'd go and there'd be no changing him. She said thoughtfully: "I think I understand how you feel. We've been a lot of places, too . . . Montana and Nebraska before Kansas. But it always looked better over the ridge. Always new country opening up, and we went." Her shoulders rose and fell and the fear, held in as she spoke, came striking back and her vexed eyes sought the street.

The unexpectedness of what she'd said gripped him, and he stared at her, silent and wondering. Why, he'd figured them both as not having seen much country, hating to move, and feeling only scorn for a drifting man. But Douthitt had been a roamer and together they'd tried the far places and the old man, weary now, had found his land.

Miles and Douthitt came running from an opening between two buildings. When they reached the wagon, Logan dropped to the ground. "Not much time."

Eyes cloudy with temper, Douthitt held back. "I'll get it over with here," he said, breathing hard.

"Get in, Matthew." Logan made his voice rough. "You can't fight now, and Jessie's here."

Douthitt took a slow, heavy step, undecided, then turned his eyes on Jessie. "You're right," he grumbled over his shoulder. Still unwilling, he hoisted himself slowly to the wagon seat. He took the reins and looked down.

"I'm much obliged to you both." A tiny point of fire burned in his eyes; it flared brightly for a moment and went out. "You're set on going. I can see that. Good luck."

Awkwardness grew on the three men. They shook hands, briefly.

This was good bye, Logan understood suddenly, and he saw an expression in

Jessie's eyes that he could not read. She waved, as she had the day of the run, and he waved back.

He watched her go then, thinking there could have been more between them. He heard Miles's voice, oddly flat, cut across the wagon's rumble: "Wonder how long it'll take Sid Traxell to locate the old man's claim. He could ask Carmire . . . maybe the Land Office."

The same worry had been massing in his own thoughts, Logan admitted silently, walking to the street. All at once, he felt a vast discontent, like a job half finished, although he reasoned that nothing really held him now. He and Barney could sell out and ride off without looking back, without obligation. And Douthitt, he kept reminding himself, had not asked for help.

Up the street Carmire's bold sign stood out, swaying in the wind and waving Logan on. Men ganged the office door. "Go ahead," Logan said.

Miles threw him a queer, narrow-eyed look. His usual easy nature had escaped him for once. He had the indifference of a man for whom the fun had pinched out, and with that missing there wasn't much left.

"Go on," Logan insisted, irritation in his voice. Miles's face reddened at the harsh tone, and instantly Logan regretted using it. Before he could speak, Miles was drifting into the crowd.

Restless and inwardly angry, Logan heeled around on the plank walk and scanned the sea of faces. They had, he saw, the look of staying people. His awareness of that rubbed along his tight nerves, gave him the singled-out feeling of being adrift. In his mouth the red dust was gritty and acrid, and the wind, so steady and promising all day, struck him with a certain raw loneliness.

He was still standing, stiff-legged and grudging, not quite understanding why he hadn't followed Miles, when he saw Sid Traxell leave the Land Office tent and cross the street to his horse. Walking fast, Frank and Jay Traxell followed him and rose to their saddles. The three of them swung out at once, pushing against the flowing crowd. Sid and Frank rode with a hard-faced intent etched in their dark features, hurrying, impatient at the delay.

Certainty rang a distant bell in Logan's mind, while an inner voice told him not to show himself. He crushed it down and with a stunned fixation saw them coming and spurring to a trot as the traffic thinned. He felt the gun hanging against his thigh. He touched it, automatically now, because he was stepping off the walk at the street's end before he fully realized his intentions.

A metallic taste was strong in his mouth. Waiting, he felt the dread building up in him. Sid Traxell checked his horse first.

"Where you headed?" Logan said softly.

A thin smile moved Traxell's mouth, brightening his eyes. "When did a drifter get interested in where a man heads?" He seemed to bite off the words.

"Right now."

Bent in the saddle, Frank Traxell kneed his horse sideways. The movement drummed a series of warnings at Logan, touched off his backward step. Frank halted, his sly glance split between Sid and Logan. Jay Traxell kept his hands on the saddle horn.

"We know where Douthitt is," Sid Traxell said. "We're goin' after him."

"This is far enough."

Sid Traxell's face, completely unafraid, was full of an amused contempt, with an urge toward violence. "I guess," he said, and the brightness in his eyes leaped higher, "you're gonna be stubborn."

Logan saw it coming then. He could almost see the action as he knew it would unfold — Sid Traxell lifting his gun and Frank shooting from the side.

Sid Traxell's hand whipped toward his pistol. He wasn't on the lightning side, for no one was in farm country. But he was fast and sure and he had the desire to kill.

Instinctively Logan fired at the shape framed high on the horse, the reports clapping close together. And with Frank Traxell's presence beating at him, Logan pivoted back.

There was another explosion, but Logan did not feel the bullet. He saw Frank Traxell jerk and slump forward on the neck of his horse. When Logan wheeled around, Sid Traxell was straining to stay upright. Suddenly he collapsed and slid from the saddle. Dust puffed as he struck, sprawled, his gun in his outflung hand. Jay Traxell hadn't moved.

His young face, tight and drawn, changed slowly. It took on an expression in which regret and disbelief struggled and then a gradual awareness, swifter now, that he'd been released from something he could never have broken by his own will. He got down from his horse, but he did not go over to Sid Traxell.

Cloudy-gray smoke hung over the street. Logan smelled the burned powder and he stared at Sid Traxell down in the dust, mouth slack with shock. Across from him

Frank Traxell lay still.

Sick inside, Logan looked away. Men pressed in, voices high. There was a stir and Barney Miles pushed through, still holding his pistol. It was all very clear to Logan now.

"Never send a man after money when things need regulatin'," Miles complained.

"You see Carmire?" Unseemly to ask here, Logan knew, but he had to know.

"Didn't even try." The devil lights in Barney Miles's eyes were gently mocking now. "And you're not going anywhere."

Logan lifted his head. He wasn't traveling; maybe he'd known it for a long time. Thinking about it, he guessed she would understand when he stared westward across yellowing fields, half dreaming, with the old desire in him so strong he could smell far country. He was lucky, mighty lucky, for it would take a roaming woman to know and hold a drifting man.

PAPER BULLETS

The whoop cut distinctly across the wind slapping the frame building. Horses drummed up from the log bridge over the river and sound seemed to roll along the hard-packed street. Tom Allard became thoughtful at his desk. He caught the eye of Harry Babb, standing in stoop-shouldered competence before the type cases.

"Visitors," murmured Tom, with a rueful grin. He glanced at his watch and stood up.

Babb had the cynical expression of a man who had observed much of mankind in fifty-odd years and retained not a single illusion. Despite that, a flicker of interest broke through his habitual indifference now. His voice came muffled from around the tattered shreds of his dead cigar, while his thin, sensitive hand kept traveling without pause between case and composing stick.

"Wonder how long old Art Swan can hold the lid on?"

"A good question." Tom stopped by the door, thinking that Harry Babb lived a lonesome life. "Have some fun tonight, Harry."

"At my age a bottle is no longer fun . . . it's medicine." Babb seemed to back off from the subject, as he did from anything that broached sentiment. He switched his attention to the make-up tables. "Ads running light."

Tom nodded wearily. For both had read the same set of tracks and divined where they were heading in a town that was slowly dying. He had his hand on the doorknob when he heard boots strike the plank walk. Then the handle turned roughly and Tom stepped back, seeing Frank Vane fill the doorway.

"Come in," Tom invited uneasily.

Vane did not bother to close the door. He circled a look of distaste around the crowded print shop, and his broad nose appeared to draw in against the smell of ink and paper. The judging eyes were bright with anger that he could not contain.

He held a newspaper; he slapped it for emphasis. "Still ranting about cowmen coming across the river to trade!"

"I've no complaints against cowmen," Tom answered evenly, "and it says so. But riff-raff's another thing. Tinhorn gamblers.

Thieves and murderers from the States. Gun sharks like the Cimarron Kid. Hide out in Indian Territory and come over here to raise their hell. And they're hurting us. We've acquired a gun town's name on this side and you know it. Oklahoma Territory knows it." He indicated newspapers on his desk. "You ought to read the exchanges."

Vane was unimpressed. "Sure, the boys have their fun. But Riverton's sliding downhill . . . remember that. I figure these riders just about keep it going. Why rile 'em? If you ask me, they're doing us merchants a favor."

Vane holstered no guns. As if he disdained them. He was in his middle thirties and he wore his dark conservative suit and white shirt and pearl-gray hat as a uniform of respectability. As if, Tom thought, he had some secret need for it.

Pride and ambition shone in Vane's alert, bold eyes. He was not an extra large man, but he could create the impression of bulk and formidable power. He also could take almost any side of an issue, Tom had discovered, and by some puzzling alchemy of character make it sound right and good for all.

"Depends." A quiet caution touched Tom. Was he getting careful, like the others? "I know this . . . homesteaders are taking their trade to Pawnee City. Some have even quit this part of the country, moved on West. They want a town free of shootings. Where their womenfolk and kids can come and a horse won't crowd them off the walks." Vane lifted a hand, but Tom went on, conscious that his voice was climbing: "Another thing. Art Swan needs help. One marshal isn't enough."

"I see no reason why we should start a war." Vane breathed in his superior manner. "Swan's doing all right. Riverton will settle down in its own way. What do you expect? It's no skimmed-milk town. No sleepy Eastern village. Thank God, we'll never be like your lukewarm Kansas towns!"

He was at once self-righteous. As if by some special insight he had detected a common danger and must denounce it. He batted the newspaper again.

"I can see you're bent on causing trouble. But I'll hog-tie you." His eyes became unbelievably cold. "Be careful what you print. No more of this."

"Get out," Tom said softly, with disgust. The pressure kicked his stomach and as Vane shouldered out, amusedly taking his time, a quick certainty flashed upon him: he means it. And yet Tom felt no great surprise.

Actually it was a relief to know.

Babb's matter-of-fact voice rubbed across the room. "The frontier brings out all the good or bad in a man. Always the bad. Vane, there, was raised on sour cream."

"Harry . . ." — Tom faced him, alive to a cold fact — "you know what's coming. You don't have to stay."

Babb stared back a moment, bony features expressionless. Then something like hurt changed the pale, ravaged face. He said gruffly — "Better make your rounds." — unable to cover up a moistness in his eyes, which was strange for him. He blinked and bent to his typesetting. As Tom started through the door, Babb called after him: "You should see Sharon Larned more! There's a fine young woman. Vane's been calling on her, I understand."

Stepping outside, Tom entered a copper world of late morning sunlight. He hesitated on the walk, thinking of Sharon Larned and momentarily held by a view that never tired him. The river's silver ribbon winding past the rough-hewn bridge and the wooded bluffs, into the mystery of space and land a thousand years fallow. Rounded hills bulging green with promise.

But when he faced the sun-blasted street, his brief exultation died. Horses were ranked before the Longhorn, Vane's place. Otherwise, the street threw back a mocking emptiness. A bad sign, he thought, a growing sign.

He moved slowly in long-legged steps, a thrust of weary discouragement nagging him. He had the sensation of battling a rising wind, and the wind pressing stronger and stronger, until at last he could no longer stand.

He placed another glance on the high-fronted buildings, and a sick regret gripped him. For he'd seen Riverton that hopeful day in April. Land-opening day. Hardly more than a year ago. Swaggering beneath its dirty tent folds. Everywhere men with the dreaming look of far country in searching eyes.

And, like a whispering vision, many of them had found it where the land bent westward into promising prairie and gentle hills, and others thought they had discovered it in the stripling town they'd begun by the river crossing. Except that Riverton had become a one-man town — Frank Vane's town.

That knowledge deeply aroused Tom, made him think of the settlement's secret workings, of men grown afraid. He shook off the feeling and waved at the bent shape of Jim Browerton in his saddle and harness shop; at Samuel McGregor, quaintly immaculate, in his dry goods store. Tom went up the street to Adam Harlow's place of business, *Genl. Mdse. & Groceries,* and found Harlow staring moodily out the front window.

"Art Swan been around?" Tom asked.

"Was earlier." Harlow's tone lacked interest.

But Tom persisted. "Think we might talk the council into hiring a couple of extra deputies for Art?"

Unease grew in Harlow's round face, a hesitancy, and he stared down. "Tom," he answered in the quietest of voices, "I read your paper. Don't push too fast."

It hurt to see Harlow avoiding his gaze. This man like a stranger. Not the Adam Harlow of those earlier days. Hawking dollar pies in a ringing voice over a cottonwood plank counter supported by two empty whiskey barrels. Helping lay the town. Eager as any man, then.

"We're losing our town," Tom insisted.

"I. . . ." A beginning protest edged into Harlow's voice. His chin tilted up. For a moment he was different. Then the brown eyes turned tired and careful and his shoulders rose and fell.

"At least we could organize vigilantes," Tom ventured hopefully. "Police the town with Art. Vane won't like it, of course, and you and I know why. Things other folks don't know about."

He stifled the impulse to mention Vane's threat. If he did, Harlow might judge that to be a personal reason for Tom's insistence.

There was a silent struggle going on inside Harlow. A reluctance.

"I'm not as young as I was once. Things have changed. You know about Vane's ambition, his mania for respectability. He'll run for the legislature before long. You know his sensitive spot . . . his past. It's also his great weakness, if people knew. For that reason he'll allow no man to cloud his name, regardless. Remember the risk . . . to yourself."

He turned indecisively to a counter, his step stiff and heavy. Although just past middle age, he looked far older, and beaten down.

A sudden compassion filled Tom. As he stood there, a keen knife of comprehension cut across his consciousness. He had waited too long. If Adam balked, so would the others.

Harlow swung around. He forced his eyes to meet Tom's. His face had a grayish cast.

Something in his tenseness said he had reached a reluctant decision.

"Tom," he began, and unwillingness slacked sickly across his features. "I hate to say this, but I have no choice. Take out my ad."

Stunned, Tom stared with disbelief. Finally he found his voice. "All right, Adam. But. . . ."

Harlow said nothing more and Tom, suddenly understanding, did not press for an answer. He could spare Adam that self-humbling. After all, it was there for Tom to see without asking. There in the ashamed, stricken eyes. Harlow abruptly stepped away, not seeming to know what to do with his hands. Tom knew immediately that he was thinking of those lost, earlier days.

In silence, Tom walked out of the store, thinking of Vane and how fast he'd moved since the paper had come out yesterday. How Vane, while ruining one man, permitted another to survive only after crushing his spirit. Breaking a man to halter, like a wild horse.

Trembling with anger, Tom moved on. He could see the shape of things and somehow he knew how it would be. So he experienced no surprise when McGregor, a man in his sixties and much too genteel for the frontier, told him: "That is how it is, Tom. I am too old to fight back. And don't blame Adam. Pity him. Pity us all, because not one of us is truly his own man."

Jim Browerton was a cripple, scrawny of build and drawn of face. One foot dragged when he walked and the knobby hump on his back gave him a look of perpetual pain. For all that, his courage had not withered.

"The Cimarron Kid himself brought me the word from Vane early this morning," he told Tom. "Not exactly an order, y'understand. Just a hint, he said, but I knew better. I didn't say a word. Guess I was too scared. Then he looked around with them dead-pan eyes of his and says . . . 'You got a nice stock here. You sure have, Jim. Good harness. Hand-tooled boots and saddles. Reckon you'd have a devil of a time fishing 'em out of the river.' He went out laughing." Browerton's eyes blazed. "That gunslinger! He can't tell me what to do!"

Tom eyed the little man, admiring his courage. It was one light in a dark day. "Don't be a fool, Jim. If he comes back, tell him you decided not to run your ad this week."

Browerton's mouth dropped. "I don't get it. How you think you'll get along without business? Better go ahead and run my ad."

"Thanks, Jim. But one fence at a time. For right now, tell him you've canceled."

"Well-l . . . if you say so." Browerton seemed relieved, and also bewildered. "You're up to something?" he asked curiously.

Tom had no answer. On the walk he could feel the wind steadily rising, and he knew that he must push against it or fall. Much like a long traveler, seeing a landmark peak jutting out of shimmering plains, he glimpsed where he was heading. The realization carried him up and down the street to the remaining stores, knowing each stop fruitless before he made it. Vane had been thorough.

Later, pausing in front of the Pioneer Hotel, he noticed men bulked before the Longhorn. Down the street a rider dallied. Thinking of Art Swan, Tom angled into the street.

Halfway across, he heard a whistle from the Longhorn crowd. It meant nothing until it shrieked again. Suddenly its insistent shrillness, its timing, struck him as peculiar. Like a signal. At the same moment, from the corner of his vision, he saw the rider spur his horse forward.

Some instinct warned Tom. He wheeled, all his senses hackling. The horseman was galloping straight at him. Tom glimpsed the blur of a dark, mirthless face. He did not realize that he was running, but he was, his long legs springing him toward the boardwalk. It loomed ahead and he jumped. And just before he landed, he felt the violent, air-whipped passage of the horse behind him, heard the rider's flung-back yell: "Jayhawker, look out!"

Anger burned in Tom. He flung himself around, expecting to find the rider waiting for him. Instead, the man was pounding off down the street, out of town. Without looking back, Tom worked his glance on the crowd. No one spoke. Yet every face told him that they knew the attempted rundown had been deliberate.

Boots sounded at the Longhorn's entrance, and Art Swan came out. He was tall and angular and walked with a cowman's choppy gait, a slow-moving man long past his physical prime, with the belt and holster lying so heavily against his lean thigh they seemed too large a burden for him. His thorny hands appeared cast in a mold of stiffness. Straw-colored mustaches drooped above a tired mouth.

Swan scouted his gaze around, muttering: "What's this?"

A man said in mock concern: "Somebody

tried to run the editor down. 'Pears Jayhawkers ain't liked around here."

"Know the rider, Kid?"

"Never saw him before." The face of the Cimarron Kid was both young and old, both cool and unpredictable. He teetered on his boot heels with a wild-running insolence. From within him leaped an inviting malice that he pushed straight at Swan. "Any more questions, uncle?"

Swan's shoulders rolled doggedly, wearily. "Reckon not. Just figured you might've recognized him."

Swan took a step, only to check up as the Kid spoke flatly, clipping out the baiting words: "You calling me a liar?" The Kid stiffened and crouched a little, and Tom read the obvious challenge. Concern for Swan stirred him.

He heard himself calling: "Hold on! Nobody's hurt."

Swan had already turned. "Look," he said patiently, "you'll pick no fight with me. Go inside . . . have yourself a drink. Cool off."

The Cimarron Kid stood rooted, faintly puzzled. A look that told Tom he had expected Swan to draw and was disappointed because he had not. There was this old bone between them, Tom knew, and it would never be buried until one shot the other.

The Cimarron Kid said in his flat, dry-wind voice: "Don't crowd me. I'm telling you, uncle." With a shrug, he strolled inside and the entire crowd followed.

Swan's old eyes trailed them. "There was a day. . . ." His low, passionate muttering broke, choked off in the terrible yearning for the vanished years, for the lost keenness of eye and the speed of hand.

He had been quite calm while he talked the Kid down. Now, Tom saw the loose skin quiver along the gray-stubbled jaw, saw the drawn hands like knotted rope. In that moment, Tom greatly admired the man — and greatly pitied him. Swan had courage, but that was about all he had left. That and an outward cool nerve that came from playing the risky game these many years.

"Watch him, Art."

"My job to."

Tom lowered his voice. "You could use some help. Anybody in mind? Some good names we could bring up before the council?"

"No man I know is a big enough fool." Swan was skeptical. "How would you get it past the council, with Vane running things? He wants a wide-open town." Gratefulness built up in the over-tired eyes. "Here you are trying to help me, when somebody in this bunch just tried to cripple you. I would advise you to carry a gun."

"You have no one in mind, then?"

"Not a soul."

Tom recognized the doggedness again. He hesitated. "What would you say if private citizens got behind you?"

"Vigilantes?"

"Yes."

Swan half groaned. "You want to blow this town sky high?" Protest lay darkly in his eyes. A dread of the future. His uncertain gaze wandered to the river and back. He said wearily: "I have my rounds to make."

He drifted away and all at once, sharply, Tom felt the day's heat weighing upon him, and a sudden shock of loneliness. It was, he sensed, the same loneliness that walked with Art Swan. He was startled to find himself wondering which way to turn.

The knowledge bothered him as he returned to the print shop. It still persisted early that evening as he entered the Pioneer Hotel. There was in him now the desire to see Sharon Larned, to sit in her parlor and feel the contentment ease over him.

"Miss Larned in?" he asked the clerk, who nodded down the hall.

When Tom rapped at the parlor door, it opened quickly and he wondered if she'd been expecting him. She drew back and said: "So they didn't hurt you?"

He walked in, aware of the blue- and rose-colored wallpaper, of the neatness of this room, and the peace of mind it gave to him. Already some of his depression had lifted.

"Did you expect them to?"

"I expect them to try to kill you. That was no accident . . . a man almost riding you down in daylight."

"Word gets around."

"It does . . . that kind. Next time they'll use a gun."

Her nearness always affected him, and it did now. He caught himself considering her intently. At first glance she seemed a plain young woman, except that she wasn't plain at all. He guessed it was her neatness.

Her cheek bones rose high and rounded and there was a substance to her tallness and her lips were full. She had inherited the hotel after her uncle's death and had come out from Missouri a few months back to manage it surprisingly well.

Her face showed a trace of disapproval now. "I wish you'd be careful, Tom."

"That's it. We've all been too careful. Too long."

"I wouldn't say that. You're shooting paper bullets in a pretty serious game."

Irritation caught him. First Adam, now Sharon, telling him to go easy. He was studying her again, not quite understanding her. Sometimes she surprised him with her perception. It was that of a woman older than her years. It puzzled him, made him wonder.

"Enough paper bullets," he said, "can awaken public opinion. That's the one thing Vane really fears. He's playing both sides and some day he'll get caught in between. You weren't here when Riverton was started. Different, then. People saw something. It's still here, if we can find it again." He hadn't realized it until now, but his tone sounded bitter and he was putting it badly.

Her gray eyes, widely appraising him, mirrored a sharpening concern. She drew her dark head back, made a small gesture with her hands.

"Tom . . . you are troubled!"

He shrugged, thinking — *Am I that easy to read?* — and said: "Nothing to worry about."

"No . . . nothing," she mocked him. "I heard about the ads, too."

He had been sitting on the divan. He stood up, shaking his head. "Adam is under pressure from Vane, and who isn't? He had no choice. I can't blame him."

She regarded him with open surprise. "You can still say that, knowing what it means, that it will ruin you?"

Her eyes were larger than he'd ever noticed before. She stood very close and suddenly tiny tremors raced through him. There was a tight string of feeling reaching out from her to him. He moved as though in a hazy, high-singing world. His arms went around her. He held her roughly. He kissed her and, for a moment, he forgot anything existed but the two of them.

"Tom, what am I going to do with you? I wish you'd stay here a while. Till dark. I wish you'd think this over before you. . . ."

He stepped back abruptly, gripped by a stab of suspicion. *Unfair,* he told himself, *and unfounded. Yet Frank Vane also called here. Was she . . . ?* He swore silently at the thought, and still he said: "You want me to quit? That's it?"

"I want you to think of yourself."

Of a sudden all the wonderful closeness between them had gone. He sensed it, and he saw the same shocked awareness in her eyes. He took his hat and walked to the door. There he paused, and, even as he spoke, he knew that he was being unreasonable.

"You mean that would suit Vane better?"

Sharon colored. "I didn't say that. You know. . . ."

He said stonily: "I think I know what you mean."

He let himself out into the hall, dismally damning himself, hearing her voice behind him as something he'd lost forever. "Tom! What are you going to do?"

He kept going. But when he reached the end of the hall, he glanced back. She stood at the door, and he could see her eyes upon him and he had the instant knowledge that there was a hurt there which he could never erase. She did not call to him again, and he turned his back. As he left the hotel, the old violent storm of feeling came shouting around his ears, and he saw clearly the peak of his destination in the distant reaches of his mind's eye. It seemed much nearer this time.

He went outside. He must have gone on a dozen steps before he noticed the blanket of silence over Main Street. The emptiness. It struck him as unusual for this time of evening, and with the Longhorn's tie racks jammed with horses. He stopped, gazing curiously, and vaguely disturbed. Then, pinpointing his gaze, he made out faces peering from the Longhorn's smoky windows, other faces peeking downstreet over the batwing doors.

Tom's glance followed their stares and he saw two men.

Boots planted wide on the planks, the Cimarron Kid stood confidently. He stood in that queer, stiffened crouch of his, and a few steps away Art Swan faced him. He looked old and gray and cornered, both thorny hands carefully at his flanks.

Tom heard the Cimarron Kid sing out: "I told you, uncle, I told you!"

Swan's answer came as an indistinct mutter of protest.

"You're yeller!" The Cimarron Kid bit off the challenging words. He spat them at the older man.

"You. . . ." Swan became doggedly erect, in strain. He appeared to summon all his faculties for one supreme effort, for the swiftness he no longer possessed.

It was over in a moment. In one terrible, helpless moment. Before Tom could move or cry out, Swan's knotted right hand jerked. *So slow,* raced Tom's mind. *So agonizingly slow and futile.*

The Cimarron Kid's right shoulder dropped a notch. His hand whipped to his holster. Tom heard the ear-blasting report, and saw Swan recoil from the bullet. He did not go down for a second or two. He seemed to sway tenaciously, as an old tree would when uprooted by a violent wind, and then he fell. He still held his pistol. He had not thumbed off a single shot.

A cloud of dirty-gray smoke was drifting away from the Cimarron Kid's six-shooter. He stared down a moment, then coolly holstered his pistol and, with a shrug, wheeled and strolled into the Longhorn.

Tom was the first across the street, and a glance told him the marshal was dead. In these last moments the tired face appeared to have softened, quietly relaxed in an expression of contented peace that Art Swan had never found on his dusty streets.

A great wave of regret rolled over Tom Allard. His throat thickened; he felt sick. He bent his head, aware that men were coming out of the buildings. Presently three men picked up Art Swan's body and carried it away.

Tom's sense of helplessness became intolerable. He had, he realized, crossed the haze of distance and reached the foot of the peak. He stood before it now. He detached himself from the milling crowd, walking fast toward the newspaper office. A man caught up and matched his strides.

It was Harry Babb, breathing hard. Something in Tom's face must have told Babb, who said finally: "When do we put out the paper?"

He knew it all along, thought Tom. He said: "Right now." He felt no excitement, just a settled resolve. "Maybe our last paper here. But it's the only weapon we have. I said it before, Harry, and it still stands. You don't have to get mixed up in this."

"Think I'd run out?" retorted Babb, then he was through the door, lighting the coal-oil lamps and slipping on his apron.

A growing outrage drove Tom to his desk. He shut the street sounds from his mind. He half closed his eyes a moment and the clarity of his thinking astounded him. All of Riverton's secrets took on a close, harsh focus. He picked up a pencil and began writing rapidly, his fury, his bitterness spilling out on the paper, burning in his words.

When he had finished the first sheet, he stood and handed it to Babb, who stepped to a type case. In no time at all it seemed that Tom was done, and was waiting as Babb set the last stick. Quickly Tom inked the type, rolled a proof, and held it up in the yellow light. Babb looked over his shoulder as he read:

The most cold-blooded killing in Riverton's violent history occurred tonight when the Cimarron Kid, long wanted by Texas authorities, shot and murdered Marshal Art Swan on Main Street.

The murder, witnessed by the editor of the Weekly Freedom Call, *was an act of deliberate provocation by the outlaw. He cursed Swan, and the marshal courageously sought to defend his good name, though it is common knowledge that his hands were all but crippled by rheumatism. Swan had no chance.*

Blame for this outrage must be placed where it belongs. The Freedom Call *editor feels it his duty to inform the public that Frank Vane, Riverton's principal businessman, is a former outlaw and has encouraged the Cimarron Kid and other members of the Wild Bunch to make Riverton their playground. It is the editor's finding that Vane is still the real leader of these outlaws, while he poses in the guise of a respectable citizen.*

Investigation by the editor also reveals that Vane has been active in purchasing homestead lands cheap from fearful settlers desirous of moving away from the vicinity of Riverton's notorious outlaw headquarters. Vane has ruled by fear, and he will continue to do so until vigilant citizens cast him out.

There was more to the story, additional details of the gunfight, Swan's record as a peace officer in the Southwest, and Vane's rise in Riverton. Tom read it with moving lips.

As an afterthought, he said: "Let's add this final paragraph." He began dictating slowly as Babb's hand fairly leaped back and forth. " 'This . . . will be the last issue . . . of the *Freedom Call.* The editor makes that announcement . . . because he knows . . . that Vane's hoodlums will wreck his shop . . . or kill him . . . just as the Cimarron Kid murdered Art Swan.' "

They set a black headline and placed the type in the page-one form, filled in the remaining space with overset and last week's ads and locked the form. While Babb inked and worked the Washington hand-lever press, Tom picked through his desk for a few personal items, suddenly feeling the finality of all this.

He looked through the window. Men stirred restlessly out there, talking in groups.

Tom stood motionless, tight-mouthed. The room grew quiet. The papers were off. He turned and met Babb's stare, catching the concern in the eroded face.

"There's a six-shooter in the bureau in my room," Babb told him.

Tom, going over to the paper stack, nodded in a way that said he knew. He said: "Better go by the alley, Harry. Be sure to leave some copies at the hotel, and avoid the Longhorn. I'll take care of it and the crowd." He hesitated. He felt responsible for Harry Babb. "Don't come back here tonight. And thanks, Harry, thanks."

Babb was fumbling with his papers, and he seemed to take a long time bunching them. He glanced up just once, and hurriedly hid that glance. Then he muttered — "Watch yourself." — and went out of the shop, through his room and the rear door.

Tom's attention stayed on the door until Babb's footsteps lost sound. He swung away, sick at heart, not liking the solitary loneness, sweeping his eyes around the shop. Every piece of equipment in this room he had wagon-hauled from Kansas. Regret piled up like bitter gall within him. For here was the end of something. It was, he recognized, like a lot of other fine hopes Riverton once had. This was a vital part of him and it would soon be smashed.

It came to him that he was dallying. He sighed softly, tucked the papers under one arm, blew out the lamps, and left the office. Pointing up the street, bright with lights now, he threw a brief look at the blurred lettering of his paper's name on the window. He moved quickly, conscious that his allotment of time shortly would be running out. He passed out papers to each knot of men he found.

Finally he stood before the Longhorn's doors. Here a guarded caution made him hesitate. He had the uneasy conviction of being utterly foolish. But even as he lingered, drawing in breath, he knew that he would go in. He pushed through the doors, into the brittle, excited humming of talk that came against him like a dark current.

He stopped, although hardly aware of it. There was a beginning stillness around him and there was a close-by pressure. He swung and saw Frank Vane at a table near the door. Vane loomed, solid and square, and Tom did not miss the impression of stored-up malice. Deeper in the broad room beyond Vane stood the Cimarron Kid, elbows hooked indolently over the bar's edge. His men flanked him.

"Want something?" Vane's voice was a falling axe, chopping apart the quietness.

Tom took a long step to the table. He said softly — "Brought your paper." — pitched it upon the table, and waited.

Contempt hardened Vane's stare. "All about the shooting, eh?" He ignored the paper and Tom caught the subtle switch at work in the man again, the elusive metamorphosis. "You brought this on," Vane stated, "by stirring up the boys. You forced poor Art Swan to fight or back down. I told you to watch what you printed. You're through in Riverton."

"I think," Tom told him, and his voice sounded overly distinct, "that we're both through. But you will never tell me what I can or cannot say."

He turned and strode straight to the entrance, feeling the hanging silence and the cold fingers kneading his spine. He barged through the slatted doors, only dimly seeing the stage pulling up at the hotel, and kept on going to his shop. Stumbling through the unlighted front office into Harry Babb's room he found the pistol in the top bureau drawer. He locked both back and front doors and posted himself by a corner of the building.

He was stationed there, the pistol heavy in his slack hand, when the Longhorn erupted men. They formed a dark huddle, as if deliberating. Then Tom, pulled back in the sooty shadows, noticed something for which there was no apparent reason. The street was empty. It had been except for the stage, he remembered now, when he had made tracks for the shop. It was only a vagrant thought, however, and quickly broken when the men advanced along the walk. They made hard-angled shapes in the greasy light, the Cimarron Kid swaggering in front.

Tom waited tensely. His body, he discovered, was not fully steady. He waited as a man would who stares in fixed fascination at his destiny marching to meet him. And in that time every muffled sound, every smell, came to him keenly. Spurs chinking. A horse's fluttering snuffle. A soft wind fanning off the prairie, cool to his hot face. His mind spun once to Sharon Larned.

Then the men reached the street's center.

He thumbed the hammer and fired, deliberately placing the shot over their heads. They drew up just a moment, scornfully, but Tom knew they would not stop. He saw flashes of flame from the Cimarron Kid's gun. Bullets chugged into the pine boards at Tom's shoulder. Suddenly shifting, he felt something strike him — something hot as fire. In the remoteness of the street he heard a woman's throat-torn scream.

He was falling. An instinct that went deeper than thought sent him rolling and twisting around, straining to bring up his pistol. He brought it up at the same moment the Cimarron Kid ran across. Tom fired, feeling the recoil kick in his hand, and the confident shape before him appeared to lose footing and fall slackly away.

A light-stabbing blackness swarmed Tom Allard. He was a swimmer struggling in swift water and no bottom under him. Just before he slipped under, an angry shouting registered distantly on his senses and he caught a glimpse of the wedged men swinging down the street. He could not be certain, because the dimness kept growing. But he thought he saw Adam Harlow, and Jim Browerton's crooked shape, and a woman. . . .

He heard murmurs. Far off at first. Like whispers. He found himself staring at a sky. It seemed unreal. Blue and rose-colored. It gave him a vaporous, detached feeling. He stirred. Pain shot up his left side, which he now learned was bandaged, and he closed his eyes against the hot irons embedded there.

"Be still, Tom. A man can't take a Forty-Five slug and expect to run foot races the same night. But you will, in time."

Harlow's round features broke through the dizziness. Tom's eyes wandered. It gave him a start to find that he was lying on the couch in Sharon's brightly lamped parlor.

There was a shuffling behind Harlow, and Tom, looking, found Browerton and Babb and McGregor. And they all seemed different in manner somehow, although he did not know why. His bewilderment grew.

Harlow was saying: "We were late enough as it was, just as we've been late about many things in Riverton. But as we came down the street, the crowd seemed to pick up like a snowball. And with the Cimarron Kid dead, the wild ones had no heart. Your paper did it, Tom. Coming out right after the Kid killed Art. Harry here let no grass grow telling us you'd gone to the Longhorn. We hurried fast as we could."

"Don't be so blamed modest, Adam," McGregor cut in gently. "You came to my store this afternoon talking up vigilantes."

"He sure did," Browerton agreed. "Once Adam swung, we all did."

Tom was grateful, and he understood about them. The change in Adam. The change in them all. And he'd been wrong, thinking they would not fight. Why, he hadn't heard this tone of talk since land-run day. He grinned at them. Until a thought made him frown.

"Vane? What about him?"

Harlow took a moment in answering. "We gave Vane his choice . . . get out, or stay and face the music. He blustered a while. I'd say two things decided him. The Cimarron Kid was finished, and he didn't like the looks of the crowd. They wanted to rough him up, Tom. Maybe string him up. So he's gone. Took the stage back to Indian Territory." Somewhere a door opened and Harlow, glancing backward, added hastily: "Plenty time later for the details."

Tom Allard was scarcely aware when they left, although he did notice Harry Babb's parting wink. He was listening to a light step crossing the room, feeling a presence. Turning his head, he saw Sharon Larned, holding bandages and a pitcher of water. She put them on a table and bent down. She filled his eyes and the tremors got him again.

She took his hand fiercely. "Tom, you're going to be all right."

He was silent so long, his throat so thick, that anxiety straightened her. Her hand dug deeper into him.

"It isn't that," he managed with effort. "But a man must eat humble bread at times. I will take mine."

Her lips were close to his ear. "Frank Vane never meant anything to me. I knew you had to fight back. Only I was afraid. Guess I didn't reckon with your paper bullets."

He could not speak at the moment. He

knew this woman would be continually surprising him with the depths of her love and understanding. And, just now, he could think only of her crying his name as she ran through the blackness.

Killer's Medicine

It made a man feel tight under the collar to hear the shuffling and muttering from the courtroom. A kind of dread touched Sheriff Orvie Tuttle as he came reluctantly to the door and looked inside. It was pretty packed, he saw, with cowmen and town-folks, and there was Murdo Quinton standing up big as daylight, telling them about the job that wasn't being done, although not mentioning any names. But everybody knew, and Orvie flushed hotly.

"Folks," Quinton was saying in his strong voice, "you all know why we're assembled here. I hesitated some time before calling this mass meeting, but we can't hold off any longer. We've got to take matters in our own hands, if the law can't do the job." He paused significantly, and there followed a burst of hand clapping and whistling.

Orvie felt a sudden tug of anger, but he forced himself to stand there, unmoving.

He was a raw-boned man with gray-streaked hair and rope-scarred hands, holding himself in, struggling for control. This was the old rivalry all over again between Quinton and himself, a feud that originated years ago, even before Judith. Quinton had won that round, too.

Half smiling and slowly bowing, Quinton lifted a broad, square hand for silence. "Friends," he said, "in my humble opinion there is only one way to correct this outrageous situation . . . organize our own posses and hunt down the Jardeen boys!"

Applause broke out again, filling the big room. Quinton looked like a man feeling strong drink. Watching him, Orvie decided he hadn't changed much, despite the years. He was just a little thicker through the shoulders, and the shock of black hair was beginning to thin.

Everything about the man gave the impression of stored-up power and driving ambition — the stout neck column and the staggering voice, the rugged features and the straight-backed manner of carrying himself a bit too proudly. But he was a roughly handsome man, in spite of his cold eyes. Yes, Murdo Quinton had done well. Several spreading ranches bore his brand. He owned the local livery stable and a growing freight concern. He'd always wanted more, and usually managed to get it.

As the racket faded, Quinton's eyes roved over the courtroom and rested on Orvie. "I see that Sheriff Tuttle is among us," he said, with the faintest trace of amusement. "It is no more than fair that he be accorded the opportunity to speak for his office."

Orvie met the gaze and held it, thinking bitterly: *He knows danged well I don't have the answers, else he wouldn't offer.* There was a hush, and eyes turned toward him as Orvie clumped to the speaker's table. His boot steps sounded unnaturally loud. He turned and faced the crowd, aware of a sea of aroused faces.

"Any man" — his voice drifted back to him, tight and strange, because speech-making was a chore — "has the right to defend himself and his property. And I have no complaint against citizen posses. But times have changed. Vigilantes were all right in their day, except when they went off half cocked. Got the wrong man. As for taking the law in your hands, maybe stringing up the Jardeen boys, if you can catch 'em, I'm against it." He paused, and his tone deepened. "Folks, I'll have to ask you for more time on this stage business."

At once a man stood up, shouting. "How

long's that . . . forever? The Jardeens have been running loose for months now." The speaker was Wes Carker, the freight company superintendent, all bones and long jaw and a quarrelsome mouth that even in smiling, had no warmth.

Orvie tried to hold his voice steady. "I'm not so sure the Jardeen boys are responsible. No evidence that. . . ."

"They killed Jim Pace!"

Turning, Orvie recognized Blue Hackett, another freight firm employee, and it came over him that Quinton had packed the crowd for a one-sided hearing.

"Nope," Orvie countered stubbornly. "Don't figure they shot Jim." But as he spoke an overwhelming sense of being cornered belted him.

"Yeah? Then who did?"

"Frankly I don't know. But we're working on it, Charlie Two-Star and I." He was, Orvie realized, a stumbling fool for being drawn in. Still, a man had to answer, he owed folks that.

"You and that sleepy Injun deputy," Hackett snorted, and sat down, his point won.

Somebody laughed, and Orvie knew that his face was burning again. He started to answer but a certain inner caution checked him. There were some things you couldn't explain to the public, such as the fact that Al and Billy Jardeen weren't cold-blooded killers like the men who'd shot Jim Pace off the box. You knew that from knowing men. Horse thieves and wild and young, yes, but the Jardeens weren't killers. You'd come within a fine hair of catching them twice, and you'd get them yet . . . later, when this stage game cleared up.

Orvie cleared his throat. "Charlie's the best tracker in Osage county, bar none. I'll be glad to talk on any other questions."

He waited in uncomfortable silence. Nobody spoke. After a moment, he went, stiff-legged, from the room. It seemed mighty quiet behind him, but for the snickers.

Lost in thought, he almost bumped Charlie Two-Star, his full-blood Osage deputy, whose black braids jiggled as he said: "Big trouble, huh?"

He had a furrowed, ageless face the color of old saddle leather and a sinewy body, wiry as a Spanish pony. He wore a Jeff Davis hat, round-topped and black and plumed with a red feather, and on his feet were rawhide moccasins. Most times, when he wasn't aboard his bay pony or taking in Indian feasts, he dozed in a chair at the sheriff's office.

Wordlessly Orvie nodded, and together they moved to the street. Any other time he'd have enjoyed the sights and smells of Antelope Springs. This was his town and he'd grown up here. Only, today, with the dust husking in and the sun shadowed by clouds, it struck him as unwelcome.

"You got letter," said Charlie, handing it across.

Orvie stuffed the envelope in a pocket and tramped down the street to his office. Not until then did he read the letter. Then, frowning, he said: "Says here the express company wants special guards through the Wildcat hills for the next stage." His scowl grew. "Must be a big cash shipment for the new bank."

Lazed down in a chair, Charlie Two-Star was admiring a beaded buckskin pouch. The bright object, scarcely wider than a man's hand, held Orvie's interest for a moment. "Now where'd you get that thing? Trade some full-blood for it?"

Charlie Two-Star looked hurt. "Medicine bag. Charlie carry all the time. Mighty good luck."

Unimpressed, Orvie said dryly: "We're going to need some medicine, all right, big medicine. Two men can spread themselves just so far in rough country." He paced to the window. "Every time it's been three, four gents, and they never stop the stage in the same place. Don't have to, because any spot's handy for a hold-up in the Wildcats. Nope" — he shook his head doggedly — "need two men to guard a stage. Or three, counting the shotgun rider."

The Osage said nothing. His interest was on the pouch, his muddy eyes bright with pleasure.

"I'm afraid," Orvie said at last, "I'll have to ask for a citizen's posse. Sure hate to, though. It's our job." Yet he knew that really wasn't it. What cut him was his pride. He'd be forced to eat crow in public and admit he couldn't handle the situation. A stab of defeat hit him, and he thought of Murdo Quinton, who would like nothing better. This day had turned sour.

"No need posse." It was Charlie Two-Star's calm, grunting voice, dragging him back. "You me good fighters." He tapped his scrawny chest. "Ride pony hard. Shoot straight."

Orvie couldn't control his grin. Sometimes you wondered about Charlie Two-Star. He had old-time notions, Charlie did, about being a warrior, and riding a pony, and being extra brave. On the other hand, sometimes you had the feeling that he wasn't some simple Indian living in the past, in buffalo days.

"Well, I'm stumped," Orvie admitted, tossing the letter in a file box on the desk. "Looks like. . . ." He never finished. Listening to the tread of boots coming along the boardwalk from the courthouse, he had a knowing feeling as he looked up. Murdo Quinton's bulky frame filled the doorway, Carker and Hackett behind him.

They stomped in as if they owned the world, Quinton getting to the point without delay. "Tuttle," he said, "you left before the party got finished. The citizens of this county passed a resolution demanding that you go after the Jardeen boys." He let the news sink in. "Now what do you intend to do about it?"

Anger clawed inside Orvie. He let it pass slowly, let his thoughts settle. "You've always bulled your way around this town, Murdo, but you'll never run this office. When I cut the Jardeen boys' sign, I'll bring them in. So far they've steered pretty clear of us. Right now there's more important work. I mean these stage hold-ups."

"So." Quinton's amused gaze ran around the office, caught on Charlie Two-Star. "Yes, I can see that you're busy with official duties." His voice flung contempt. "Two-Star here generally can be found asleep in the office, and you've been sticking close to town." His eyes grew hard and he asked softly, pryingly: "Could it be because Judith has opened a dress shop in town?"

There it was again. Raking up the past and rubbing it into a man's hide. For a moment Orvie saw Quinton through a red haze. Finally he answered: "Murdo, that was settled long ago." That was true, though Orvie had never forgotten Judith.

Quinton's face altered swiftly, as if he'd said too much.

"What you got there, chief?" Wes Carker was staring curiously at Charlie Two-Star.

"Medicine bag. Sacred things."

"Some tomfool doodads to catch badmen, eh?"

"Maybe so."

"Let me see them."

The Indian's mahogany eyes turned to weathered stone. "Bring Indian good luck, bad for white man." He shook the pouch ominously; it rattled.

Carker's laugh rolled out. "Sounds a little like nuggets." He was pleased with his joke, but his interest rested intently on the buckskin before he lifted his gaze.

"Maybe so." Charlie Two-Star possessively jammed the bag inside his pocket.

Quinton had stepped to the door. Over his shoulder he told Orvie — "People are going to hear about your lack of cooperation." — and walked out.

A sinking feeling and a sense of bewilderment kicked hard at Orvie's stomach as they stalked off. Always he and Murdo Quinton had been on opposite sides, from that day when powerful young Murdo had held Sylvester Jenkins's head under too long in the Salt Creek swimming hole. Orvie had jerked Murdo back and pulled the sputtering Sylvester out on the bank. Then Murdo had beaten Orvie until he had to crawl to his pony. Judith Carlton entered later, and Murdo had won again.

For all that rivalry, Orvie knew, much of it at first had been the natural desire of coltish young men to outdo each other, nothing more. He harbored no bitterness, because bitterness only soured a man's soul. Except sometimes he thought he caught more than mere dislike in Murdo's iron voice, in Murdo's eyes. Other times it was just a feeling you had, too vague to understand exactly. It was kin to the sensation you might have in timbered country when you're riding alone — wind on your back, making your nerves stringy, when you know a rider is somewhere behind, stalking you.

Orvie had noticed it once more, only stronger, a few weeks back when Judith returned to open a dress shop in Antelope Springs. Judith was legally free of Murdo Quinton, after staying a year in Rocky City, another county town. There was talk for a while. Orvie himself had wondered about the breakup. Judith seemed to avoid him and naturally he hadn't pried.

Looking out his office window now, Orvie could see her shop. He never went over there, because he could tell she'd rather be left alone. So he had to be content with seeing her at a distance on the street. Even so, he often caught himself looking that way, wondering about Judith after all this time. It made him feel futile and regretful, older than he was. Maybe if he weren't so easygoing, if he'd spoken up when they were younger. . . .

Unease stirred in Orvie. He stepped outside, walking to the street's end before he turned back. He was preoccupied, slowly retracing his steps, when he happened to glance up and see her. She was a slender woman, still young, with the sun striking flecks of gold in her yellow hair as she came along the walk with a package in her hands.

Her nearness always affected him, and he awkwardly touched his hat. " 'Afternoon,

Judith." He thought she was going on as usual. Instead, at the last moment, she paused, and Orvie found himself wanting to stop.

"Orvie," she said lightly, "it's a good thing we don't have street posts in this town. You had your head down and weren't even looking much."

"Just thinking," he said, smiling. "It comes hard for me. Guess you know I'm not exactly in good standing around here." He held his hat in his hand. Raw-boned and kind of uneasy, he stood there and hoped his eyes didn't betray his admiration too much.

"It isn't that, really." She shook her head and he marveled at her freshness. Time, he saw, had treated her gently, as if it had generously endowed her as a young woman and then quickly forgotten her. She had the same blue eyes, wide and lively, and the same full mouth and rounded face. *She'll never get old,* he thought, *if she lives a hundred years.* Suddenly he looked away, for he knew he'd been staring.

"I was at the meeting." Judith said it so quietly that he wondered if she'd noticed the obvious. "Everybody was. I thought it unfair, the way they. . . ." She seemed to catch herself. "Politics, too, I suppose."

All at once he realized she was attempting to tell him something. In the next moment, he also knew she'd never tell him now. She was already moving away, saying evasively: "I have to hurry this material over for Missus Hensley to see."

She was gone and he became aware of a sudden regret.

The feeling lingered as he paced back to the office. Charlie Two-Star hadn't budged. He was slumped in a chair, his Jeff Davis hat pulled low over shuttered eyes. Remembering the express company's letter, Orvie took a pencil stub and in his labored scrawl wrote an answer confirming an escort for the next incoming stage.

Finished, he said — "Charlie." — and grinned as the old Osage blinked and came awake.

"Ride this over to Rocky City," said Orvie. "I'm telling the express company that we'll have guards handy when they enter the hills." He frowned and added: "I didn't say how many, though."

Charlie Two-Star was at the door when Orvie's voice halted him. "Want to keep this under our hats. Got enough trouble for two men."

The Indian nodded and scuffed out in his moccasins. Presently Orvie heard his pony clattering out from the corral behind the office. Orvie shook his head, half grinning at a sudden thought. This was the month of June and the Osages were dancing and feasting in the Wildcat hills. Might be that Charlie, on his return trip, would stop and visit briefly, maybe talk over old times with the Osages who'd been with him on the agency police force. That was before white man's law, when armed Indians escorted the tribal agent to Kansas and back with the government annuity payments.

After some moments, Orvie heard a racket down the street. It grew, with voices calling. Going to the window, he saw horses ranking in front of the livery stable. Murdo Quinton was shouting orders again. Soon the horsemen formed and trotted toward the sheriff's office.

Orvie's shoulder muscles bunched as he went to the door and waited. They made a solid mass, every man armed, with Quinton leading them.

As they halted, Quinton sang out: "You coming?"

It was more of a command than a question.

Orvie swung his glance over these men. He knew them all, and many of them were friends of long standing, but grim- and determined-looking now. Jim Pace had been a popular man, so he knew that it hadn't required much urging by Quinton to send them riding after the Jardeen boys.

Wearily Orvie shook his head. "Nope." There was a deepening stubbornness in him. "Figure there are more important chores. You boys want to ride around the country, go right ahead. Just don't hang anybody up to dry."

A rider shifted uneasily. "Come on, Orvie, saddle up."

"Don't beg him." Quinton's tone was dry. "He's kind of set on town these days." His gaze took on a jeering amusement, and something under the surface of the cool eyes went beyond that. He lifted his reins and the others drummed after him.

Orvie just stood there. It was human nature, he admitted ruefully, to blame a known badman for every unsolved crime in the country. Trouble was that sometimes the wrong man ended up swaying under a cottonwood.

Afterward, he walked thoughtfully to the corral and saddled up. An hour later he was riding into the massive Wildcat hills, along the rutted stage road that led to Rocky City. As he rode over timbered ridges, following rocky, twisting turns, he fixed in his mind the most dangerous places, where the stage must slow to a walk and timber and brush flanked the way.

When he thought of only Charlie Two-Star and himself, his doubt increased. Every bend offered opportunity. There was one spot in particular, where the road dipped across a rock-bottomed stream, climbed tortuously, and turned up a steep slope through the crowding blackjacks. Once, faintly on the wind, he heard drums in the distance, and he knew the Osages were dancing.

When the sun dropped in flames behind the far western ridge, he made camp beside a cool creek and cooked bacon and coffee. He slept there, rolled in his blankets. Next morning he angled slowly back toward Antelope Springs. Nothing was really settled in his mind, nothing bettered by this punishing ride. Around mid-morning a stringer of dust took shape ahead of him. A faint curiosity worked in him as he rode on. Approaching closer, he noticed a light team pulling a rig with a man and woman aboard.

He felt a quick stab of surprise, because the woman was Judith. The driver reined up. Orvie looked at her, at the rig. It was loaded with a trunk and valises.

He forced a grin. "Fine day for traveling."

He returned his glance to the piled baggage, vaguely bothered by the meaning there.

She pulled her lips together, and he had the impression that she would have avoided him again. Her hat brim threw shadow across her cheek bones, across the pools of her eyes. "A long ride," she said without enthusiasm.

The evasiveness puzzled Orvie; it also annoyed him for some reason. And when the driver impatiently shook the reins at a nod from Judith, he heard himself saying in a wondering way: "You leaving again?"

"Wait," Judith told the driver. She turned, squarely facing Orvie, so that he looked into her eyes and saw the obscure hint of something in them. But it was gone in a moment. "I've closed the shop. I'm going to Rocky City for a while."

That was all, although somehow it wasn't all. "Well." He was at loss for the right words, feeling clumsy before her. Regret piled against him like a weight. He tried to sound casual. "No need of that, Judith. We need a dress shop in Antelope Springs. Shows the town's growing up, progressing. Maybe you'll be coming back soon." He wanted to say more. He wondered if his concern showed in his face, in his voice.

There was the barest trace of feeling in

her face. It wavered there, indecisively, and he saw a look of resolution grow in her fine eyes. With an awareness for the driver beside her, she said: "I don't know." She gave the driver a swift look. "Orvie, be careful."

At that, she faced back, the driver grunted the team forward, and Orvie watched her go with a sense of loss. His eyes fixed on Judith's straight, slim back.

Slowly Orvie headed for Antelope Springs. The feeling of defeat stayed with him as he unsaddled and entered the empty office. He'd hardly gone to his desk when a passing townsman stuck his head in the doorway. "Posse's back. Drew a blank."

"Figured they would," said Orvie, without interest.

"They're going out again."

"Let 'em ride the fat off good horseflesh." He turned his attention to some new reward posters received in the mail. He was only dimly aware of when the man left, for his thoughts kept tracking back to Judith, her reluctance to talk before the driver. He was going through the rest of the mail, scanning letters and trying to impress the information in the reward notices on his memory, when it came to him.

He sat very still. The driver worked at Quinton's livery barn, a new man hired just a week or so ago. Orvie weighed the meaning and ended by shrugging if off. Judith had simply hired the rig to take her to Rocky City. The little flicker of concern with which she'd spoken was merely at saying good bye to an old friend. Feeling a mite foolish, he dismissed the whole thing and made himself finish the mail. Oddly enough, he couldn't find the express company's letter in the box — not that there was any need for it except for filing purposes.

He did not see Charlie Two-Star that day or the next. He would have to speak to that Indian. He must be out feasting and showing his tail feathers at some dance, while office business went begging. But Orvie really had an affection for the wrinkled little deputy. For all his outwardly sleepy unconcern, he always had reasons for his absences. At times he'd vanish for several days, unless on assignment. He would go into the frowning hills, observing and tracking any strange stock, storing bits of details away in his patient mind, things a white man would overlook.

Orvie spent half a day finding a whiteface bull, reported stolen, which had gone strolling across two creeks and half a dozen fences.

Riding in, he saw Charlie Two-Star's bay

pony drowsing in the corral. Inside, Orvie found the Osage eased down in a chair, snoring, hat tilted over his face. His blue cotton shirt was gray with trail dust, his rusty trousers showed slept-in wrinkles.

Irritation edged Orvie's voice. "Wake up, Charlie!" Finally the chocolate-brown eyes winked open. The Indian yawned.

"How was the feast?" Orvie inquired with sarcasm.

Charlie Two-Star's face was so much wood, but Orvie persisted with: "Long time just to Rocky City and back."

The coffee-hued gaze didn't change. "Uhn-huh. Long time. Feast plenty good. Plenty talk. No sleep."

"Remember," said Orvie, his good humor returning, "we pull out of here early tomorrow. Y'know, Charlie, sometimes I'd as soon talk to a tree."

Charlie Two-Star made no answer, and presently Orvie saw him take out the medicine pouch and study it. After a time the little man rose and went down the street. He returned soon, carrying a small package. Without any explanation, he stepped to the gun-rack room. He seemed in deep thought as he closed the door.

He stayed so long that curiosity stirred Orvie, who slipped over to listen by the door. He caught a faint shuffling, then a pause, and then both sounds repeated. There was nothing else. Minutes later, when the deputy came out, he was empty-handed. This time he had a settled, satisfied look. He took his customary chair and fixed his gaze on the wall, a mask of indifference dropping across his face.

Somehow the Indian's usual silence rubbed Orvie's nerves today, so he took to the street and walked it. He was at the far end, talking grass and water with two passing riders, when he saw Charlie Two-Star turn in at the freight office. He was still there when Orvie went by.

There wasn't much sleep that night for Sheriff Orvie Tuttle. He kept seeing the close timber and the rocks and the rough trail road, the stage slowing down and masked men spurring out from the trees. Common sense told him he should swear in more men, take them along tomorrow. But his stubborn pride always broke in, overriding the gamble he was taking.

The worrisome thought hung in his mind depressingly as he rode along the Rocky City road in the gray of early morning. And Charlie Two-Star offered no relief. The Osage was more silent than usual. He rode like a man needing sleep, uninterested in the country around him. Orvie threw him an occasional covert glance, but, when he attempted to draw him into conversation, all he got in return was a brief grunt.

They came to the eastern rim of the tangled hills, where the stage road entered the up-and-down land, and halted to await the stage. Orvie rolled brown-paper cigarettes and watched the road. Charlie Two-Star, he observed with irritation, sat lumped on his pony, silent, impassive, eyes blinking under his hat brim.

Toward late morning Orvie made out the stage in the distance, bumping and swerving behind four horses, the wheels spinning up dust.

Some minutes afterward, the driver hauled up and called through a cloud of grit: "Where are the guards?"

"We're it," answered Orvie.

The man's eyes bugged. He exchanged a concerned look with the shotgun guard on the box, then swung around again. "But we understood there'd be a big bunch." His glance moved critically over Charlie Two-Star, slouched indifferently in the saddle. "My gosh, Sheriff!"

Orvie snapped back — "We'll get you through." — and wished he were as confident as he tried to sound. He had pistol and carbine, but they'd need a generous helping of luck.

"You'd better," the driver answered grimly, slapping a metal box beside him. "We're loaded this trip." He moved his shoulders. "Well, come on, we can't turn back. Got passengers aboard."

As the driver yowled and the stage shook forward, Orvie's eyes wandered to the windows and the faces there.

He stared, a wave of surprise going through him, for there sat Judith Carlton, waving at him. He waved back uncertainly. The stage rattled past him and he spurred to keep up. He'd talk to her once they stopped, although they weren't likely to do that until they reached Antelope Springs because the driver was pushing the horses.

Still wondering, Orvie sided the stage and motioned Charlie Two-Star to the other flank. For an hour or more they proceeded like that, climbing and dipping, across an occasional patch of prairie.

Gradually the country grew rougher, and Orvie's sense of dread deepened. The round-topped hills became rugged shoulders of limestone outcrops and dense stands of scrubby blackjacks. The stage crawled up these strewn slopes and came jolting and weaving down the other side. Heat layered the shallow places, and dust whipping up from the wheels choked a man's throat, burned his eyes and nostrils.

Orvie rode with his careful glance tracking along the timber edges, to the side of him and beyond. He figured they were halfway through, going well. Only it seemed too easy. Even after they lumbered past two points where stages had been stopped before, Orvie couldn't breath easier.

It happened without any warning, when the stage dropped down and clattered across the rocky stream he remembered. The driver's voice shocked the horses lurching forward, and they made a sharp twisting turn up the face of the steep slope. The black timber closed in the tortuous trail road.

For a while the stage struggled on, swaying and weaving, until there was suddenly a slowing down among the lead horses, a faltering up ahead. The driver yelled hoarsely.

Then Orvie saw the rocks piled high, blocking the road. His eyes clung there for a moment too long. He turned instinctively toward the trees on his left. He knew it now, trying to bring his pistol around and feeling the coldness on his neck, knew that he was late, outfoxed. He felt it behind him.

"Keep 'em up!"

A sick regret brought Orvie fully around. All the actors of his bad dream the night before stood menacingly before him — masked men who'd spurred from the timber and rushed up from behind as the stage halted.

"Drop it! That saddle gun, too!"

Orvie hesitated, weighing his chances. He had none, so he dropped the pistol and next the carbine, watched them spin down uselessly. At almost the same moment, a rider near the coach grunted a command to the guard, who let his shotgun fall away. Voices came from the other side, harsh, prodding voices. Horses moved and Orvie saw Charlie Two-Star, hands high, kneeing his drowsy pony around.

He seemed unconcerned, half indolent, as indifferent as if he were slumped down in his office chair, save for one difference. The beaded buckskin medicine bag hung from his neck on a string of rawhide, making a bright splash of color against his dusty shirt. He had put it on as he rode beside the stage, Orvie thought wretchedly. For good luck!

"You passengers . . . get out!"

Judith Carlton and a moon-faced drummer, white to the gills, stepped from the coach. Her face looked tight, held in, but she kept her shoulders straight, her head high. Just the sight of her gave Orvie a jolt of helplessness.

"Throw down the box!"

The same man had spoken each time, his voice coming roughly muffled through his red bandanna. Orvie sought the voice in his memory; it meant nothing. There were four riders in all, one big man sticking close to the timber's edge. All were dressed plainly, and were even riding unbranded horses. In a few minutes they'd be lost in these hills without a trace.

"I said throw it down!"

The driver had hesitated, his gaze accusingly on Orvie. With a shrug he picked up the box and heaved it down, heaved it angrily at the feet of Orvie's horse. It clanged on rock. The horseman motioned with his pistol, and the drummer, eyes pale with fear, hurried over. Grunting, he lifted the box to the gunman's saddle.

Orvie thought they'd go then, galloping off through the timber. But the hoarse-voiced rider, box balanced across his saddle, dallied. His glance swung, and there was contempt in the way he canted his head, in the slow searching he gave Orvie. Next his attention slid to Charlie Two-Star, went past him, and all at once raked back. The eyes narrowed.

"Come on!" the big man close to the timber called nervously. Two of the bunch swung toward him.

But the nearest outlaw ignored the summons. His heavy gaze still centered on Charlie Two-Star, dwelling there scornfully. He growled: "That plaything around your neck, Injun. We'll just take that along with the money."

Charlie Two-Star stiffened, alarm showing in the leathery features. His mouth barely moved. "Medicine bag . . . no take."

The gunman answered by roughly edging his horse closer, waggling the pistol. "Hand it over."

With unwilling slowness, the Osage drew the loop over his hat. For just a moment he looked regretfully at the pouch, and Orvie could see his reluctance growing.

"Hurry up!"

Charlie Two-Star started to pass it across, and suddenly he paused. "Keep sacred things, huh? You take rest." The coppery eyes were wistful, almost pleading.

Now the outlaw hesitated, a hesitation he broke with a brief laugh of contempt. "All right . . . but move!"

Charlie Two-Star nodded, pleased as a child. He was smiling, rather thinly. But,

Orvie saw, it wasn't exactly a smile, more of a tightening of the lips as he opened the bag.

The following moment was brief and savage, fast as the flash of powder. One instant Charlie Two-Star was slowly burrowing his hand inside the pouch. In the next flick of time he was no longer smiling. He pointed the pouch at the outlaw and there came a popping sound. The outlaw lurched and made a crying noise.

Orvie was not aware of movement. He sat like a spectator, frozen, and now he was flinging off, his hand scooping up his pistol. He turned as the two men angling for the woods shouldered back, guns swinging. Orvie's bullet took the first rider high. He made a swaying grab for the saddle horn. His companion reined away.

It was quiet for a space around the coach. There was violence off in the timber, a horse running somewhere fast, some scattered shots, some more whooping. Orvie threw a look around him, saw Judith, and hurried over. He put his arm around her and she did not pull away.

In a haze of wonder, Orvie noticed Charlie Two-Star. He held the pouch and a Derringer. That small package — now the sleeve gun — why, he'd had it in the medicine bag all the time. He looked at the nearest man on the ground, groaning and stirring a little, not hurt much. As Orvie watched the outlaw pawed at his mask.

Then Orvie stared, for the wounded man was Wes Carker. The knowledge brought another quick thought. "Two got away!" Orvie yelled suddenly, starting for his horse.

Charlie Two-Star just shrugged. "They come back. Purty fast."

That checked Orvie in his tracks, heeling him back, his bewilderment growing.

Slouched in the saddle, Charlie Two-Star calmly considered the timber, his lazy manner strangely confident, unconcerned.

Orvie felt annoyance; it climbed demandingly. "Let's go!" he said, and stepped toward his horse again.

Still Charlie Two-Star did not stir. But interest deepened in the muddy brown eyes. "Coming now," he said.

Breaking through the timber, fanned out around two white men, came mounted Indians — perhaps a score or more. They were old-time Osages, Orvie saw, carrying carbines and war clubs — Osages of Charlie Two-Star's time, gray and wrinkled.

And suddenly Orvie understood, before the deputy grunted proudly: "Indian police. Fight purty good. Beat white-man posse."

Pieces of this puzzle began falling into place as the Osages swarmed from the timber with Murdo Quinton and Blue Hackett, the freight firm employee, under guard. At the same moment it came to Orvie that the fourth man down over there looked like the livery hand who'd driven Judith to Rocky City. Orvie also saw much more, very clearly. He remembered Quinton so all-fired eager to point an accusing finger at the Jardeen boys, Quinton urging posses off chasing shadows. Pretty darned smart.

Most of the pieces fit. Yet. . . .

In a somewhat mellowed irritation, Orvie asked: "Charlie, wonder how they knew this shipment was coming in today? Y'don't suppose somebody picked up that letter in the office?"

For once Charlie Two-Star seemed flustered. It only lasted a moment or so, however. The ageless face became wistful, the picture of injured innocence. "Sometimes strong wind come up. Blow mighty hard."

"Yeah," said Orvie, grinning, "blew it right down the street into the freight office. Unusual."

He stopped, watching Charlie Two-Star sadly examining the tiny bullet hole in his buckskin medicine pouch, then shake the contents into the palm of his hand. There were several round stones, an eagle's claw, a dried owl's head — nothing more.

Just one piece of this puzzle was left unjoined now.

Orvie found Judith Carlton standing by the coach. He saw her look once at Murdo Quinton and turn away, her face drawn, remembering. She seemed to be trying to erase the thought of all the bad years, the years she'd tried to build happiness with Murdo Quinton and couldn't.

But as she faced him, Orvie saw her expression change. He saw the sunlight fully on her face, and a light in her eyes he thought maybe had been there a long time, only he hadn't seen it.

She stood very close to Orvie Tuttle, and she was saying: "After I left Murdo, he threatened to kill you if I gave you any attention. I thought it best if I left. I couldn't tell you why that day on the road, with Murdo's man driving."

But she'd come back to tell him the one thing he wanted most to know. And right now he was thinking of the good years left them, and of how young he felt.

SUMMER OF THE BIG DIE

Riding past the house, Wes Crawford could feel the run-down shabbiness of the scattered ranch buildings. It hadn't bothered him last fall when Lily came, for his hopes had been high then. Sun-cracked and bleakly gray, the place was an ugly reminder of plans blasted by fickle weather. There'd been the long, harsh winter, and now the dust and heat of a grass-killing drought kept hanging on.

He was in no hurry and he rode slowly inside the corral of warped jack-oak poles, the clanking of the windmill grinding in his ears. He watered the gelding and unsaddled over by the horse shed. As he forked loose hay, he stared at the ribs of the empty grain crib. Then his head came up and he paced through the hot wind across to the house, where the cottonwoods threw out black patches of shade.

Before going in, he glanced up at the

cloudless, copper sky, sliding toward dusk now, and a little shudder touched him. He stepped inside.

She was bending over the wood-burning stove. Against the yellow light of the coal-oil lamp her face was flushed and shining. She looked up and straightened, the round, full shape of her blouse rising and falling as her hands worked.

"Supper's ready," she said.

Awkwardness came on him and he was weary all through, not wanting to tell her what he'd seen today. Always like this, at the wind-up of his long fence-riding rounds, they would talk and always the talk drifted to short water and grass and lank cows.

"The Pretty Water is gettin' down," he said. "But no more than I expected and it's never dried up. We've had dry spells before."

He spoke with a forced good humor that he didn't feel. He thought of Sol Beeson's invitation that morning as they squatted in the thin shade of the blackjacks where the Saddle Rock spring seeped. "Dance at Beeson's place tomorrow night," he said. "I figured we might go."

She nodded, her eyes searching his face, and abruptly he wanted to reach out for her. Instead, he dippered water from the bucket on the wooden stand and washed the dust from his face with a noisy, grunting relief.

He was reaching for the roller towel when he heard her say — "Wes." — and something told him that she'd been figuring again.

He pulled out a chair at the table before he spoke. "Farley?" he asked, low and even. He knew his own face was showing his resentment and he could see the color climbing in her cheeks. At that instant she looked drawn thin again. It dug into him that maybe she'd worked harder than he'd realized.

"Why, yes. How'd you guess?"

He tried to smile. "I can read the signs." The smile vanished. "We've been over it before . . . a couple of times."

All at once she sat down across from him and he caught the faint, clean scent of her hair. "Wes," she said breathlessly, "I'm just trying to help us. John Farley rode over to ask me again. He wants me to take my old job back . . . teach the next term in Mesa. School starts in two weeks and he has to know right away. It isn't much, but it'll help us get by here. You've said yourself that we're burned out this year."

"Not yet," he said in a flat, stubborn voice. "This drought'll break soon. They always do. And I thought we'd turned down Farley for good." Tight-lipped, he stopped talking, trying to think of the right way to say it. "You're a town girl, Lily. I know that and I know this is a hard year on a woman . . . any woman."

"That's why I want to help." She leaned forward, her face upturned.

Last fall he'd have told her that having her here was what counted. The thought turned him awkward and stiff again. What he wanted to say was that it took two people — a man and his woman. But he couldn't straighten out in his mind what he felt, and he was straining against a rising bitterness.

"You're helping plenty," he said. "What'll people say if you move into town? That you had to because I can't make it for us out here." He swallowed hard and he knew he was getting it mixed up. "I've got my pride, Lily."

He saw the gray eyes widen, heard her voice high and aroused.

"And I have mine! What if people do talk? It's nothing to be ashamed of, and it's only for a little while . . . this fall. You're wearing yourself out while I just watch. I don't feel that's enough."

"Maybe," he heard himself saying bitterly, "I'm just now gettin' it. It'd be easier for you in town. Maybe you could have some of the things you don't get here." His voice was rough-edged and he said: "No . . . I don't want you to go. We'll make out here."

He saw the swift change in her face. She seemed to shrink away from him, to shut him out. Quickly she got up and Wes stood with her. It rushed over him miserably that he hadn't meant to say it that hard. Trouble was the town job had long been a sore subject between them. It had been ever since Farley had offered it last winter, and the wedge between them had grown as the drought sharpened tempers.

"Lily," he said, taking a step.

"Don't touch me!"

She jerked away and stood there, rigid and hurt, not looking at him. He could hear her rapid, broken breathing. He was groping for the right words, the words that wouldn't come. But smooth talk had never been easy for Wes Crawford, a big-boned, drawling man with rope-roughened hands. Then she turned and was gone into the other room. Everything was empty and wrong inside him when he swung outside.

It was almost dark, with the strong-scented smell of the dry prairie grass keen on the climbing wind. A wind that was like a hot tongue licking against his face. The words he had said whipped back at him, the clumsy, hurting words, and he saw himself big-handed and rough and awkward. Lily was right. They were burned out and the place he'd slowly built up was slipping back to dust. Yet — he ground around stubbornly — her way wasn't a man's. It wasn't false pride for a man to stiffen and fight back in the only way he knew. He found himself searching the beginning of the faintest suspicion in his mind. Was this her way of easing out of a poor match?

With a sudden self-disgust, he realized that wasn't fair thinking. Still, the thought kept sliding back, dark and ugly, hitting at his pride. He hadn't really told her how bad it was. Gaunt, bony-ribbed stock was bawling and some dying around the mud-cracked water tanks. In places the creek had dried down to shallow holes, even in the deep stretches where the Pretty Water ran past the Trawler range. He'd seen it again today, the water green and murky and the flat rocks showing. The horse ranch of Murdo and Tharp Trawler held a heap of memories, none of them pleasant.

Their headquarters was a shack cabin and scattering of lean-to sheds and rickety corrals in the rough hills across the creek. It was there that Wes, then a deputy marshal saving his pay for the ranch on the other side, had caught the brothers with stolen horses. On Wes's testimony they had drawn five-year sentences in the penitentiary at Concho. One day they'd finish their time. They'd come helling back. They'd come looking for him. He'd got that in Mesa's crowded courtroom after the trial was over.

Grim-mouthed and surly, Murdo and Tharp stood sullenly between deputies Ed Bowdre and Tom East, the shock and disbelief showing on the brothers' dark faces. As Wes was walking past, Murdo's head jerked and Wes halted. He was aware of the thick quiet, the restless shuffling of boots, as if everybody waited for something.

"We ain't forgettin' you," Murdo grunted, letting the words sink in. His heavy-lidded eyes seemed to narrow in their sockets, to flicker their hatred, and he swung his square and solid shoulders.

"They used to hang hoss thieves," Wes snapped. "You got off easy. You can cut your time down by good behavior."

Murdo's bushy mouth was working. "Yeah," he sneered, "that'll help."

Murdo was the waspish one, Wes remembered. A dark, moody man, he made decisions for the brothers, and Tharp followed them with a blind and reckless devotion. Tharp was weak, unpredictable, dangerous

— and yellow. He tried to mimic Murdo's swagger, Murdo's tough talk, although he didn't have his brother's nerve. He was thin-faced and bony-shouldered, with restless, smoky eyes and skinny hands that were never still.

"We'll remember," Tharp joined in, his voice a raspy imitation of Murdo's.

"Good enough," Wes gritted. "I don't hold grudges. But when you get out, remember where the fence lines run. My grass takes in the Pretty Water past your place . . . your range is on the other side. Remember that."

"Come on, Murdo," Ed Bowdre spoke up irritably. "Long ride to Concho. Mind your ways and we'll forget the cuffs, but let's go."

It happened all at once, like something long held in suddenly bursting. Murdo shuffled his feet, turned reluctantly with the deputies behind Tharp. Murdo took a slowing step, with his shaggy head lifting. He stopped, boots planted wide. In one jerking, hating motion he wrenched around. Wes saw the big fists knotting.

"Damn you," — Murdo drove his voice at Wes — "you better stay primed! We'll be back quicker'n you think!"

"Shut up, Murdo!"

It was Ed Bowdre's alarmed voice. He was reaching for his gun when Murdo lunged and flayed out murderously. Wes ducked and threw up his arms. Too late he felt the rocky knuckles smashing across his chest, his face. Pain sliced through him, and, as he tilted back, off balance, he saw Tom East struggling to hold Tharp.

But Murdo had torn free. He was rushing in, bull's head lowered, the short, stocky arms swinging. Tharp had thrust his short, long frame in front of Bowdre and the deputy was punching violently to break through to Murdo.

Abruptly Murdo's face was blurred, close in, the sweaty body smell strong. Wes twisted and shot a fist along the sloping line of the bearded jaw. There was a choppy *thunk.* Murdo's head canted up, surprise springing across the eyes. Around Wes was the shouting and stamping of the pushing-in crowd. He saw Murdo, wild-eyed and grunting, boring in recklessly. Then Bowdre's gun barrel was slashing downward. It cut a short, wicked arc. Metal cracked on bone and Murdo sagged to his knees.

Something sick turned over in Wes. It flashed through him that the Trawlers would blame him for this, too. He watched Murdo wilt like an axed steer, his stubby-fingered hands gripping the long-haired head that ran red. Now Bowdre and East were slapping on handcuffs and hurrying the Trawlers through the crowd. A moment later, Wes heard Murdo's high-pitched, furious voice, almost a scream: "We'll be back!"

After three years, flashes of the courtroom fight still wandered through his mind. Lately, in his low moments, he had found himself studying ahead to the time when the Trawlers would return, studying about guns — the worn Colt he'd put away when he quit the law-dog game and the old Winchester coyote gun. He was frowning, thinking of Murdo and Tharp, as he saddled up the following evening.

Silent, he and Lily rode toward Sol Beeson's ranch. They were angling across hill-rolled country under a star-scattered night. It reminded Wes of other nights last year, when they had first married, when the smell of the coming-on fall was strong and bracing. Only there was a dryness now on the wind, and the horses kicked up dust that gritted between the teeth.

Lily hadn't mentioned the school job again. Yet Wes knew it hung in her mind. He sensed it in the silence as she waited for him to cinch up. He caught it in the cool surface of her eyes, the voiceless reproach, the unspoken bitterness. When she took the reins and slipped her boot in the stirrup, Wes moved to give her a hand. Swiftly Lily was in the saddle before he could more than touch her. For a second, while his hand fell away, he felt the brushing lightness of her and her woman's softness. She turned her face from him and she beat him out of the corral. He swung up, letting the gelding foot alongside.

"You're quick," he said.

"Quick," she asked, "for a town girl?" — and rode ahead.

Bundled behind her was an extra skirt. She'd change to it as soon as they got to Beeson's, and he remembered last year the pride he'd felt in her when they'd gone to their first dance there. Later, the realization of his own untractable boots and how, after two dances, he'd left her to the waiting, more sure-footed cowboys, while he talked weather and cows and markets with the older ranchers.

Wes heard the violins before he could make out the shapes of the drawn-up wagons and the horses hunched around the brightly lighted ranch house. The music came high and scraping, thin on the wind. It gave Wes a quick-running warm feeling, a feeling of belonging to these people. To the leather-faced men and the uncomplaining women. It struck him as a sort of half-wild defiance to bad weather and lean times.

When they dismounted among a chattering cluster of ranch kids, he saw an expression of eagerness on Lily's face in the streaky light. Leading the horses off, he heard a small girl's voice, pleased and astonished.

"It's Miz Lily!"

There was a stampede of feet rushing across the hard-packed earth, the sound of young, excited voices. He saw Lily go inside, trailed by the kid bunch.

Coming back from the corral, Wes stood a moment in the lantern light off the long porch. A tall man walked over from the shadows, brushing back his thicket of stringy white hair.

" 'Bout time," chided Sol Beeson, looking uncomfortable in his fresh shirt. "Now I get to dance with Lily."

"You'll have to hurry." Wes laughed. "I aim to stomp some myself tonight."

"There'll be a speakin' first," Beeson drawled. "Before we bed the kids down in the wagons. John Farley's little girl, Della."

Beeson drifted inside and Wes heard the fiddlers break off. When Beeson announced the reading, Wes moved upon the porch. Looking in from the crowded doorway stood John Farley, a mild man, running to heft who liked his ease. He turned and grunted.

Wes said: "Howdy."

Farley looked at him questioningly. "You and Lily make up your minds?"

"Guess so." Wes nodded, surprised at the regret he felt. "Lily's goin' to stay on the ranch, John. She'd like to help, though."

"Why, sure," said the big man too quickly. "Don't blame you." But Wes caught the disappointment. "We'll miss her. The kids like her."

Inside, a girl's clear voice was reaching out and Farley turned to listen. In a few minutes, the recitation was over. There was a following outbreak of clapping and voices murmuring, and then Wes saw Lily standing with Mrs. Farley and the Farley girl running across to take Lily's hand.

Farley swung on Wes, chuckling. "See . . . what'd I tell you? Lily's got a way with kids. That's the piece Della learned from Lily a year ago. She remembered every word," he said proudly.

Beeson waved at the fiddlers. Boots tapped the rough floor and the music commenced, loud and catching and stirring. Womenfolks began streaming from the house, herding the children to the wagons. Wes saw a grinning cowpuncher from the LX outfit stop and face Lily. Her arms came up and she was smiling as they swung out to join the forming circle of dancers. Wes stepped back in the shadows, hearing the caller's hoarse voice bawling the rapid changes. After a while Beeson came up, and then Farley eased over.

Listening to their talk of poor grass and scarce water, Wes found himself only half attentive. Somehow it all seemed unimportant tonight. His mind was inside with Lily. When another rancher joined them, Wes left and went inside.

He heard the music stop and he searched out Lily and moved toward her. Just then the music started again and he hurried. Her eyes were fully upon him, and he thought she was going to wait for him. Then, with a cool smile, she turned deliberately to the LX man. Suddenly Wes stood alone with the dancers circling, with the clumsiness dragging through him. Walking stiffly to the porch, he knew it was her way of hurting him.

He avoided the knot of huddled ranchers and tapered up a cigarette. Shoulders hard-angled against a porch brace, he stood watching the bright, glittering pattern of the dry-winded night. Men's voices drifted across to him. From the wagons he heard the whispering of the bedded-down ranch kids, restless on their quilt pallets. It struck him that the children liked Lily. He'd seen that and he'd been proud in an unshowing way. Slowly he felt something like regret, something like the first ravel of doubt. The thought came to him swiftly now, changing him. Maybe he ought to let Lily go.

He stayed outside till the music slowed and snapped off, till the sky turned milky gray, till Lily came out and the men and the women walked tiredly to their wagons and horses.

Riding home, he said — "You had a good time." — thinking of the LX man and the flush of pleasure on her face as he swung her. "Those kids, too."

Her voice, at first drowsy, became alert, sharp. "The children made it good, Wes," she said with a kind of bluntness, and he knew she meant it.

They rode home in the thinning half light. She went at once to the house while he unsaddled. He took his time, lingering over the chore, pitching extra hay to the horses. His mind was made up when he finished.

He went, slow-footed, to the house. Lily came in from the back room and crossed to the stove to start coffee. Abruptly he wanted to get it over with.

"I been thinkin," Wes began, trying to make his tone easy. "I think we better take Farley's offer. Not much time left and he might find somebody else. I'll ride over this afternoon, tell him to pick you up in a buggy."

A thickening silence followed — save for the quick rush of Lily's breathing — that Wes broke by saying: "Guess you'll want to take most of your things."

She stared at him in astonishment, and he tried to smile. He failed miserably, watching the bewilderment in her heat-drawn face.

"Why," she demanded, "why'd you change your mind?"

Wes shrugged. "We're burned out. I figure this is the best way. No place for a woman here."

Looking at her, he had the odd and unreasonable impression that she didn't believe him. That she didn't want to go. He thought she was going to come to him and he felt a hard, pent-up pounding deep in his chest.

But she said tonelessly — "I'll start getting ready." — and walked away from him. In that moment she looked very straight and dark, with a pride and composure he'd never fully noticed before. He heard her moving in the other room, heard her light step on the rough flooring as she went about her packing.

Her image kept jumping in his mind during the ride to Farley's ranch. He was thinking of the solitary days to come, of the house dark and silent when he rode late.

Wes found Farley cooling under the cottonwoods. "You're pushin' that hoss hard." Farley grinned, hoisting up his huge bulk. Wes saw the flicker of interest in his eyes. "Lily change her mind?"

Wes nodded. "If it ain't too late."

"There's others," Farley said with a shake of his head. "But I been holdin' out for Lily. The kids are set on her. You saw that last night."

"She'll be ready early tomorrow. You'll need a buggy. There's a light trunk and some other things."

"I'll be there before noon. Now, you're gonna light an' eat."

"Much obliged," Wes said, turning his horse. "It's late."

Farley gave him a close look. "No trouble is there?" he asked. "You know, Wes, you oughta carry a gun again. The Trawlers'll be back one of these days. You don't want to get caught empty-handed."

"I know," Wes said wearily. "But they still got time to serve."

He was gone before Farley could go on, leaving him standing there with a troubled frown on his round face.

He was cutting the Mesa road when he noticed the rider coming from town. Wes pulled up when the man waved frantically and kicked his horse to a run. Wes recognized Sol Beeson's lank shape in the saddle. Watching him push the horse, Wes wondered at the hurry. Beeson's eyes were excited when he came up.

"Wes!" he called out. "You heard?" And before Wes could answer, he blurted: "The Trawlers broke out at Concho! Shot up a guard, got clean away! Everybody in town's talkin' about it. Nobody's seen 'em yet, but you know damn' well where they're headin' . . . they're lookin' for you!"

"I just came from Farley's," Wes said. "He hadn't heard."

"He will tonight. There's a school board meetin'."

Wes hadn't moved. He felt a sort of numbness crawling through him. Now that he knew it was coming, certain and soon, half the dread had gone. And something else stirred him. It was a kind of relief. At least Lily was leaving.

"I'll be watchin'," Wes said with a casualness he didn't feel. "If they're smart, they won't head back here. Not with the whole country lookin'. Maybe they'll just ride on."

"The hell they will! An' you know better. Now, look sharp. Start packin' a gun. Murdo's bull-headed and Tharp's crazy wild." Beeson slapped his saddle for emphasis. "They'll hit here."

"Damn' fools if they do."

Beeson's mouth tightened cynically. "That's easy for Murdo," he snorted. "But he's after you. You . . . you want me to send a couple of hands over to your place?" Beeson's grin was grim. "Might need 'em."

For a second Wes was tempted. Call on your neighbors. They'd come loaded. But something told him that it wasn't their worry, and then Lily would know, too. "I'm obliged," he said. "But I'll make out."

Beeson's mouth tightened cynically then, muttering, and Wes rode on. Topping the last knuckled ridge, he saw the light from the house. In the purpling darkness, it thrust a yellow finger under the giant cottonwoods, black and towering and swaying against the skyline. Far off, where the wild hills massed in hunkering knots, a coyote lifted a lonesome howl. Shuddering, Wes rode down the slope. It came on him that a light was a simple and needed thing for a hungry man riding in after dark, with the wind just beginning to cool the faded grass.

Tonight he didn't pause at the door, for he knew that the time for such mooning foolishness was past. He came in quietly, into a house already showing signs of emptiness. She was folding dresses and aprons, placing them in a barrel-topped trunk.

"Farley will be here in the morning," he told her.

She turned a tense, expressionless face. "I'll be ready," she said, her hands busy.

At daybreak he paced stiffly to the corral, the wash of sleeplessness low and heavy in him. How, he thought, did you tell a woman good bye — a woman who wanted to leave? A town woman? He walked back to the house and ate his breakfast, the food flat and dry in his mouth. He was buckling on the worn gun belt when he remembered the old Winchester carbine.

Bleakly he guessed he'd need it, too. Still loaded, it reared up in the corner where he'd left it last spring after calving time. He turned with the saddle gun in his hands. He caught Lily's eyes on him, straight and questioning.

"Something's worrying you," she said. She stared at the pistol, at the Winchester.

"What . . . ?"

"Coyotes," Wes snapped.

"First time you've mentioned any since last spring."

It stabbed through his mind that he should have taken the carbine out first thing when he got up. Now there were questions — questions he couldn't rightfully answer.

"Spotted a big one early this morning," he said, the sound of his voice flat, unconvincing. "You keep it handy. Use it if you see one around the place. Save me the trouble later."

She stepped back, the wide-set eyes narrowing on the gun.

"It's loaded . . . ready to go." He levered in a shell, the click sharp in the room, and he pushed the gun toward her. "You've shot it a couple of times."

But she held her hands back, tense and tight against her, doubt and confusion drawing on her face. He saw revulsion, too, and her hands fluttered nervously. Shuffling and clumsy, he leaned the carbine against the table.

A moment later, he stood at the door.

"I'll be back before you leave," he said in a loud voice. He wondered if his cramped face gave him away. For he'd thought it all out. He wouldn't be here when Farley came for her. Easier that way.

He saw her lips move. He thought she was about to speak and he hung back, waiting. Instead, she grew slowly rigid, shutting him out, and her mouth turned firm, stubborn, proud.

Almost blindly he heeled around and outside. The knotted feeling was balled up inside him. Afterward, he took his look from the slope north of the house. He couldn't be sure — but, for the briefest instant, he thought he saw a flutter of movement at a window, a face. Swinging back, he knew that John Farley would be on time.

Late morning caught Wes angling through a thick stand of jack oaks above the Trawler place. It was a thin chance, he realized, that Murdo and Tharp would dodge back here. First glance showed the corrals empty. Nothing stirred around the weed-grown cabin and sheds.

Looking at the tangled pole corrals, he figured Farley would be there now. He'd be grunting and laughing, full of good humor. And Lily — well, he guessed she'd be glad to go. That was what really hurt. She wanted to go, and the sign said she wouldn't be back.

After half an hour of watching, Wes's restlessness drove him out of the hot timber.

There was a recklessness sawing at him as he rode up to the cabin. He had the Colt out when he slid down and kicked open the door. The place was a littered nest of old clothes, dishes, broken rope, and leather pieces. A black rat padded swiftly across the dirt floor. With the closed-up, musty smell strong in his nostrils, he swung up and headed south, killing time now. Past noon he crossed the rock-bottomed Pretty Water again.

He'd delayed long enough. He saw that coming on the road to Farley's ranch. There were narrow-rimmed tracks — Farley's buggy — going and coming back. Something slipped away from Wes then, all the harshness and blame for her that he'd held deep in his mind.

It seemed a long time before he rode down the slope and saw the cottonwoods weaving. He reined up, his glance touching the out-scattered sheds, windmill, and single corral this side of the silent-looking house. It ran through him that he was mooning again, that a solitary man ought to hold himself in. With a dull aimlessness, he walked the gelding forward. He felt the animal's muscles bunch and the gait quicken as they approached the corral.

Inside, Wes stepped down. He was moving, flat-footed, toward the horse shed when he heard it. A clicking sound sharply cutting across the dismal clank of the windmill's gears. But he took another step before he wheeled. Before it flashed coldly on him that he was too late.

"Turn around, Crawford!"

It was a hoarse, hating voice, one that Wes knew even as he heeled back, his hand dragging down. Murdo and Tharp Trawler stood posted behind him at the edge of a shed wall. Wes saw the hard shine on Murdo's bushy face, saw the leveled Colts, and his own hand froze.

"We're back," Murdo mocked savagely. "Only sooner. Good behavior, by God!"

Wes raked in a long ragged breath. "You're damned fools to show up here. Everybody's lookin' for you."

"Plenty o' time," Murdo sneered, "an' we won't be here long. You're easier'n I ever expected. Why, you rode up here daydreamin' . . . not even lookin.' " His rough, arrogant voice shaded off, pleased. "You didn't spot our horses 'cause they're outta sight in a shed. . . . All right, Tharp, he's yours. You been wantin' 'im!"

Tharp's lips flattened. His glance slid briefly to Wes, back to Murdo. But the yellow was showing through. It flicked in his jumpy, almost begging eyes, in the uncertain droop of his bony shoulders.

"Go on . . . damn you!" Murdo bawled at Tharp.

It fanned out fast. For a moment the Trawlers stood rooted. Then Tharp was spinning, driven by Murdo's voice, and Wes saw his chance. It hit him that he'd have to choose. That Murdo was the waspish one. Wes swung the gun up. He heard his bullet strike the half-turned Murdo. He saw Murdo stumble, desperation straining in him before he buckled and fell. Pivoting on Tharp, Wes knew there wasn't time.

There was a sharp crack in Wes's ears. All at once Tharp doubled up. His pistol raveled down, kicking up a whiff of dust as it hit. Dimly Wes knew it wasn't his bullet. He seemed to stand in a thin, unreal mist. He heard the windmill still grinding. He stood, spraddle-legged, and his own Colt was heavy in his hand. Murdo lay sprawled forward. His square body was very still. Tharp had quit moving.

Something tore into Wes, a sudden knowledge. He whipped his glance around. Almost before he knew it, he was running toward the house. He saw the door swung open, black, empty. And, for a second, he had his doubt. But when his boots struck the steps, he saw Lily standing back in the room.

She was holding the Winchester uncertainly, like some strange thing. She looked at him, not moving. Then her slim fingers loosened and the saddle gun clattered on the floor. She was coming to him, saying in a dim voice: "Wes . . . I couldn't leave. . . . You didn't come back, and then those men came up to the shed."

"Farley tell you?" he heard himself asking.

She was hard and shaking against him, her voice lost, muffled, and he felt the held-in feeling inside him go. But he knew — and it was running through his mind that the bad year was beginning to turn.

Hide Hunter's Prize

Time-worn, the hills still shoulder up from the rolling face of the prairies. There's the notched landmark cleaving the first knuckled ridge. There's the broad, shallow valley, a stout fence closing it in, with the creek running crookedly through black timber. Buffalo — only a lonesome sixty-odd now — crop the thick grass. As the shaggy, ponderous beasts move, there's a flash of color — a white buffalo.

It's a pleasant place, summer-quiet, still safe. But Will Teague saw it long ago, fence-free, contested, and troubled. He saw it when the tolling boom of hide hunters' Big Fifties rolled flatly off the wind to the west — when defiant Pawnees whirled gaunt ponies in the valley. . . .

Shep North cocked his long-haired head and sniffed the hot, dry wind. "I don't know," he said in a muttering voice. "Don't even smell right no more. Time for 'em to be moving north to the Platte."

Last summer, Will remembered, the unmistakable signs of plenty of buffalo had been the teeming flies, hatched from thousands of rotting carcasses, and the sickening smell. They had done mighty good last season, the three skinners and Shep North and Will Teague. There'd been $6,000 Teague and North split after the buyers had paid off.

But this summer the bobbing sea of black, lumbering, hump-backed animals was suddenly drying up. Looking for better shooting, Will had led the hide outfit down from Kansas to the Indian Nations. It was risky traveling, but he was skirting the rim of the forbidden Pawnee country.

"Reckon I know," North shook his head regretfully. "Too damn' many hunters. Why don't people quit crowding? Then there'd be enough hides for everybody."

He was past middle age with bony hands and feet, with gray eyes washed pale and squinting. He was worn thin, his sharp face stitched with sun-brought wrinkles. He looked sour and cantankerous till he grinned, then the good humor broke to the surface.

"Enough for Injuns, too?" Will asked.

"Yeah." North's leather-hued face was

almost wistful. "Even Injuns." But his eyes showed his doubt, his plain worry. "The plains tribes claim there'll be game long as the big medicine bison ain't killed off. That's the white buffalo . . . somethin' a man sees once in a lifetime, if he's lucky."

"Somebody besides Injuns'll go hungry this winter, Shep. The buffalo's gone . . . shot out. Never thought we'd see it. Figured us hunters was just takin' the natural herd increase. Too bad. We've sure had a bunch of fun."

The old hunter swung around stubbornly. "This season's been full of bad luck from the start," he complained. "Lost Nick Tarman second day out. And now you got to take on this Blaze Dealey. Why'd you do it, Will?"

"He's a good killer."

"So I hear." North spoke with a grunting, deceptive softness, plainly suspicious. "Funny how none of Todd Sloan's outfit came back. Dealey claimed the Pawnees jumped 'em, killed the whole bunch while he was out hunting." His voice grew thoughtful: "Nobody would sign Dealey on this summer . . . nobody but you."

Will felt himself flushing. "If there's any buffalo, he'll find 'em."

"Maybe," North said skeptically. "Only

ninety hides are in the wagons. Skinners ain't pegged out a robe in a week."

Shep North had raked up his own doubts, Will knew, crossing over to the makeshift camp where the three skinners squatted and played cards in the thin shade of a wagon. But there hadn't been any choice at the time.

Tuck Barton, the boss skinner, looked up from his greasy cards. "Skinnin' knives are goin' to rust, Will," he grumbled, big-knuckled hands fidgeting. "It looks as if this trip won't pay for salt. Guess I'll be behind a plow come next spring."

Irritably Will let his eyes search the vast bone-littered plains. A rider was angling for camp. It was Dealey on the run, square and thick in the saddle. He had pulled out early that morning looking for buffalo, while North and Will had escorted the wagons to the next rendezvous west of the Arkansas.

"Here's work comin'," Will grunted. No man rode that fast out here unless there were buffalo.

Dealey raked a lathered horse over to the wagons. He pulled up, his wide-boned face excited, flushed.

"Buffalo!" he called hoarsely. "East of here . . . let's go get 'em!"

The skinners dropped their cards, jumped

up. Barton's eyes were hard-bright and Will caught the hungry look. "How far?" Will asked.

"Eight . . . ten miles."

"East, you said." Will frowned, turning it over in his mind. "Across the Arkansas. That'll put us smack into Pawnee country."

Flat suspicion stirred in Will, sudden and sharp. He remembered the skeptical tone of North's muttering voice. He was thinking of Todd Sloan's wiped-out crew on the Arkansas.

"Came to shoot buffalo, didn't you?" Dealey sneered. He looked at the skinners for approval and Will heard their quick grumbling.

"Sure," Will said coldly, "but I don't like my skinners in Pawnee country with a river at their backs."

"We're willin'," Barton spoke up. "How are we goin' to make wages here?"

Will stared at them. It came to him that he'd have a hard time holding the outfit together if they didn't find buffalo pretty quick. At 25¢ a hide, skinners needed volume to share in the pay-off.

"Hitch up, then," Will said with reluctance. "But stick close. I hate to see a young man lose his hair." When North joined them, Will said: "What'd I tell you . . . Dealey's spotted a bunch."

"He's ridin' a damn' smart horse." Without another word, the hunter stalked, stiff-legged, to his gelding.

They rode out under a fire-baked sun, the hollow rumble of the wagons far-carrying. They struck across a flat, grass-thick prairie, limitless south and west, oddly silent. With his Sharps .50 jolting it the long saddle holster, it grew on Will that the buffalo, like the Indian, was being forced into the broken hills, across the river. Only the real protection lay still deeper eastward, where Will could see the rough line of timber massing on hunkering slopes — Pawnee country.

Watching the wagons ford the shallowing Arkansas, Will felt a nagging dread. He pressed his lips together and his memory fled back.

It had started in Dodge City just before the crew trailed south for the season. His luck had been running high that night. Blaze Dealey's bearded face had stood out across the tight, smoky circle of curious men knotted around the table. Will had won the pot from the fancy-vested sharper and, with pockets bulging, had backed out the door of the dive, the silence suddenly heavy and ominous. It came to him later that Dealey had ducked out before the last hand. Will had turned down the murky street. Before he'd gone a dozen steps, he heard the running tap of boots behind him. Swinging around, he had seen the glint of light on the gambler's gun barrel. He remembered his own instinctive lunge for his weapon, the racketing shot, the gamester swaying, falling. Then Dealey had stepped from the shadows.

"You," he had growled, accusing, "you murdered him."

"Murder!" Will had stepped back. "I beat him square. He was coming at me."

"Reckon I seen," Dealey had said with a shrewd flatness. "You drawed first. Looks like your word against mine . . . and you just killed a man. Could be right serious if we don't get together."

Realization had traveled through Will in a sharp shock and he straightened. He had felt a forced-on weakness, but he fought against it stubbornly. The shooting was self-defense, he had reasoned, and he could prove it in court. Yet maybe he'd have trouble if Dealey had set his head, because a hard-handed rough justice was reaching out across to the wild, far-off prairie towns. Anyway, Dealey could delay him and the crew for costly days, even weeks. Five miles outside town the men were camped, ready to move. And with the buffalo thinning out and the hide gangs hurrying to get the jump, time meant everything.

"The hell with you." Will had punched his pistol forward.

"Get held up here and the other outfits'll beat you to buffalo range." Dealey's voice had been a heavy drone, biting and pushing into Will's mind. "Ain't like it used to be. Just the early-bird hunters'll make hide money this year. If you want to get out fast, better cut me in with your bunch."

Behind them there had been a shout and boots pounding along the hard-packed street.

"We got two killers now," Will had protested.

"Suit yourself."

There had been rapid movement pressing him from up the street and Will had jerked. He had seen figures, heard boot heels thudding, coming on. Aware that he was doing a foolish thing, he had grunted — "Come on." — and had run to his horse. Dealey had been siding him as they galloped out of town.

It was breaking daylight when they rode into the stirring camp. At once, Will caught the dark, frowning reproach as Shep North's faded old eyes took in Dealey. Taking him on was a mighty crazy move, Will realized, as the wagons groaned up the slanting, timbered riverbank and crawled upon the flattening land.

"Over there," Dealey pointed after a while. Will waved the wagons to a halt.

Eastward, he saw the slash in the hills, the beginning of a shallow valley. Now the three of them trotted ahead, dismounted, and climbed a grassy knoll. As Will looked down, something like regret touched him, twisted deep down and caught. It was the biggest band they'd spotted this season. About a hundred head, he figured, and an inner voice told him that they wouldn't be bunching any bigger. No more thick, dark masses blacking the country far as a strong-sighted man could see. No more creaking, hide-loaded booty wagons.

Dealey licked thick lips in his brush of a beard. Will looked at him and said in a matter-of-fact voice: "Wind's right . . . straight to us."

They fanned out, keeping low, set up rest-sticks with the Sharps' long muzzles resting in the notches. Dealey's rifle boomed first, eager, deadly. A stub-horn bull with a chin mop of stringy hair shuddered, sank to his knees. Suddenly the buffalo broke their lumbering, nodding gait. Smelling blood, they started milling around the bull, pawing and bellowing, viciously hooking the brown-black carcass.

It was blind, stupid instinct that Will had watched work but few times even during the peak years of the plains slaughter. This was the beginning of unusual circumstances — a stand made to order for the cool, experienced hunter. Keep blasting the outside animals, Will remembered, knock off any buffalo starting to bolt the herd. Keep them milling in the doomed, confused circle. Don't shoot fast enough to overheat your rifle barrel.

Will could feel the tightness of rising excitement in his throat. He kept aiming back of the shoulder blade for the lungs, aware of the booming grunt of the Big Fifties. Once he thought he heard the faint drumming of a horse behind him. Once his smarting eyes picked out a flash of something, but lost it in the smoky haze, the churning black bodies. He fired and jerked the breechblock down and reloaded till his arms ached, till the gunpowder smell was acrid. Like shooting beef in a pen, he thought, and, glancing across the strewn prairie, he knew that some of the fun had gone out of this for him.

Finally, when he quit and looked up,

bone-weary and red-eyed, he saw several cows and bulls scrambling off to the east at a heavy-bodied run. Shep North was still firing methodically and Dealey, his broad back turned, was blasting the runaways. Then Will saw the calf, awkward on trembling legs, running to keep up with a wounded, laboring cow. Something about that calf riveted his attention.

Will hunched forward, staring. It was a white calf. It flashed over him then that he was looking at that rarity of the plains — a white buffalo. Big medicine to the superstitious, bison-worshiping Indian. Big money to the lucky hide hunter. One white robe would bring a fancy price, a season's payoff in one shot.

He was figuring as he squinted along the hot barrel of the Sharps, when a movement in the corner of his eye brought realization that he wasn't alone any more. Jerking around, he saw the old Indian — lank-bellied, bony-ribbed, with sunken cheeks in a thin, hungry face. Will also saw the Indian's gaunt pony now cropping grass with the hunters' horses, but otherwise the prairie was empty.

Empty-handed, the Indian was peering fixedly at the stretched-out carcasses. He stepped a few paces, lips moving.

"Buffalo about gone," he grunted regretfully in a dead-toned voice. Will saw him straighten as his eyes picked out the calf. He half turned, the prominent cheek bones stretching the skin drum-tight, and Will caught the pleading expression in the saddle-colored eyes, in the wrinkled, year-bitten face.

"Mebbe you let white buffalo live. So buffalo no die . . . come back."

"Get out of here!" Will called harshly, waving him off.

With a feeling of lost time, Will swung back to the Sharps. The Indian stood with his glance swinging back and forth from Will. About a hundred yards away Will saw the cow and calf moving away slowly. He lined up the white, bounding shape. He started to pull the trigger, held up, clamped down again, then took a deep breath. It wasn't the harmless, hungry-looking old warrior with his crazy talk about the buffalo coming back. It was something more, a vague, troubled reluctance rolling through him.

Oddly furious, Will let the rifle sag down. As he raised up, he heard Dealey's coarse, recognizing yell. Wheeling toward the sound, Will knew that the hunter had sighted the calf, too. He saw Dealey frantic with haste, pushing in a cartridge. Almost before he knew it, Will was running. He saw the Big Fifty swinging and he threw up his arm. He felt the darting pain as his forearm smashed against the barrel and the rifle went off. It whoomed in his ears with Dealey's startled, rumbling curse.

"You crazy?" Dealey roared. "That's a white buffalo!"

"I know." Will's mind was spinning and from the rim of his vision he saw the cow slow to a stumbling, broken walk. He heard his own voice now, choked and strange: "Let 'em go . . . we got enough."

For a swift second, Will saw the blank astonishment in the weather-toughened face, now the streaking fury. "I'm going after that calf." Dealey's voice was a challenge. "By God, I am!"

"You won't today. We owe it to the skinners to hold up. No good strung out this way."

"You can't stop me."

As Dealey spoke, he was swinging the Sharps with a pawing hand and Will ducked. He heard the barrel swish wickedly past his face, then he was lunging. He drove into the man, felt the framework of solid shoulder muscles. Dealey dropped the rifle and they were rolling over the grass, Will punching wildly with his fists. A knee ripped across his belly. Half blinded from the flooding pain, Will hit the raging face. His knuckles made a chopping, squashy sound. The hunter kicked out with both boots, the sharp heels scraping and ripping across Will's chest. As Dealey fell back, Will swayed, fell on him coming up. Dealey's fists were lashing out, but Will slugged him across the thick neck, the broad, bushy-haired face. All at once the power seeped out of Dealey's chunky body and his fists slackened. He lay on the grass, panting, red-eyed, shaggy.

"Get out!" Will groaned. His wind came in ragged, racking gulps. He was aware of Shep North running up, the will to kill in the old hunter's face.

Will waved him off, watching Dealey push up painfully. Dealey scrubbed a skinned hand across his bloody, swelling mouth. "I got hides out there," he complained.

"You'll get your share . . . back in Dodge. Now straddle that horse."

Dealey's eyes shifted to North's slanting rifle, back to Will. "Never was much of a hand to argue with a Big Fifty." He shuffled his feet, his voice strange-sounding. "But could be you'll see me before you get to Dodge."

When Dealey reached down for his Sharps, Will heeled half around, looking. The cow had collapsed and the calf was nosing the black, sprawled shape.

Will said — "Grab a rope from the wagons, Shep . . . we'll bring that calf in." — and watched Dealey's halting, interested gaze. Will hurried him. "Go on! Come back and I'll kill you!"

Wordless, Dealey limped, slow-footed and deliberate, to his horse. He rode south without looking back.

"He sure left easy-like," Will heard North's worried voice. "Too damned easy. Ain't like him to give up."

"You mean . . . what?"

North nodded. "Injuns or renegades. Maybe both. Same as happened to Todd Sloan."

"That Injun's looking, too."

"He's seein' big medicine and he wants that calf. Reckon he ain't the only one."

After North loped back from the coming-up wagons, Will took the rope and they rode out to the white calf. Will caught it on the second throw. He dragged and pulled it to where Tuck Barton had halted the hide wagons.

"One walking hide, Tuck," Will announced. "Tie him up."

Barton gave the animal an amazed look, faced Will. “That old Injun,” he said nervously. “He rode off fast. Got an idea we’d best get the skinning over quick.”

Nodding, Will jogged out among the glassy-eyed bodies, through the gathering bloody smell. Last season and the years before, when the prairies swarmed with life, he would have counted a stand-kill hungrily, thinking of what the buyers would pay. It was big business and the market was high. A hunter had the feeling of supplying something. Hadn’t Sheridan himself said wipe out the Indian’s commissary, so the country could settle up? But now he felt a waste and no pride.

“Eighty-seven,” he told North, riding back.

Skinners and hunters worked till dark. Straight knives for ripping down the hairy bellies and slitting the stumpy legs, curved knives for skinning. Soon Will’s hands were bloody to the wrists. Afterward, they made camp, pegged and stretched the green hides, boiled tongue, and fried humped meat. When the fire was chunked up, Will heard the long, drawn-out howl of wolves wrangling over the bloated, sun-rotted meat.

“Can’t cross the river till daylight,” Will decided.

North kept looking and cocking his head. "I'd be willing to risk it right now," he grumbled, "but we couldn't make it. Not with the skinners fagged out. You don't peel the hides off eighty-seven head just by rolling up your sleeves."

Will figured it was around midnight when the hunter nudged him, muttering: "Can't see a thing . . . black as the inside of a cow's belly."

Stiff-muscled, Will got up and felt the catching pain wash across his chest and arms. The fire had died down to a dull cherry-red. It cast in blurred outline the sleeping skinners under the far wagon, showed the square shape of the restless, stamping calf tied to a wagon wheel. Will circled the camp, came back, and squatted down. It was a black and formless world, with the night sounds working and simmering off the cooling prairie. He watched the darkness till his eyes burned, listened till his ears seemed to merge all sounds into an indistinct humming.

At last he saw the start of a faint glow in the east, a rift in the inky blackness. He went stiff as he heard a noise, faintly beating. It slackened, faded out, and he thought of antelope running free. When it was streaky light, he looked around. Relief crawled through him and it occurred to him that it was time to roll the wagons. He swung his glance once more, then froze.

A horse seemed to rise out of the murky ground, a vague hulk looming in the fast-scattering light. There was a high-pitched yell — like a signal — as Will grabbed up the Sharps. He heard horses in rolling, violent gallop. Rifles cracked and he saw the spitting flashes, heard the *tunk-tunk* of lead slamming the wagon sides. Shep North pitched up from his blankets, howling at the skinners.

Will was pulled in against a wagon wheel, the jarring tremor of the hoofs across the ground making a knot in his stomach, when he recognized the steady boom of Big Fifties. Now he saw the riders. Ten or twelve strung out loosely — white men. One rider cut away, angling for the outfit's horses. Will knocked him down. That was Blaze Dealey's hoarse voice out there, he realized. Around Will was the blast of Shep North's buffalo gun. Reloading, Will heard him bawl belligerently: "Stay down!" There was a wild slash of shots from the other wagon where the skinners had forted up. Dust and smoke smell were close and strong, and Will knew that the hide crew couldn't last this way.

North yelled and Will whipped around.

He heard a whooping from the east side of the camp. It was a shrilling racket, a hoof-drumming clatter, coming from out of the valley. Something balled up inside Will as North squalled: "Injuns with 'em!" Horses were plunging around the wagons. Will heard a choked-off yell of pain from the skinners' side.

He jumped up, but North jerked him down, cursing.

Flattened out, Will saw the Pawnees' naked, shiny, coppery bodies weaving on bareback ponies. Will sensed an odd slackening among Dealey's men. They milled in confusion, tried to wheel clear. There was a frantic, broken rattle of buffalo guns.

The firing dropped off.

Will saw the Pawnees were not a part of the attack on the wagons. Will's mouth dropped open as a skinny Pawnee pulled a man off his horse. The Indian's knife flashed once, briefly, and slanted down. Dealey's bunch was shattered, his men dead in the dust, or they had fled out across the prairie. Then Will saw the bony old Indian on the gaunt pony. He gripped a short-barreled Winchester. There was a long-bladed knife at his belt.

A horse broke down heavily in front of Will's wagon. He saw Blaze Dealey spinning up and running, saw him halt and look at the wagon. Will swung his Sharps. He hesitated when Dealey yelled. The man's hands went up and he rushed over to the wagon.

"You," Will said slowly, "you better get out of the country for good this time, Dealey."

"I'll go." Dealey's voice was a jerky grunt and he kept his eyes on the Pawnees. "Just keep them Injuns off me."

Shep North made a muttering sound and Will saw the old Indian staring at the white buffalo. But Will noticed that the Pawnee was only half watching the calf. The muddy-brown eyes seemed to jump and flick, looking beyond Will, and then he was jerking the rifle.

"Look out, Will!"

It was Shep North's frantic voice. Wheeling around, Will heard the stunning, ear-ringing report. Thick clouds of powder smoke hung in the cold morning air.

Dealey stood close to the wagon, swaying drunkenly. The pistol slanting on Will spilled from his hand, and Dealey fell in a bent-over, reluctant sprawl.

"Don't ever turn your back like that," Shep North complained angrily.

"I know . . . now," Will said.

His eyes were on the old warrior. Shep North was a rigid shape beside Will. Across the camp by the other wagon the two skinners, their faces drawn and white, supported Tuck Barton. The Indian hadn't spoken. He didn't have to. His glance had strayed to the white calf, fixed with an awed and hungry look. This wasn't a begging Indian, Will knew. It went beyond that. There was something that few white men understood, maybe. But Will thought he understood.

"Go ahead," Will heard himself saying. "Take the white calf. He's yours. I guess you've earned him."

The Indian's braided head jerked up. "Me take 'im," he grunted. "Now buffalo come back some day. Plenty buffalo. Maybe you come back, too."

He slid from the pony, ran to the wagon. He whipped out the knife and slashed the rope halter. As the calf stood there, spraddle-legged, the Pawnee slapped him across the rump and the calf ran off.

Will was silent, his mouth dry and pinched together hard. Watching the running calf, with the Pawnees following and singing in a low chant now, he knew in the back of his mind that the buffalo wouldn't come back and that he wouldn't be back. . . .

■ ■ ■ ■

Will Teague never came back. Time-worn and rugged, the hills still shoulder up from the grassy floor of the prairie. Nobody remembers the skinners and long-haired Shep North and Will Teague. Gone are even the oldest men of the Pawnees who rode their stringy ponies through the gunsmoke curling around the wagons. But the story of the fight has been handed down, revived on feast days. And the buffalo didn't die. There's a lumbering, shaggy band cropping the valley grass of the government reserve, and when they move lazily from the timber you can see a white buffalo.

ACKNOWLEDGMENTS

"The Mystery Dogs" first appeared in *Antaeus* (Spring/Summer, 1977). Copyright © 1977 by Fred Grove. Copyright © 2010 by Lucile Grove for restored material.

"The Deadly Friends" first appeared in *Dime Western* (5/53). Copyright © 1953 by Popular Publications, Inc. Copyright © renewed 1981 by Fred Grove. Copyright © 2010 by Lucile Grove for restored material.

"Satan's Saddlemates" first appeared in *New Western* (5/54). Copyright © 1954 by Popular Publications, Inc. Copyright © renewed 1982 by Fred Grove. Copyright © 2010 by Lucile Grove for restored material.

"Hostage Trail" first appeared in *Texas Rangers* (4/57). Copyright © 1957 by Standard Magazines, Inc. Copyright © renewed 1985 by Fred Grove. Copyright © 2010 by Lucile Grove for restored material.

"Comanche Son" first appeared in *Boys'*

ABOUT THE AUTHOR

Fred Grove has written extensively in the broad field of Western fiction, from the Civil War and its postwar effect on the expanding West, to modern Quarter horse racing in the Southwest. He has received the Western Writers of America Spur Award five times — for his novels *Comanche Captives* (1961) which also won the Oklahoma Writing Award at the University of Oklahoma and the Levi Strauss Golden Saddleman Award, *The Great Horse Race* (1977), and *Match Race* (1982), and for his short stories, "Comanche Woman" (1963) and "When the *Caballos* Came" (1968). His novel, *The Buffalo Runners* (1968), was chosen for a Western Heritage Award by the National Cowboy Hall of Fame, as was the short story, "Comanche Son" (1961).

He also received a Distinguished Service Award from Western New Mexico University for his regional fiction on the Apache frontier, including the novels *Phantom Warrior* (1981) and *A Far Trumpet* (1985). His more recent historical novel, *Bitter Trumpet* (1989), follows the bittersweet adventures of ex-Confederate Jesse Wilder training Juáristas in Mexico fighting the mercenaries of the Emperor Maximilian. *Trail of Rogues* (1993) and *Man on a Red Horse* (1998), *Into the Far Mountains* (1999), and *A Soldier Returns* (2004) are sequels in this frontier saga.

For a number of years Grove worked on newspapers in Oklahoma and Texas as a sportswriter, straight newsman, and editor. Two of his earlier novels, *Warrior Road* (1974) and *Drums Without Warriors* (1976), focus on the brutal Osage murders during the Roaring 'Twenties, a national scandal that brought in the FBI, as does *The Years of Fear* (Five Star Westerns, 2002). Of Osage descent, the author grew up in Osage County, Oklahoma during the murders. It was while interviewing Oklahoma pioneers that he became interested in Western fiction.

The employees of Thorndike Press hope you have enjoyed this Large Print book. All our Thorndike, Wheeler, and Kennebec Large Print titles are designed for easy reading, and all our books are made to last. Other Thorndike Press Large Print books are available at your library, through selected bookstores, or directly from us.

For information about titles, please call:
(800) 223-1244

or visit our Web site at:
http://gale.cengage.com/thorndike

To share your comments, please write:

Publisher
Thorndike Press
10 Water St., Suite 310
Waterville, ME 04901